THE RED HERRING

Recent Titles by Sally Spencer from Severn House

THE DARK LADY
DEAD ON CUE
DEATH OF A CAVE DWELLER
GOLDEN MILE TO MURDER
MURDER AT SWANN'S LAKE
THE PARADISE JOB
THE SALTON KILLINGS

THE RED HERRING

A Chief Inspector Woodend Novel

Sally Spencer

This first world edition published in Great Britain 2001 by
SEVERN HOUSE PUBLISHERS LTD of
9–15 High Street, Sutton, Surrey SM1 1DF.
This first world edition published in the USA 2002 by
SEVERN HOUSE PUBLISHERS INC of
595 Madison Avenue, New York, N.Y. 10022.

British Library Cataloguing in Publication Data

Spencer, Sally, 1949–
  The red herring
  1. Woodend, Chief Inspector (Fictitious character) – Fiction
  2. Police – England – Fiction
  3. Detective and mystery stories
  I. Title
  823.9'14 [F]

ISBN 0-7278-5707-X

Typeset by Palimpsest Book Production Ltd.,
Polmont, Stirlingshire, Scotland.
Printed and bound in Great Britain by
MPG Books Ltd., Bodmin, Cornwall.

F or most people in the declining mill town of Whitebridge, the fear was not an immediate thing. Their heads were not pounding as they switched off their wireless after hearing the announcement. Their hearts didn't race as they put on the kettle to make a soothing cup of tea. They noticed no tremble in their legs as they stepped outside for a breath of northern industrial air. The simple truth – and they liked *simple* truth in Whitebridge – was that it hadn't really begun to sink in yet.

In a way, they were like victims of a rail crash, who know their train has hit something, but have yet to fully grasp the implications. But however much they might have wanted to, they could not remain in ignorance for long. Slowly and steadily, like fog rising from a murky river, the reality of the situation began to engulf them, until they were encompassed by panic.

It just couldn't be happening, they told themselves from the centre of that panic.

The Russian leader – the bald-headed man who'd banged his shoe on the table at the United Nations – could not have put missiles on Cuba. And even if he had, the American president – who was so handsome he might have been a film star – could not have retaliated by placing a tight naval blockade around the island.

It just couldn't be happening because both those things were virtually acts of war. And the world couldn't afford a war – not now there were nuclear weapons capable of

1

vaporising millions and millions of people in seconds.

Yet it *was* happening. The chickens had all come home to roost. The wind had been sown, and whirlwind was about to be reaped. The two most powerful men in the world were each writing a suicide note, both for themselves and for the rest of humanity.

Had any of these worried citizens of Whitebridge been told that only a few hours after the paralysing announcement there would be a man in their midst – a man faced with the same prospect of the impersonal destruction of his whole race as they were facing themselves – who would somehow find the will and the energy to destroy a *single* soul in a highly personal and brutal manner, they would have thought it incredible.

But he did – and he would!

One

Captain Wilbur Tooley of the USAF stood in front of the mirror straightening his necktie and examining his face closely for signs of ingrained Southern Baptist guilt.

'Who's giving the class tonight?' asked a voice behind him.

It was not a question he welcomed, and Tooley swallowed hard. 'The woman, I think.'

'Which woman? The pretty redhead? The one we met in church?'

Doing his best to freeze his face into a mask of innocence, Tooley turned round to look at his wife. Mary Jo had been pleasantly plump when he'd married her, but since then she'd given birth to their two kids and had never managed to lose all the extra weight she'd put on during pregnancy, so that now she was looking more and more like a round rubber ball.

'Yeah, she's the one we met in church,' he agreed.

'And what's the class on?'

Tooley shrugged his thin shoulders. 'I'm not exactly sure, honey. I think it's something about Britain searching for a new role now she's lost an empire.'

'Sounds dull.'

'It probably will be.'

'Do you have really to go?' asked the round rubber ball.

'It's something officers are expected to do,' Tooley replied.

'But what if something happens to you tomorrow?' she asked. 'What if you don't come back? Do you realise this could be the last night we ever spend together as a family?'

Yes, he realised it. And yes, he knew that he ought to spend the time with his family. But it wasn't what he *wanted*.

'You shouldn't talk like that,' he said. 'I've got enough on my mind when I'm in the air, without having to worry about family problems.'

Mary Jo's eyes moistened. 'I'm sorry,' she said.

'Forget it,' Tooley told her – but he was thinking: How can I be such an *asshole*?

'Could you at least promise to come home straight after class?' Mary Jo asked.

Tooley shook his head. 'I can't,' he lied. 'There's a ton of stuff going down. I might be needed.'

'You're needed *here!*'

'I'm sorry,' Tooley muttered, echoing his wife.

And he was. Sorry that his high principles could so quickly be overruled by his more basic instincts. Sorry that he was not half the husband he had once thought himself to be.

Verity Beale slowed down as she approached the main gate of the air-force base, but before she had come to a complete halt the guard stepped out and waved her Mini through.

As she drove between the lines of Nissan huts which had been erected hastily during the war – and still survived to defend the fragile peace – she felt as if she were trapped in a tunnel she did not like, but from which there was no turning back.

When had it all started, this journey through the tunnel? she wondered.

Was it when she'd first decided that a conventional career in a City law firm was not for her? Or had it been while she'd been watching the images on television of Allied planes flying supplies into a besieged Berlin?

She supposed that it didn't really matter now. The tunnel was there, and she had to take whatever steps were necessary – however distasteful they might be – to keep on moving through it.

'You're doing a good job,' she tried to reassure herself. 'A worthwhile job. A job not many people could do well.'

But even in the narrow confines of the Mini, the words sounded hollow to her, and she could not help wishing that, just once in a while, she could be *herself* and say what she *really* thought.

She pulled up in front of the large hut which served as her classroom on two nights a week. Through the window she could see several rows of American airmen already sitting down and waiting for her.

Most of them were little more than children, she thought – even younger than she was herself. And yet they each had under their control a weapon of war which could have wiped out the mighty forces of Genghis Khan with the single push of a button. It was frightening – all the more so because there was a distinct possibility that one of these young men was not at all what he seemed.

As she walked into the lecture room, she was aware of heads turning and eyes following the gyrations of her body. It was not a new experience for her. She was well aware of the fact that with her flaming red hair and firm figure she was what the Americans called 'a looker'. Indeed, if she hadn't been 'a looker', she'd never have been assigned this particular task.

She reached the front of the hut, mounted the podium, and turned to face her audience. There were gaps tonight, she noted – gaps left by men who would already be in the air.

'I'm flattered that so many of you tonight have decided that I'm a bigger draw than Mr Khrushchev,' she said.

They laughed, as she'd expected them to. But there was a nervousness in their laughter – and that was only to be expected, too.

She scanned the room and saw Wilbur Tooley – skinny, earnest Wilbur Tooley – sitting right at the back, trying his best to look at her as if she were his teacher and nothing more. She had arranged to meet him later and was already steeling herself to slip into the role he expected her to play.

If I'd gone into the law, as Daddy wanted me to, she thought, I'd have spent my days standing up in court and pleading the innocence of clients I knew damn well were guilty. Would that really have been any better than what I'm doing now? We're all whores – in one way or another!

She cleared her throat. 'The British Empire,' she said, underlining her words with her tone. 'In 1945, at the end of World War Two, there wasn't a politician in Britain who didn't believe that the Empire was as solid and durable as it had ever been . . .'

The atmosphere in the public bar of the Drum and Monkey was even more subdued that night than it had been when the English football team had been beaten by the Argentines or the cricket team thrashed by the Australians. And there was good reason for it. After defeats, there was always the chance of a comeback, but if either Mr Khrushchev or President Kennedy once pressed down a finger on the nuclear button, there would *be* no next football season, and instead of playing for the Ashes, the cricket team stood a fair chance of becoming – literally – ashes themselves.

The general gloom seemed to be shared by the man and woman occupying the corner table. The man was big, in every sense of the word – large head, broad shoulders, hands the size of shovels – yet there was a gentleness about his eyes which somehow served to soften what would have otherwise been a blunt face. The woman was blonde, younger than her companion and had a prettiness which was not quite English.

Anyone watching them would have known immediately that they were not married, but might have suspected, from the intimacy they seemed to share, that they were having an affair. And in a way, they were, though their mutual affection stemmed from the fact that they were both in love with the same job.

'Are you thinking about the missile crisis, sir?' the woman asked.

The man, Chief Inspector Charlie Woodend, nodded. 'I went through six years of war so that when I had kids, they could be sure of a decent future, Monika. Well, I've got a kid now – my Annie – an' it doesn't seem right that somethin' happenin' the other side of the ocean could snatch that future away from her.'

'If there *is* a war, we'll be a prime target in this area, won't we?' Detective Sergeant Monika Paniatowski asked.

'Aye, thanks to the aircraft factory an' Blackhill air-force base, we certainly will,' Woodend agreed. 'It's a real bloody mess, isn't it?'

'Whose fault do you think it is?'

Woodend shrugged. 'Nobody's. An' everybody's. Khrushchev didn't put them missiles on Cuba because he actually wants to fire them at America. They're only there as a bargainin' chip – somethin' he's prepared to give up if Kennedy will promise never to invade Cuba. But if Kennedy does make that promise, it'll look as if he's only backin' down because he's weak.' The chief inspector stopped to light up a Capstan Full Strength. 'Have you ever played poker, Monika?'

Paniatowski grinned. 'Yes, I've played it. How else do you think I could afford to run a car like mine on my salary?'

Woodend returned her grin, though he did not really feel very cheerful. 'Then if you're a player yourself, you'll know what I mean when I say it's mainly a game of nerve and bluff.'

'Of course.'

'The cards you hold in your hand are important, but often they're not *as* important as how far you're prepared to go with them. Your aim is make your opponent drop out as early as possible. But sometimes that doesn't happen. And sometimes the stakes get so high that none of the players feel they can back out – whatever it costs them.'

7

'And you think that's what's happening over Cuba?'

'That's right,' Woodend replied solemnly.

Paniatowski took a sip of her vodka. 'Look on the bright side, sir,' she said.

'An' what might that be?'

'You always fret when we've not got much work on, but by tomorrow morning we might have a nice gruesome murder to distract us from any thoughts of the end of the world.'

'Aye,' Woodend agreed, perking up a little. 'Aye, I suppose there's always a chance of that.'

Two

Nobody now remembered why, when the Second World War broke out, it was decided to construct the air base close to the edge of an aspiring forest known locally – whatever it said on the Ordnance Survey maps – as Dirty Bill's Woods. But someone, somewhere, obviously *had* taken the decision, and so, though the runway was some distance from Dirty Bill's, the main entrance to the residential section of the camp was less than a hundred yards away from the first line of trees.

The guard on duty at the main gate that night liked the fact that the wood was there, since it provided a distraction from what was otherwise a very boring duty. Sometimes he would imagine that Jane Mansfield, wearing an impossibly skin-tight dress, was lurking behind one of the oaks, waiting to ambush him and demand that he give her what no other man in the world could supply. On other, less fanciful, occasions, he contented himself with merely watching the cars containing courting couples turn off the road which ran through the wood and carefully negotiate their way between the gaps in the trees until the occupants were far enough away from the road to get down to serious business.

There was a car there that night. He'd seen its headlights just after he had lifted the barrier to allow the good-looking dame with the flaming red hair into the camp. Which meant, he calculated, that the couple in the car had been humping for nearly an hour now. He envied them. Or, at least, he envied the man – as he envied any man getting his rocks off while he himself was forced to stand by the guardhouse, defending Western civilisation.

The sentry turned to face into the camp, and saw a number of men emerging from the lecture hall. So the redhead had finished talking about English dukes and princes – or whatever the cockamamie subject had been that night – and now the aviators were heading for the luxury of their club. It usually irritated the guard that they led such a pampered existence, while a p.f.c. like himself was not even allowed through the door, but tonight he was not so sure that they had got the best deal. Come the morning, and those guys could find themselves flying over enemy territory under hostile fire, and by one of those reversals of fate would find themselves shifting abruptly from a situation in which they didn't know they were born to one in which they wished they never had been!

One of those pissant Brit automobiles – the redhead's black Mini – was approaching the gate. The guard stepped forward to raise the barrier. Instead of saluting, he gave the driver a wide grin, and felt a slight thrill run through him as she grinned back.

The Mini roared off into the night, but instead of lowering the barrier again, the guard began to slowly count to ten. He had reached seven when the Chevrolet Invicta appeared. Now there was an automobile, he thought to himself. Its engine was seven times the power of the vehicle it was following, and the Mini would have fitted into its trunk.

As the Chevrolet drew level with him, he came to attention and snapped off a tight military salute. The driver returned the salute. The Mini had already reached the woods, turned a bend in the road, and disappeared from sight. The Invicta followed it and a few seconds later, the car which had driven off the road earlier reappeared and set off in the same direction. It seemed as if everybody was getting their rations that night – except for the poor sap who'd been ordered to man the main gate.

The sentry gazed into the darkness for a moment, then wondered if he dared risk lighting a Camel.

'You lucky bastards,' he said softly to the three now-departed vehicles. 'You lucky, lucky bastards.'

Most of the other kids in her class would be watching television by now, Helen Dunn thought. But then most of the kids didn't have a father like hers. There was no point in telling Squadron Leader Reginald Dunn that she had finished her homework, even if she had, because he had got it fixed in his mind that his daughter needed to study for two and a half hours every night – including the weekends. And even though Miss Beale had told him she looked tired in class and probably needed to get to bed earlier, he had remained inflexible in his belief.

'You get nowhere in this life without discipline and determination,' he had told her often enough.

He had a way of making her feel a failure even when she *did* manage to do well.

'There are no prizes for coming second in anything,' he'd say. 'And no excuses, either. If you push yourself harder than anybody else, you'll do better than anyone else.'

'But what if I don't care about doing better than everyone else?' she'd once dared to ask him.

And he had glared at her hard enough to melt her slim body down, and said, 'After all the sacrifices your mother and I have made for you, you owe it to us to be the best. But more importantly, you owe it to yourself.'

He had said the same to her sister, Janice. But he couldn't say it any more, could he? Not now Janice was dead.

Helen grieved for her sister a great deal, but there were times when she thought that of the two of them, Janice was the luckier. Through death, Janice had found a way to escape from their father's incessant demands. Through her death, she had achieved some kind of victory.

Keeping one ear open for the sound of her father's footsteps

11

on the stairs, Helen made her way stealthily over to her chest of drawers. The squadron leader inspected her room regularly – almost every nook and cranny of it – yet she had still managed to achieve two small victories of her own in spite of that. The first victory had been constructing a hiding place at all. The second had been what she kept hidden in it.

She opened the top drawer as quietly as she could, and slid the neatly folded underwear to the front of it. Then, with infinite care, she removed the false back to the drawer and took out her prizes – a costume-jewellery bracelet, a Collins pocket English-Spanish dictionary and a cigarette lighter. None of them were of any use to her: she would never wear anything so obviously trashy as the bracelet (even if she dared), she did not speak Spanish and she felt no desire to smoke.

That didn't matter. What *did* matter was how she'd acquired them. She had stolen them all from shops in Whitebridge. She, the younger (and only surviving) daughter of Squadron Leader Dunn, was a thief. And though she knew now that she would never be brave enough to tell him – though she was aware that her other thefts, the ones which *had* been discovered, had put her in another's power – she could not bring herself to regret it.

Her revolt over, Helen sighed, returned the treasures to their hiding place, and looked down at her history book again. Miss Beale was giving them a test the following morning, and she knew it was not enough to get the top mark – she would have to score a mark which was *easily* the top.

The Spinner Inn stood on the edge of a small village several miles from Whitebridge. In the past, it had served as a post house for mail coaches and as a watering hole for drovers and shepherds on their way to the big markets in Manchester. But those days were long gone, and now it relied for its trade on after-hours drinkers and couples who would prefer to have their rendezvous far away from the prying eyes of their friends, neighbours and – most especially – their husbands or wives.

It was the pub's isolation which had recommended it to the two men sitting at the furthest table from the bar. But even so, it did not seem to be quite isolated *enough* for the one in the green corduroy jacket, and as his companion – a man with thinning brown hair and heavy schoolteacher glasses – outlined the final arrangements, he let his eyes dart nervously round the room.

The other man broke off his exposition, and sighed. 'For God's sake, Roger, pull yourself together!' he said.

'It's easy for you to say that,' Roger Cray replied. 'You don't have anything like as much to lose as I do. You're not a married man. You don't have any of my responsibilities.'

'And it's precisely *because* I'm not married that I'll be running the bigger risk,' Martin Dove argued.

'How do you work that out?'

'Because after it's happened, suspicion will be bound to fall on people like me first. Whereas nobody will ever suspect that you—'

'I don't want to do it,' Roger Cray said, trying to sound firm and failing miserably.

'You're lying,' Dove told him. 'You want to do it just as much as I do. You're *burning* to do it. Do you realise how long we've been planning this – how long we've been relishing the thought of it?'

'I—'

'Months, Roger! Bloody months! And now, just as we're on the point of achieving everything we wanted, you're starting to get cold feet.'

'Can you blame me?'

Martin Dove frowned. The man was coming to pieces, he thought. He needed to say something quickly to distract him – something to temporarily turn his mind to pleasanter, safer subjects.

13

'How's the car?' he asked. 'Still having that trouble with your cylinders?'

The change in Cray was almost immediate. The tension drained from his face, and a blissful smile replaced it. 'I had two valves replaced, and now she's running like a bird,' he said. 'I told you she was one of the first few ever produced, didn't I?'

'Yes, you did.'

There was very little that Cray hadn't told him about his 1953 Armstrong Siddeley Sapphire, Dove thought sourly. Ever since he'd inherited it from his uncle, it had been one his main subjects of conversation.

'Like a bird,' Cray repeated. 'You know what they say – "It's the car that's built to standards of a plane".' He laughed. 'If only some planes were built to the standards of that car.'

He had mellowed enough to be brought back to the main purpose of the meeting, Dove decided. 'So we're all right for tomorrow, are we?' he asked.

Cray looked worried again. 'It's a big risk,' he said.

'Of course it's a big risk,' Dove replied. 'But think of the *rewards*. Think of the *satisfaction*.'

'Think of the fact that we could spend the rest of our lives in prison,' Cray said heavily.

'And wouldn't it be worth it, if we did?' Martin Dove countered.

'I don't know.'

'Well, I do. This is something we've wanted passionately – both of us. And if we don't see it through now, we'll both regret it to our dying day.'

But Roger Cray was no longer listening. Instead, he was gazing in horror at the pub door.

'What's the matter?' Martin Dove.

'Have you seen who's just come in?'

Dove turned towards the door and saw the woman with the long red hair standing there. 'Oh my God!' he groaned.

14

Verity Beale was as horrified to see the two men as they were to see her. Who would have thought that they'd choose this pub – in the middle of nowhere – to meet?

She glanced nervously over her shoulder. Her date would arrive in a couple of minutes, and it was as important that he didn't see these men as it was that *they* didn't see him.

She took a deep breath, and wandered over to the men's table. 'Martin! Roger!' she said, feigning pleasure. 'I never expected to see you two here. I didn't even know you were friends.'

'Didn't you?' Martin Dove asked, making it sound almost like an accusation.

'We . . . we don't know each other that well,' Roger Cray mumbled. 'We're just casual acquaintances. Ran into each other completely by chance. And we . . .' he glanced down at his almost untouched drink, '. . . we have to be going now, don't we, Mr Dove?'

'I . . . er . . . yes, I suppose we do,' Martin Dove agreed unconvincingly.

The two men rose awkwardly to their feet, gave Verity Beale a farewell nod, and headed to the door.

Verity watched them leave. She had had her suspicions about both of them individually, but never of them together. It was certainly a development she would have to investigate more thoroughly in the morning. But right now, she had another task on her hands. For the moment she could only hope that they had left the car park by the time the big American car arrived.

Once in the car park, Roger Cray gave full vent to the panic he had been trying to control whilst he was inside the Spinner.

'That's it!' he said, in a voice which was almost a scream. 'The whole thing's off.'

'Because we saw Verity?'

'Of course it's because we saw Verity!'

'There's no reason she should connect us with what's going to happen,' Martin Dove said soothingly.

'The second she hears about it she'll connect it with us!' Cray babbled. 'You could tell by the way she looked at us that she knew we were planning *something*.'

'I'll deal with her,' Dove said firmly.

'What do you mean by that?'

'Don't worry about the details. I've promised I'll deal with her, and I will. I'll do whatever's necessary.'

The evening rolled on. At ten to eleven, the landlord of the Spinner rang last orders. By a quarter past eleven, when most of the customers had left, he slid the bolt across the door to seal in the last few, illegal drinkers.

It was at around twenty-five to twelve that Verity Beale, who seemed to have been deep in thought – not to say, troubled – downed the last dregs of her drink and announced it was time to leave. The landlord followed her to the door, and opened it for her.

'Your feller didn't stay long,' he said.

'No, he had to get back home,' Verity replied.

'Married, is he?' the landlord asked.

'Not that it's any of your business, but yes, he is.'

The landlord shook his head. 'You're wastin' your time knockin' about with married men. You're a good-lookin' lass – why don't you get yourself one that's unattached?'

'And why don't you stick to pulling pints?' Verity asked.

'Fair point,' the landlord agreed.

Verity Beale stepped out on to the forecourt, and heard the door shut behind her. It was as she was walking to her Mini that she noticed someone standing in the shadows. She didn't know who it was at first, but as she drew closer, the shape took a more distinct form and she felt her heart sink.

'Have you been out here waiting for me?' she demanded.

'Yes.'

'Why?'

'Because we need to talk.'

'There's nothing to talk about.'

'Don't you realise what risk you're putting yourself at?' the man asked.

Verity fumbled in her handbag for her cigarettes. 'Maybe I am,' she agreed, 'but, as I've just told the landlord back there, what I do is my business and nobody else's.'

The man stepped forward. 'You're wrong,' he said. 'You're so very, very, wrong.'

Three

There was nothing unusual about the way in which Jed Buckley started the next day. He was up before dawn, as he always was in October, and by the time the farming report was due to come on the wireless he was, right on schedule, sitting at the kitchen table with a plate of ham and eggs and a cup of tea in front of him. It was then that things started to go *abnormally*, because instead of the expected farming report he found himself listening to a BBC announcer talking, in a flat, unemotional voice, about the Cuban missile crisis.

Buckley, like most of the other farmers he knew, had never thought much about politics. When the government had told him it was necessary to go and fight the Germans, he had gone – with little enthusiasm, but without complaint. When the Chancellor of the Exchequer periodically raised the duty on agricultural fuel, he merely shrugged and told himself that the folk in London would never really understand the hardships of farming. But this, he recognised, was different. This was just about as serious as things ever got.

He no longer had any appetite for his food, and took the remains of it to the barn, where he tipped it into one of the buckets of pig swill he had mixed up the night before. That done, he picked up the buckets and made his way across the farmyard towards the sty.

It was when he was halfway across the yard that he realised something was wrong, though it took him a few more steps to work out exactly what that something was. Though there was a clamour from the sty, as there always was this close

18

to feeding time, the clamour on that particular morning was not directed towards him – the bringer of food – but seemed to be focused on the *inside* of the sty, instead.

Buckley wondered what could have brought about this change in their behaviour. Perhaps the pigs, some of the more sensitive of the farmyard animals, had picked up on the general tension in the air, he thought. Perhaps, though they could never be expected to understand the concept of a nuclear holocaust, they had still managed to grasp the concept that existence was teetering on the edge of oblivion.

He passed the cowshed, and heard his Herefords lowing. Somewhere to his left, his prize bantam cock was crowing loudly, to proclaim his power over his feathered concubines. One of the dogs barked. One of the cats slunk stealthily behind the tractor in search of unsuspecting prey. But there was no sign of the pigs' pink snouts poking out over the top of the fence as they stood on their hind legs and urged him on.

He reached the sty, and looked over into the pen. The pigs were not jostling around their trough, but instead stood in a tight bunch in the centre of the pen. Buckley puzzled over what was making them act so strangely. Then one of the sows shifted position – and he saw what was, undoubtedly, a human leg.

The pails clattered to the ground, spilling the swill everywhere. The farmer pulled back the bolt on the gate and rushed into the pen, waving his arms and shouting almost hysterically.

The pigs squealed, but were reluctant to give ground. Buckley, screaming at the top of his voice now, lashed out with his foot. The fat porkers grunted in protest, but finally retreated to the edges of the pen.

The farmer looked down in horror. There was a woman in the frozen mud – a woman with long red hair. A piece of cord was wrapped tightly around her neck, and she was unquestionably dead. He didn't think he knew her, but it was impossible to say for sure, because the pigs had been working on her for some time – and now all that was left of her face was bits of bone and gristle.

DCI Woodend watched the covered stretcher being manoeuvred into the back of the ambulance, then lit up what *should* have been his second or third Capstan Full Strength of the morning, but was probably closer to his tenth.

'I don't like this, Monika,' he said.

'It's not the kind of thing I enjoy seeing just after breakfast, either,' Paniatowski agreed.

'That's not what I mean,' Woodend said. 'You know how I work. I like to know where the victim was killed. I need to root around the scene of the crime, a bit like the pigs. In this case, I've no idea where the crime took place – an' what's even more troublin' is that I don't know why she was brought here.'

Monika Paniatowski looked beyond the pigsty to the sloping field which led down to the road. Half a dozen uniformed constables were criss-crossing it, their eyes fixed firmly on the ground. Standing at the edge of the field, watching them intently as they searched, was DI Bob Rutter. Apart from the police, there was nobody around – which was hardly surprising since the nearest village was a couple of miles away, and the nearest town of any size at least four or five.

'You see what I'm gettin' at?' Woodend asked.

'Perhaps the killer murdered her near to his home – or even *in* it – and thought that if the body was discovered there, it would be likely to draw attention to him,' Paniatowski suggested.

'Yes, it wouldn't be the first time the body's been moved for that reason,' Woodend agreed. 'But I think you're missin' the point, Monika.'

'Am I, sir? So what *is* the point?'

'He doesn't want her found near his home – fair enough – so he drives her out into the countryside. But why not just leave her on the side of the road? Or else drive her to somewhere much more secluded? Why run the risk of carryin' the body across a field to dump it in the pigsty?'

'Maybe he thought the pigs would destroy the evidence.'

'Well, they've certainly tried their best to do that. But he can't really have expected them to swallow her without trace. Which brings me back to my original point. Dumpin' her somewhere she wouldn't be found in a hurry makes sense. So does gettin' rid of her body as quick as possible. But what he did achieved neither of those aims.'

One of the constables bent down to pick something up, then made his way over to where DI Rutter was standing.

It's a handbag, Paniatowski thought excitedly. They'd found the victim's handbag!

Rutter took the bag off the constable, and carefully opened it up. He put his hand inside, and pulled out what looked like a small red booklet.

'Seems as if we'll be able to put a name to the victim before long,' Paniatowski said.

Woodend nodded. The killer must have known the handbag would be found, he thought, which meant that he didn't care that the victim would soon be identified. So again, why run the *bloody* risk of carrying her all the way to the pigsty?

Rutter, the red booklet still in his hand, made his way over to where his boss and the detective sergeant were standing.

'According to her driving licence, her name was Verity Beale, and she was twenty-six years old,' he said.

'If that *is* her driving licence,' Paniatowski said.

Rutter shot the sergeant a look of pure dislike. 'What chance do you think there is that anybody else would drop their handbag in the middle of nowhere?' he asked.

'Stranger things have been known to happen,' Paniatowski countered.

'But they don't happen very often,' Rutter said cuttingly. 'That's precisely what makes them strange.'

Woodend looked from the inspector to the sergeant. The

first impression anyone got of Rutter was of smartness. Smart haircut, smart suit, smart shoes and smart eyes. A young man who was going places. With Paniatowski, what you noticed was the fact that her nose was a little too big and her mouth a little wide – which was a long way from saying that she could walk across a room without the gaze of every man there following her. And like Rutter, *she* had smart eyes, too.

'What's the address on the drivin' licence?' the chief inspector asked.

'Ruskin Road, Woolwich,' Rutter answered.

'But she's not lived there for a while,' Paniatowski said.

Rutter glared at her. 'How do you be so cocksure sure about that, Sergeant?'

'That skirt she's wearing was in Fred Ball's summer sale at the end of August. I nearly bought it myself.'

'And you're saying that Fred Ball's was the only place in the whole country she could have bought it?' Rutter asked sceptically.

'The blouse and jacket were on sale as part of the same ensemble,' Paniatowski told him matter-of-factly. 'I didn't think they quite went together – that's why I didn't buy them in the end. The chances of any other retailer offering exactly the same combination must be about a million to one. If you don't believe me, why don't you ask your wi—'

She stopped suddenly, as if she would willingly have bitten off her own tongue. People forgot that Maria Rutter wasn't like most women, Woodend thought – forgot that though she had a baby now, and was coping exceptionally well with all the difficulties that had brought her, she'd still been totally blind for over two years.

'I'm . . . I'm sorry, Inspector,' Paniatowski mumbled.

'Forget it,' Rutter said brusquely. 'Maria doesn't want your pity.' Then *he* began to look a little ashamed, too. 'It's an easy mistake to make,' he admitted. 'I've been guilty of it myself a few times.'

'So we think the victim was livin' locally, do we?' Wood-end asked, turning the conversation back on to the investigation.

'It's what I'd put my money on,' Paniatowski replied.

'Then it shouldn't be too hard to trace her, should it?'

A young constable who'd been searching one of the outbuildings made his way uncertainly towards them. He came to a halt when he drew level, and looked from Rutter's face to Woodend's – then back again – as if he were uncertain which of them he should speak to.

'What is it, Dobson?' Rutter asked.

'One of the lads was sayin' that you've found the victim's driving licence, sir.'

'That's right.'

'So you know who she is?'

'Why the interest?'

'It's just possible I might know her.'

'Assuming that the licence belong to her,' Rutter said, giving Paniatowski a quick glance, 'then we believe her name was Verity Beale.'

The colour drained from the constable's face. 'Oh, my God, it's true,' he moaned.

'So you do know her?'

The constable nodded. 'When I saw she had the same hair as Miss Beale, I thought there might be a chance, but I never really believed . . .'

'Tell us about her,' Woodend said gently. 'Did you know her well?'

'More know *of* her,' the constable said. 'I've got a nephew at King Edward's Grammar, you see – my sister Linda's lad. I've been up to the school a few Saturday mornin's to watch him play football, an' she was usually there. She's . . . she *was* one of the teachers, an' I rather . . . an' I rather . . .'

'An' you rather fancied her?' Woodend suggested.

The constable nodded. 'Yes, sir. I know it sounds a bit sick now, but I'd no idea she was goin' to end up . . .'

'Tell me about her left knee,' Woodend said.

'I . . . I beg your pardon, sir.'

'Her left knee, lad. I noticed somethin' distinctive about it, an' if you fancied her, you'll have noticed it too.'

'She . . . she had a scar on it,' the constable said, reddening. 'It was quite attractive, actually . . . I mean . . .'

'What kind of scar?'

'It was a bit like a crescent moon.'

Woodend turned to Monika Paniatowski. 'That's a positive enough identification for me,' he said.

'Me, too,' Paniatowski agreed.

Four

T he King Edward VI Grammar School stood, appro-
priately enough given its position in the educational
hierarchy, near the top of a steep hill. It was flanked on
one side by large, detached houses, and on the other by
Whitebridge Corporation Park. Though it could trace its
origins back to the sixteenth century, the oldest buildings
on the school site dated back only to the nineteenth. These
edifices – for there was no other way to describe them – had
all the ornate pretentiousness of Victorian civic architecture.
The newer extensions, on the other hand – added as the school
expanded and science became almost as important as Latin –
had about them a blandness which was positively post-war
utilitarian. The complex would, therefore, never have won
any architectural prizes, but for the aspiring burgers of
Whitebridge, the opportunity to have their children educated
at 'Eddie's' was a prize in itself.

Woodend had known the school when he was growing up,
though only as a result of walking past it on the way to his
elementary school, an institution where you were taught the
basics, then kicked out to fend for yourself when you turned
fourteen. Now, for the first time in his life, he found himself
standing in the entrance hall of the hallowed institution,
surrounded by shelves of sporting trophies and long strip
photographs of generations of privileged schoolboys.

He leant closer to one of the photographs, examined the
grinning, confident faces of the pupils, and found himself
wondering whatever had happened to all those boys. Had they

conquered the world, as they had once so clearly believed they would? Or were they now assistant bank managers and head wages clerks, administering their small empires from musty offices far from the centre of things? And did it really matter one way or the other? Because if the American president and Russian premier both refused to back down, then not only their careers, but their world, could go up in smoke.

A large oak door swung open, and a grey-haired woman in a grey knitted twin-set appeared.

'The Headmaster will see you now,' she said, as if she were conferring a great honour on him.

Woodend turned to Paniatowski. 'I hope you haven't been caught smokin' behind the bike sheds again, Monika,' he said *almost* in a whisper, before striding into the headmaster's office with his sergeant at his heel.

The headmaster was about his own age, Woodend guessed. He had silver hair and a stiff military bearing. He was probably the kind of ex-soldier who, if you asked him, would say he'd had 'a good war'.

As if there was any such thing, thought Woodend, who had served six years in the poor bloody infantry.

The headmaster extended his hand to both the chief inspector and his assistant, then gestured them to sit in a pair of straight chairs which faced his impressive teak desk.

'My secretary informs me that whilst you wished to see me, you were not prepared to inform her of the nature of your visit,' he said in a deep, plummy voice, which Woodend could well imagine ringing impressively round the school assembly hall. 'Could I enquire as to the reason for your reticence?'

'She wouldn't have liked what I told her, an' I didn't see any need for her to get her knickers in a twist until she absolutely had to,' Woodend replied.

The headmaster arched his left eyebrow in a most significant manner. 'I beg your pardon?' he said.

'When I want the rest of the people in this buildin' to learn why I'm here, I'd like to be the one who tells them,'

Woodend replied, as if he were really giving the headmaster the answer he'd sought. 'I believe you employ a teacher called Verity Beale.'

'She is a member of my staff, yes.'

'An' you don't happen to know if she's at work today, do you?'

The headmaster waved his hand in an airy gesture of dismissal. 'I'm afraid you'll have to ask my deputy about that. He's the one who deals with the day-to-day matters of school business.'

'How long has Miss Beale worked for you?'

'Since September.' The headmaster paused. 'Before we go any further, would you mind telling me why you're asking these questions?'

'All in good time, sir,' Woodend said. 'Miss Beale's not from round these parts, is she?'

'No, she's from London. What's the problem? Is she in some kind of difficulty?'

'Do you usually employ teachers who come from so far away?' Woodend asked.

'This school has an enviable reputation to maintain. In order to ensure it does, I employ good teachers *wherever* they come from. And Miss Beale *is* a graduate of Cambridge University.'

'Do you employ many women?'

'I think you've already met my secretary. In addition, most of the kitchen staff—'

'I mean women *teachers*.'

'I have, from time to time.'

'How many of your teachers are women at the moment?' Woodend asked, almost expecting the headmaster to reply that he would have to ask the deputy about mundane details like that.

'She is the only one at the moment,' the headmaster said.

'Doesn't she find it difficult, working in an all-male school?' Paniatowski asked.

'Don't you find it difficult working in an almost entirely male police force?' the headmaster countered.

'Difficult enough,' Paniatowski agreed.

It didn't seem to be the answer the headmaster had been expecting, and for a moment it threw him off his stroke. 'Miss Beale is a highly competent teacher,' he continued, after another moment's pause, 'though I will not deny her path is made smoother by the fact that we expect certain standards of behaviour from the boys in this school. From the girls, too, for that matter.'

'Girls?' Woodend repeated. 'Did you say *girls*?'

'Indeed, I did.'

'Well, I'll go to the foot of our stairs,' Woodend said.

'I'm afraid I don't quite follow you.'

'I never thought I'd live to see the day when Eddie's would allow *girls* through the door. When did this revolution happen? Why haven't I read about it in the papers?'

The headmaster grimaced. 'We admit a limited number of girls as a courtesy to the Air Force,' he said. 'Several of the officers at RAF Blackhill have their families with them, and since they naturally want to make sure their daughters attend a *good* school, we are asked to accommodate them.'

'But only officers' daughters?' Woodend asked. 'Not the kids of the enlisted men?'

'Naturally not,' the headmaster agreed. 'We have to draw the line somewhere. And now, Chief Inspector Woodend, I think I really am going to have insist that before you ask me any more questions, you tell me *why* you're asking them.'

'There's been a murder,' Woodend said bluntly.

'Miss Beale!'

'It's possible it's somebody else – but we don't really think so, do we, Sergeant?'

'No,' Paniatowski said. 'We don't really think so.'

The headmaster seemed shocked, Woodend thought, but not in the way most people did when they were told of a murder.

He tried to pin down what was wrong with the other man's reaction. The average feller-in-the-street's initial emotion was usually disbelief, he decided. There had to be some mistake, the feller's expression would say. Of course people got murdered – he understood that – but not people he knew personally. There was simply no way that could have happened.

The headmaster, on the other hand, looked like a man who had put his life savings on a sure winner at Doncaster, only to see the bloody horse fall at the first fence.

'This . . . this is terrible news,' the headmaster said.

'Aye, it is,' Woodend agreed. 'Now I don't want to disturb the runnin' of the school any more than I have to, but I will need to talk to your staff as a group – an' probably individually as well – sometime durin' the course of the mornin'.'

'Of course,' the headmaster said abstractedly.

'So if you could make the suitable arrangements . . .'

'Ask Mrs Green to take you to see my deputy,' the headmaster said. 'He will do whatever's necessary.'

Woodend looked at Paniatowski, then stood up. 'Well, thank you for your co-operation, sir, and we'll try not to—' he began.

'Yes, yes,' the headmaster said impatiently. 'Now if you'll excuse me, I have a great many matters to attend to.'

And all of them apparently more important than the murder of one of his staff, Woodend thought.

When he reached the door, the chief inspector turned around again. The headmaster was just reaching for the phone – but when he saw Woodend looking at him, he let his hand fall back on the desk.

Five

Elm Avenue was located on the edge of Whitebridge, far away from the old mills and just high enough above the town centre to make it unlikely that any but the strongest wind would carry the smell of hops from the town's three breweries into the residents' lounges. The houses were all solid Edwardian semi-detacheds, with bow windows and stained-glass designs over the front doors. The front gardens of many of them had been paved over, but the one which belonged to Number Twenty-Seven not only had a handkerchief-sized lawn but also boasted a model windmill and several garden gnomes angling, futilely, in a small, fish-less pond.

Rutter walked up the path and rang the bell. The door was answered by a blue-rinsed woman in her early sixties who was wearing a floral pinafore and an expression of self-righteous satisfaction.

'My husband told me never to buy anything from the door, and I never have,' she said.

Rutter gave her what he'd heard described around the police station as his 'boyish grin', and produced his warrant card.

'I'm not selling anything, Mrs Hoddleston,' he said. 'You *are* Mrs Hoddleston, aren't you?'

'Yes, I am.' The woman squinted at the card. 'What's this all about, Inspector . . . Inspector Rutter?'

'I believe you take in lodgers and—'

'Not lodgers as such,' Mrs Hoddleston said hastily, but firmly.

'I thought—'

'I do occasionally have paying guests, just to be accommodating, but I always declare it on my income tax statement.'

'And you currently have a Miss Beale staying with you?'

'Oh, is that what it's about? Her!' Mrs Hoddleston glanced quickly up and down the street, as if suspecting that some of her neighbours might be spying on her. 'Well, if it's Miss Beale you want to talk about, then I suppose you'd better come inside.'

Mrs Hoddleston's lounge was not small, but the abundance of furniture – overstuffed armchairs, sideboards and highly polished display cabinets – made it seem as though it were.

Rutter sat in one of the armchairs, his knees jammed up against the coffee table and a cup of tea balanced in the palm of his left hand. 'I get the distinct impression from your tone earlier that you were almost expecting a visit from the police,' he said.

Mrs Hoddleston sniffed. 'I wouldn't say I'd be expecting it, but after the way she's been carrying on, I'm not exactly surprised.'

'Carrying on?'

'I've been taking paying guests into my home since just after my husband died,' Mrs Hoddleston said. 'Never more than one at time, you understand, and even then, only young ladies from refined backgrounds. You won't find any commercial travellers staying here. I'm not in business.'

Rutter suppressed a grin. 'Yes, I can quite see that,' he said.

'On the whole, I've been very lucky with my guests. One of them was learning to be a bookkeeper. Another taught the violin – though never in this house, of course.'

'Of course not.'

'They led quiet lives. Occassionally, if I invited them, they'd come down to the lounge to watch television with me, but most of the time, when they were in the house,

31

they kept to their own rooms. On the whole, I've been very pleased with my young ladies.'

'But not with Miss Beale?'

'I thought she was going to be *highly* satisfactory at first. She has a good job at the grammar school, and one of the first things she asked me was whether there was a Baptist church nearby. I'm Church of England myself – my husband was very upright, a pillar of St Steven's, and sadly missed – but I like to be tolerant in these matters, so I didn't hold her interest in the Baptists against her.'

'Very understanding of you,' Rutter said.

Mrs Hoddleston sighed. 'Yes, I thought she would be the perfect paying guest at first.'

'And what happened to make you change your mind?'

'Mainly, it was the hours she keeps. Mr Hoddleston, when he was alive, always said that early to bed, early to rise, makes a person healthy, wealthy and wise. Of course, he never became wealthy, and he died when he was only fifty-three, but even so, he had a point.'

'Of course he did,' Rutter readily agreed.

'I don't expect my guests to live by the same rules I was brought up with – this is the nineteen sixties, after all – but you do still have to have certain standards, don't you?'

'She came . . . she comes in late?'

'She does indeed. Well after midnight, sometimes.'

'The buses stop running at just after eleven,' Rutter said. 'Does she have a car?'

'Yes. A black Mini. But she often leaves it here when she goes out in the evening.'

'So how does she get back?'

'She's brought,' Mrs Hoddleston said, lowering her voice.

'Brought?'

'I hear cars in the street, just before she opens the front door.'

'Cars?' Rutter said, pouncing. 'Plural?'

Mrs Hoddleston looked a little embarrassed. 'I'm not one

to spy on my guests,' she said. 'To tell you the truth, I'm usually in my bed by the time Miss Beale gets home.'

'But?'

'But several times I *have* got up and looked out of the window, and let me tell you, I've rarely seen the same car twice.'

'You didn't happen to take any of their numbers, did you?' Rutter asked hopefully.

'No, I most certainly did not,' Mrs Hoddleston replied, sounding a little offended.

'But perhaps you noticed the make and model of some of them?'

'There was an Armstrong Siddeley Sapphire which dropped her off a couple of times.'

'That's a bit of an unusual car,' Rutter said. 'Are you sure that's what you saw?'

The woman nodded. 'Oh yes. Definitely. My brother, who lives in Halifax, has one. He drove it all the way over here once – just to show it off. Mr Hoddleston, my late husband, wasn't at all impressed. He said a Morris Minor should be good enough for anybody. And I agreed with him,' she sighed again, wistfully this time, 'though I do have to admit, there was *something* about that Sapphire.'

'Is Miss Beale usually noisy when she comes in?' Rutter asked.

'Not especially,' Mrs Hoddleston said, reluctantly. 'I mean, when the house is silent, every noise carries, doesn't it? But no, I wouldn't say that she makes more noise than most people would. It's just that I don't like to think what she's been up to until that hour of the night.'

'So she doesn't bang into the furniture, as people do when they've had too much to drink?'

'Certainly not!' Mrs Hoddleston said. 'That's one thing I would *not* tolerate. But I suspect that even if she hasn't been drinking herself, she's been in places where drinking takes place.'

'What makes you think that?'

'When she goes out to work in the morning, she's always sensibly – respectably – dressed, but she often takes a carrier bag with her, as well as her briefcase.'

'So?' Rutter said.

'I thought you were supposed to be a detective. She's taking a change of clothes with her. Dresses usually. I don't specially look, but I can't help noticing. One of them I saw was purple!'

'Shocking!' Rutter said, then, noticing the hard stare he was getting, he quickly added, 'Do you have any other complaints about her?'

'We share the bathroom, more through necessity than choice. I've never had any trouble with the other young ladies, but sometimes, after *she's* used the bathroom, the smell is dreadful.'

'Perhaps she has stomach problems,' Rutter suggested.

'I beg your pardon?'

'If she leaves the bathroom smelly—'

Mrs Hoddleston blushed. 'Not that kind of smell,' she said. 'If it had have been, I'd never have mentioned it. What I'm talking about is *scent*.'

'Scent?'

'I use a little lavender water myself. Lavender water and violet are thoroughly respectable scents for a lady to use. But what Miss Beale sprays on herself . . . well, it wouldn't be out of place in a . . . in a . . .'

'In a house of ill-repute?' Rutter suggested.

'Yes! Exactly! And we're not used to that kind of thing in Whitebridge, you know.'

'Anything else?' Rutter asked.

Mrs Hoddleston hesitated for a second. 'She changed the lock on her bedroom door,' she said. 'None of my other young ladies have thought it necessary to do that.'

'How do you know she'd changed the lock?' Rutter asked.

'What do you mean?'

34

'Presumably, to have made such a discovery, you must have tried to get into her room.'

'I . . . er . . . yes.'

'And why would that have been?'

'I . . . er . . . noticed a spot of damp on my bedroom wall. I wondered if there was a similar problem in Miss Beale's room. She was out at school, so I thought I'd just pop in and check. My key didn't work.'

'And did you mention it to her?'

'I didn't see how I could, really.'

No, you couldn't, not without revealing you'd been snooping around, Rutter thought. 'I'm afraid I have some bad news for you,' he said aloud.

'She's not been arrested, has she?' Mrs Hoddleston asked, clearly alarmed. 'It won't be in all the papers that she's been living under my roof?'

'I'm afraid it might be, but not for the reasons you seem to fear,' Rutter told her. 'You see, though we can't be absolutely certain yet, we think she may have been murdered.'

'Oh, the poor girl!' Mrs Hoddleston said. 'I'd never have wished that on her – but as my late husband often said, those who live by the sword shall perish by the sword.'

Six

The staff room in King Edward's Grammar School was on the second floor of the original Victorian building, just about as far from the playground as was possible within the school complex. But even so, the sound of eight hundred boys expelling their surplus energy while they had the chance was enough to produce a persistent background hum like the engine of a cruise liner.

As was usual at break time, the room was full of teachers, standing in small groups and sipping cups of strong, warm tea. Unlike most mornings, however, the conversation that day did not centre on complaints about the administration or anecdotes relayed by teachers hoping to demonstrate their own prowess in the classroom. Instead, they were concerned with the man in the hairy sports jacket who had been seen leaving the headmaster's office but, as far as anyone knew, had still not left the school.

'His name's Woodend,' said Lew Etheridge, the head of craft. 'Local man originally, but until recently he's been based down in London. Not one of our old boys, is he, Dennis?'

'Certainly not,' replied Dennis Padlow, the head of languages. 'If he had have been, he'd have been a pupil here at the same time as I was, and I'd have remembered him. Besides, the headmaster in my day was Killer Culshaw, and he'd never have stood for one of his boys considering the *police* as a career.'

'The question isn't where he was educated, but why he's

here *now*,' said Martin Dove, with an edge to his voice which could have been either irritation or tension.

'Maybe he's got a son he wants to enrol,' Lew Etheridge suggested.

'Too late in the year for that,' Dennis Padlow said dismissively. 'I think he's here in a professional capacity.'

'Professional capacity!' Etheridge repeated. 'What kind of professional capacity? As far as I know, there hasn't been a burglary.'

'Perhaps that air-force girl has been caught shoplifting, again,' Padlow suggested.

'The man's a *chief inspector*, for God's sake,' Martin Dove said. 'I know neither of you have a high regard for the intelligence of the local constabulary, but even Whitebridge Police wouldn't waste a chief inspector's time investigating a case of petty larceny.'

A tall, almost gaunt, man with piercing eyes drifted up to the group, and stood uncertainly on the edge of it. 'Have any of you chaps seen Verity this morning?' he asked.

'No, but that's hardly surprising, is it?' Lew Etheridge asked sourly. 'She's had more days off sick than she's had working. That's the trouble with these highly educated women. They think they're far too good to roll up their sleeves and get down to an honest day's graft.'

The gaunt man gave him a reproaching look. 'That's hardly fair, Lew,' he said. 'The damp climate around here doesn't suit everybody.'

'I know it doesn't, Simon,' the head of crafts countered. 'But I'd like to bet all her little illnesses don't stop her drawing a full pay packet at the end of every month.'

The gaunt man looked as if he was about to say more, then turned and walked away.

'That was a bit harsh, wasn't it, Lew?' Dennis Padlow asked.

'Well, I'm sick of her not pulling her weight,' the head of craft said. 'And I'm sick of Simon Barnes jumping to her

defence every time anybody says anything about her. If he
wasn't so busy acting like a love-sick puppy whenever she
walks into the room, he might start to see what I mean.'

'Still, there was no need to be rude,' Padlow commented.

But in a way, he was glad that Etheridge had spoken as he
did – because that had served to drive Simon Barnes away.
And it was a view which the other members of the group
secretly shared, too. There was something odd about Barnes.
Not that there was anything wrong with a man having religion
– they all, more or less, believed in God – but there was no
need to be as intense about it as Simon Barnes seemed to be.
True, he didn't ever try to force his beliefs down their throats,
but whenever he was in their company they always felt as if
he were judging their conversation and somehow finding it
trivial and unworthy.

'Did any of you happen to see that play on television last
night?' Lew Etheridge said.

'The one with the busty blonde in the low-cut dress in it?'
Dennis Padlow asked.

'That's the one. It was *so* low-cut that it's a wonder they
didn't spill out when she bent over.'

'If you ask me, it won't be long now before they're
showing everything they've got on the telly,' Padlow said,
with considerable relish.

Bob Rutter stood in a public phone box at the end of Elm
Avenue.

'How did you get on with the landlady?' Woodend asked
him from the other end of the line. 'Was she a bit tight-
lipped?'

'No, far from it,' Rutter replied. 'In fact, I think I might
have preferred it if she'd been a trifle more reticent.'

'Reticent!' Woodend repeated, and Rutter could almost see
him rolling the word around his mouth. 'That's one of them
big words – like marmalade – isn't it? So she came on a bit
strong, did she?'

'To hear her talk, you'd think Verity Beale was the original scarlet woman,' Rutter said.

'Well, maybe she was.'

'I don't think so,' Rutter countered. 'Mrs Hoddleston's the kind of woman who thinks that playing marbles is a sign that you're in league with the devil and all his works.'

'Still, she must have based her ill-founded opinion on *somethin'*,' Woodend pointed out.

'Miss Beale seems to have had a fairly active social life,' Rutter said cautiously. 'According to Mrs Hoddleston, she was out till all hours of the night, and it wasn't always the same man who brought her home. One of them even brought her home in an Armstrong Siddeley Sapphire.'

'Shockin',' Woodend said, in mock horror. 'I don't know what the world's comin' to. I really don't.'

'You want me to pursue that line of inquiry further?'

'You can chase up the Sapphire driver if you like – there can't be too many of them in Central Lancashire – but since I'm in the school at the moment, I'm best placed to do most of the checkin' on her recent activities.'

'So what do you want me to do?'

'You get yourself back to the station, an' see what you can dig up on Miss Beale *before* she decided to grace Whitebridge with her presence.'

'No sooner said than done,' Rutter told him.

Helen Dunn had been buoyed up by the news that Miss Beale wasn't in school that morning. It wasn't that she didn't like the history teacher – she did, and sometimes she found herself desperately wishing that, despite what had happened, they could be *real* friends – but the fact that Miss Beale was away meant there would be no test, which in turn meant that she had temporarily avoided the possibility of failing to live up to her father's expectations again.

The feeling of mild euphoria had sustained her all the way through to break time, but once she had stepped into the playground the familiar feelings of isolation and depression began to assail her. She was a stranger in the school. More than that, she was *strange* – at least as far as the local boys were concerned. It was not her fault she hadn't been brought up in Whitebridge, she thought. She couldn't be blamed for the fact that while Cyprus and Germany were just names to the boys, they held vivid memories for her.

She should have been able to get on better with the few kids from the base, because at least they shared the same experiences. But there was a problem there, too. On the base, the officers and their wives mixed socially – but also cautiously. Even drunk, the flying officers and flight lieutenants had to be careful what they said to a squadron leader – especially when that squadron leader was Reginald Dunn. And somehow this attitude had been communicated to their children, so that Reginald Dunn's daughter was not merely another girl in their eyes, but an extension of the situation which existed on the base.

There were times when Helen saw herself as the maiden of the old legends, bound tightly to a post and constantly menaced by the dragon who was her father. But the maidens in the pictures were tall and beautiful, with long slinky hair. She, on the other hand, was skinny and, at her father's insistence, had her hair cut almost like a boy's. So even if there had been a knight in shining armour riding around and searching for someone to whisk away, he would have taken one look at her and then gone in search of a girl more worthy of rescue.

She brushed a tear away from her eye. Perhaps there was hope yet, she told herself without much conviction. Perhaps, somewhere out there in the wide, wide world, there was a short-sighted knight errant who would ignore the surface look and see her as she really felt she was inside. And if he could do that – if he could make that great imaginative leap – then perhaps he would take her away from the dragon who dominated her life.

Seven

The deputy headmaster's office at Eddie's was considerably smaller, and much less impressive, than the headmaster's study. It was also, Woodend thought as he looked around him at the stacks of paper resting on every available surface, much more like the sort of place where the real work of running the school was done.

The deputy's name was Walter Hargreaves. He was about the same age as his boss, though without any of the other man's crisp starchiness. He had a pencil-thin moustache and slightly hollowed cheeks. His pale blue eyes could probably look amused and preoccupied with equal success, though at that moment they merely seemed wary.

'The headmaster's told you what's happened to Miss Beale, has he?' Woodend asked.

Hargreaves nodded gravely. 'Yes, he has. It's a shocking thing to have occurred.'

But he looked no more shocked than the headmaster had, Woodend thought. If there was any difference at all between his reaction and his boss's, it was that Hargreaves seemed to be a little more fatalistic about the murder.

'It will come as a blow to the staff, too,' the deputy continued.

'I'm sure it will.'

'Which is why, with your permission, Chief Inspector, I'd like to announce it at the end of morning school. That way, they'll have the whole of the lunch hour to absorb the news and pull themselves together again. Would that be acceptable?'

41

'Sounds reasonable to me,' Woodend agreed. 'What can you tell me about the dead woman?'

'About her background, very little,' Hargreaves said. 'Her personal record will be on file in the secretary's office, but I haven't seen it myself.'

'That surprises me,' Woodend said.

'Does it really?' Hargreaves asked. 'I can see no reason why it should. The headmaster makes all the appointments in this school. I'm not really concerned with what the staff have done in the past, only how they perform once they're here.'

'And how *did* Miss Beale perform?'

Hargreaves's eyes flickered. 'You'll have to speak to her head of department if you wish to know how good she was at imparting her knowledge of her subject,' he said.

'You give the impression of a man who has his finger on the pulse of this place,' Woodend told him, 'but you certainly haven't shown me any concrete evidence of it yet.'

Hargreaves looked away. 'My main concern is how well teachers impose discipline, and Miss Beale's class control was more than adequate.'

'Was she reliable?' Woodend asked.

'I suppose so.'

'You don't sound too sure.'

'Young teachers like Miss Beale don't always know how to pace things at first.'

'You couldn't spell that out for me, could you?' Woodend asked.

'They throw themselves into their lessons with an enthusiasm which is commendable but also very, very draining. They go home exhausted, which means that they are rather vulnerable to infections.'

'What you're really sayin', in a round about way, is that she'd had a lot of time off work?'

'No more than some other young teachers I've come across,' Hargreaves said evasively.

'Couldn't be that she'd been burnin' the candle at both ends, could it?' Woodend asked.

'She did do extra classes outside school, if that's what you mean,' Hargreaves said.

'It wasn't – but tell me about it anyway.'

'This school is very highly thought of in the area, and that means that the teachers who work here tend to be highly thought of, too. So when any organisation such as the technical college needs part-time lecturers in the evening, they contact us first, to see if any of our staff are willing to take on the work.'

'So Miss Beale was workin' at the tech?'

'No, I merely mentioned the technical college as an example. Miss Beale gave some classes at the Blackhill Air Force base.'

'I thought she was a history teacher,' Woodend said.

'She was.'

'So why would any of our lads, who we're relying on to bomb the hell out of the civilised world, need to know about Henry VIII an' his six wives?'

Hargreaves laughed, though it sounded as if he were unsure whether Woodend was joking or not. 'She wasn't teaching "our lads",' he said. 'She was giving a general cultural orientation course to some of the officers in the USAF who share the base with them.'

'I see,' Woodend said. 'An' how often did she give these cultural courses of hers?'

'Two or three nights of the week, I believe.'

'Now that *is* interestin',' Woodend said.

'What is?'

'From what you've told me, Miss Beale was missin' school because she kept gettin' ill, which, as the man who runs things, must have made life a bit difficult for you.'

'It's always a little awkward when a member of staff is

43

away,' the deputy head admitted. 'It means asking other teachers to take her place, and they work quite enough hours as it is.'

'An' if I remember rightly, you said the reason young teachers get ill is often because they're exhausted.'

'That's right.'

'So why didn't you take it on yourself to have a fatherly word with Miss Beale?' Woodend asked.

'I beg your pardon?'

'She was obviously findin' it a strain, which meant that she was also puttin' a strain on you an' your staff. Why didn't you have a word with her – suggest that she cut down on her outside commitments?'

Hargreaves looked a little uncomfortable. 'It's not very easy to tell other people how to run their lives.'

'Even if the way she ran hers was damagin' the efficiency of the school you're responsible for?'

The deputy head shrugged. 'I probably *would* have had a word with her if it had gone on for much longer,' he said, 'but I wanted to give her a chance to find her feet.'

'What about her social life?' Woodend asked. 'How did she get on with the rest of the staff?'

'You could ask them,' Hargreaves said.

'I will,' Woodend replied. 'But first, I'm askin' you.'

'This is a very traditional school,' Hargeaves told him. 'Quite a number of the teachers were pupils here themselves. Most of those went to single-sex Oxford or Cambridge colleges to earn their degrees, and then came straight back to King Edward's to teach.'

'Strange,' Woodend said.

'Not at all,' Hargreaves countered. 'They – and I myself am one of them – consider this a very special institution, a place where excellence is encouraged, a shining beacon which—'

'You're startin' to talk just like a school prospectus now,' Woodend interrupted.

The deputy head grinned abashedly. 'I suppose I am,' he agreed.

'Anyway, the main point you were makin' is that a lot of your staff don't like women,' Woodend continued.

'No, I wasn't saying that at all,' the deputy head protested. 'Most of them are married and have children of their own. All I meant was that they're not used to dealing with women within their working environment.'

'So how are they gettin' on with the girls from the base that you've taken in?'

Hargreaves smiled. 'It's not always easy for them. Some of the comments they've got used to making in front of a class of boys are, shall we say, inappropriate, now that there are a couple of girls in the room. But they're learning to adjust to the situation. This school has survived for so long mainly because it's learned to adjust to changing times.'

'Let's get back to Miss Beale,' Woodend suggested. 'You were sayin' that she wasn't very welcome in the staff room.'

'I was saying that some of the old boys here were slightly uncomfortable in her presence. But not all the staff, by any means. Some of them got on very well with her.'

'Could you give me an example?'

'Simon Barnes, one of her fellow historians. I believe they went to the same church, every Sunday.'

'Oh, she was a God-botherer, was she?' Woodend asked.

The deputy head gave Woodend a long, speculative look. 'I wonder how much of this crass, blunt Northern image you project is the real you, Mr Woodend,' he said.

Woodend smiled. 'More of it than you might think,' he replied.

Roger Cray sat in his office at the British Aircraft Industries' Blackhill plant, staring at the reports which lay on his desk in front of him. But though his eyes moved along the lines of words, and up and down the columns of figures, he was taking none of it in – and when his phone rang, he jumped like a startled rabbit.

With a slightly shaking hand, he picked up the receiver, and said, 'Yes, who is it?'

'It's me,' said a voice on the other end of the line.

'What the hell are you doing ringing now?' Cray demanded.

'I'm ringing now because it's when I *can* ring,' Martin Dove said. 'I'm not an executive like you, able to pick my own time. I was in the classroom until ten minutes ago – and I'll be back there in another ten.'

'Yes, of course. I'm sorry,' Cray mumbled.

'I was just calling to make sure we're still going ahead as planned,' Dove told him.

'Going ahead as planned!' Cray repeated. 'After last night!'

'Last night was unfortunate,' Dove conceded.

'It was more than that, it was—'

'But we've got things timed too tightly to let that upset us. If we don't do it now, there's no telling when we might get another chance.'

He was right, Cray thought, as he felt his hands start to sweat. Damn him, he was *right*!

'If we do go ahead with it, we're going to have to be careful,' he said.

'We were *always* going to have to be careful,' the caller replied. 'Let's make sure we've got the details straight, shall we?'

'All right.'

'I'll be standing by the statue of William Gladstone, halfway up the park, at exactly twenty minutes to one. I've deliberately taken to going there most lunchtimes, so if some of the other teachers notice me going, they won't think it's anything out of the ordinary. As for people in the park – in this weather, there shouldn't *be* any. But it's better to be safe than sorry, so you just walk past me without looking at me. Then, when you get to the top of the path, turn around as if you've walked far enough and decided to go back to your

Sapphire. If there's *still* nobody around, keep your hand by your side but waggle your fingers. That'll be the signal for us to meet in the bushes. Have you got that?'

'Of course I've got it! I'm not an idiot, and we've been through it half a dozen times.'

'It's very important you do it exactly as I've outlined it,' Dove said, as if Cray had never spoken. 'Very important – because later, when it's all over the papers, anybody who's seen us together might remember and start to put two and two together.'

'I know.'

'We can do this,' the caller said. 'We *have* to do it. We *need* to do it.'

'Yes,' Cray admitted dully. 'We *need* to.'

'I'm standing on the dockside of the American military base at Guantanamo Bay, Cuba,' said the voice of the reporter from the wireless in the police canteen. *'It is still night here on the other side of the ocean, and under the floodlights I can see groups of women and children, holding a few hastily packed belongings and waiting for the ship which will take them away from what could, potentially, become a very dangerous place indeed to be.'*

Bob Rutter lit up a Tareton cork-tipped cigarette, and looked around him. The normally noisy canteen had fallen silent, and all the officers there were staring up at the wireless as if that were, in itself, an aid to them hearing better.

'Simultaneous with the departure of these military dependants, the base is awaiting the arrival of three battalions of US Marine reinforcements,' the reporter continued. *'Out at sea, eight hundred miles from the island of Cuba, the American Fleet is preparing to establish what* it *says is a "quarantine line", but which the USSR claims is a military blockade and tantamount to an act of war. As Russian ships steam steadily on towards this quarantine line, the governments in Washington and Moscow hold their breaths – and in this,*

*they have much in common with their own people, and with
the peoples of the world. This is Paul Townshend, handing
you back to the studio.'*

'Why the bloody hell can't the Reds stay where they
belong?' demanded a middle-aged uniformed constable on
the next table to Rutter's. 'Because they're out to conquer the
whole bloody world, that's why,' he continued, answering his
own question.

'I don't see why the Russians can't have missiles on
Cuba if they want to,' his companion replied. 'After all,
the Americans have got missiles in Turkey, haven't they?'

'That's different,' the first constable said. 'The Yanks
haven't put them in Turkey just to protect themselves –
they've done it to protect us as well.'

'Protect us? The Russians haven't got any interest in little
England,' the second constable scoffed.

'That kind of remark shows just what an ignorant, unin-
formed bugger you really are,' his partner countered. 'Have
you ever heard of a feller called William Vassall?'

'No, I can't say I have,' the second constable admitted.

'I thought as much. Well, for your information Vassall
used to be a clerk at the Admiralty. An' I say *used to be,*
because yesterday he was sentenced to eighteen years behind
bars for spyin' for just them people that *you* claim don't have
any interest in little England. An' he's not the only one, not
by a long chalk. There's Reds in the trade unions, an' Reds
in the government. It wouldn't surprise me if there were Reds
in this very station – and pretty near the top, as well.' The
constable suddenly noticed who was sitting at the next table,
and began to look distinctly uncomfortable. 'No, I take that
back. That's probably goin' too far,' he added lamely.

Rutter stood up. 'If you're wondering if I overheard your
conversation, constable, then I have to tell you that I did,'
he said.

'I'm sorry, sir, I got a bit carried away,' the constable
mumbled.

'There's no need to be sorry for your views, because, unlike the Russians, you've got a perfect right to express them,' Rutter told him. 'If anyone should apologise, it's me – for eavesdropping on your conversation.'

Without waiting for a reply, he turned and walked towards the exit. The average bobbie in Whitebridge was not known for his interest in current events, he thought. But then they didn't see this particular crisis as something that was happening far away from themselves and their interests – they saw it as a possible lead-up to World War Three! With strategic military targets like the Blackhill aircraft factory and British-American air-force base only a few miles from Whitebridge, they were worried for the safety of their families.

And they had every right to be – he was bloody worried himself!

Eight

Verity Beale's naked body was stretched out on the table, with several of her vital organs lying in stainless-steel dishes beside it. Monika Paniatowski braced herself as she looked down at it, conscious that the uniformed constable in the corner – who was only there because the law required an officer to be present at every autopsy – was watching her closely.

In her early days on the force, Monika had felt it was unfair that she should come under such scrutiny; unfair that while her male colleagues were allowed to look a little queasy when observing a cadaver, she was not – because she was a woman, and even the slightest twitch on her face would be taken as proof positive that women should have nothing to do with murder investigations. Now she regarded such an attitude as merely one more in a long list of obstacles she would have to leap over in order to prove that she was not just a *good* detective – she was one of the *best*.

Doctor Pierson, a hacksaw in his hand, looked up from his work. 'Just you here, Monika?' he asked cheerfully. 'Isn't Cloggin'-it Charlie bothering with this one?'

'He's busy up at Eddie's,' Paniatowski replied. 'What can you tell me about the stiff?'

The doctor placed his bloody hacksaw on the table, and lit up a cigarette. 'Aged about twenty-six or twenty-seven,' he said. 'Very fit, very strong. Almost an athlete's physique.'

'She must have put up quite a struggle when she was being strangled,' Paniatowski said.

'She could have done if she'd been conscious – but she wasn't. There's a bump the size of a duck egg on the back of her head.'

'Any idea of what was used to hit her?'

'More than an idea. It was a brick. An Accrington red brick, I'd say, though that's really up to your forensic boys to establish for certain. We found traces of it embedded in her skull.'

A brick! Paniatowski thought in disgust. Not a Papuan headhunter's axe or stonemason's hammer, but a bloody brick!

And how many of them were there lying around in Lancashire, just waiting for murderers searching for a suitable blunt instrument? Millions!

'What else have you got?' she asked.

'She wasn't killed where she was found. From the bruising which occurred after death, I'd say she'd been driven there, probably sitting in an upright position. Now that's a grizzly thought, isn't it?'

Very grizzly. Paniatowski lit up one of her own cigarettes and inhaled deeply. 'Time of death?' she asked.

'Sometime between eleven last night and one o'clock this morning. She last had something to eat at around six o'clock. A cheese sandwich liberally smeared with sweet pickle.'

'Anything else in her stomach?'

'She'd been drinking shortly before she died.'

'To excess?'

'Depends what you'd call excessive, Monika. Three or four gin and tonics, which probably wouldn't have that much effect on somebody with her build and general fitness. What I can't really tell you is whether she had them *before* – or whether she had them *after*!'

'Before or after what?'

'Oh, didn't I mention that?' the doctor said, sounding surprised. 'She had sexual intercourse sometime during the course of the evening.'

At the mention of sex, Paniatowski noticed, the uniformed constable in the corner of the room ran his eyes quickly up and down her body, then sniggered to himself. She could easily imagine what he would tell his mates when he was back in the canteen.

'An' when the doc mentioned sex, Sergeant Panties shivered all over. You can tell she's cryin' out for it herself.'

'Is something the matter, Monika?' asked Pierson, who'd clearly missed the constable's reaction. 'You surely weren't expecting her to still be a virgin, were you? Not in this day and age? Not now there's the miracle birth-control pill so freely available?'

The constable sniggered again, no doubt refining the story he would recount later. Paniatowski decided to ignore him.

'No, I wasn't expecting her to be a virgin,' she told the doctor. 'Not particularly, anyway. What about the sex? She wasn't forced, was she?'

'Definitely not. It was consensual, and, I would say, it was also rather energetic.'

The smirk on the constable's face was widening by the second, and even when he saw that Paniatowski was looking straight at him, he made no attempt to hide it.

'Would you mind coming over here for a second or two, Constable?' Paniatowski asked.

'Me?'

'You're the only constable I can see in this room.'

The man stepped hesitantly forward, but stopped when he was still a fair distance from the table. He was perhaps a couple of years younger than Paniatowski, and his air of superiority – which he probably thought it was natural for a man to feel in the presence of a mere woman – was rapidly draining from his face.

'Yes, Sergeant?' he said.

'Is this the first autopsy you've attended?' Paniatowski asked.

'Well, yes,' the constable admitted.

'Then come a little closer,' Paniatowski said. 'I don't think you can see things clearly from where you're standing.'

The constable took another tentative step.

'Now, as you can observe, the doctor has sliced off the top of the skull, pretty much in the way you knock off the top of your boiled egg in the morning,' Paniatowski explained, in a dry, clinical voice. 'That funny piece of meat he's taken out is, in fact, the brain.' She pointed to a spot in the centre of it. 'If it was *your* brain – assuming you have one – then that's the place where all your dirty thoughts would be born.'

The constable's skin was turning a light shade of green.

'Now, according to regulations, what the doctor's *supposed* to do before he stitches her up again is to put the brain back in,' Paniatowski continued. 'But that's a bit of a fiddle, and the brain's not going to be much use to the dead woman now, is it? So as far as Doc Pierson's concerned, it's much easier just to use newspaper as padding instead. You normally use the *Manchester Guardian* for the job, don't you, Doctor?'

'That's right,' Pierson said, deadpan.

The constable's green colour had deepened.

'You'll . . . you'll have to excuse me,' he gasped.

Then he clamped his hand tightly over his mouth, and rushed in the direction of the toilets.

'It'll be a while before he fancies an egg for his breakfast again,' Paniatowski said.

The doctor shook his head in wonder. 'Wasn't that a bit unnecessary, Monika?' he asked.

'Perhaps it was,' Paniatowski conceded. 'But I find it helps to keep me sane if I can hit back at one of the sniggering bastards occasionally.'

The wall phone rang. Pierson picked it up, listened for a second, then handed the receiver over to Monika.

'That you, Sarge?' asked the voice at the other end.

'Yes.'

'About the car you were lookin' for? The victim's black Mini? We've found it.'

'Where?'

'On the car park of a country pub on the way to Sladebury. The Spinner, it's called. We're there now.'

'I'll be right over,' Paniatowski said.

Once he'd been connected to the switchboard at Woolwich Police Station, Bob Rutter identified himself and asked to be put through to the duty inspector. He was told – just as he'd expected to be – that the duty inspector would ring him back, and the call was indeed returned a couple of minutes later.

'So you really *are* a copper,' said the caller, who identified himself as DI Cyril Hoskins.

'You get a lot of crank calls being made down your way, do you?' Rutter asked.

'More than enough. I had a bloke ringing me up last week claiming to be the Pope.'

'Maybe he really was,' Rutter suggested, grinning.

'Nah,' Hoskins said dismissively. 'Not unless His Holiness has acquired a south London accent since the last time I heard him on the telly.' He paused. 'Do I detect a bit of a London twang in your dulcet tones?'

'Well spotted,' Rutter said.

'So what are you doing up there in darkest Lancashire, among all those Northern barbarians?'

'Trying my best to teach them a little civilisation,' Rutter said.

'And are you having much luck?'

'Not so as you'd notice.'

Hoskins chuckled. 'From the ones I've met, I'm not at all surprised. So what can I do for you, Bob – it is Bob, isn't it?'

'That's right, Cyril, it is,' Rutter agreed. 'The thing is, we've had a nasty little murder on our patch, and it seems that, until recently, the victim was living on your manor. I was wondering if you could cut through all the red tape and do us a bit of legwork.'

'We're always glad to oblige other forces whenever we can,' Hoskins said cheerfully. 'I'll put some of my boys on the job right away. What's the victim's name?'

'Verity Beale.'

'And what's the last address you have for her in Woolwich?'

'Ruskin Road.'

There was a sudden pause, as if the other man had remembered something which he *should* have recalled a lot earlier.

'Are you still there?' Rutter asked.

'Er . . . yes. Sorry,' Hoskins replied. 'You did say the victim's name was Beale, didn't you?'

'That's right. Verity Beale.'

'You're sure about that?'

'I've talked to several people who know her by that name, and it's what's on her driving licence.'

'Hang on for a minute.'

There was the sound of the phone being laid down, followed by the noise of several drawers being opened.

'Sorry about that,' Hoskins said, when he came back on to the line a couple of minutes later. 'Bit of a local emergency came up as we were talking, but it's been dealt with now. You say this woman's name is Verity Beale and she lived in Ruskin Road?'

How many more times does he want me to repeat it, Rutter wondered. But aloud, all he said was, 'Correct.'

'We'll look into it, like I said we would,' Hoskins told him. 'The only problem is, we're a bit short-handed at the moment, so I can't promise you we'll get on to it right away. Would the day after tomorrow do you?'

'We are investigating a murder here,' Rutter pointed out, 'and you know yourself that the more time that's allowed to lapse, the less chance there is of getting a result.'

'True,' Hoskins agreed reluctantly, 'but we are very

55

undermanned, you see. I could probably get you something tomorrow, which is still a lot quicker than if you went through the official channels. Will that do you?'

'It'll have to, won't it?' Rutter said, trying not to sound too ungracious – but without much success.

Nine

'I realise that the announcement of this tragic event must have come as a great shock to all of you here,' the deputy headmaster said.

He paused for a moment, and ran his index finger across his pencil-thin moustache.

'A great shock,' he repeated. 'But as callous as this might sound, I think we must all accept that, even in the face of it, normal life still has to go on.'

Positioned just behind Hargreaves's shoulder, Woodend scanned the faces of the audience the deputy head was addressing. All these teachers were strangers to him, and most of them would remain strangers, but there were a few, his instincts told him, whom he would have much more contact with before this case was over. He had already picked out two of them – men who, by their reactions to the news, stood out from the rest of the group.

One, a thin, gaunt-faced young man, seemed absolutely stricken. The other, slightly older and wearing heavy-framed glasses, had initially adopted the same look of surprise and disbelief as his colleagues, but soon he was glancing nervously down at his watch, as if he had a pressing appointment which was far more important than anything he might hear about the violent death of a woman he had worked with.

'In just over half an hour the bell will ring for the start of afternoon classes,' the deputy headmaster continued, 'and once it does, I must ask you to remind yourselves that you have been entrusted with the education of several hundred young minds, and that that must be your first duty and consideration. Are there any questions?'

One of the teachers raised his hand, almost as if he were back on the pupils' side of the classroom, and when Hargreaves nodded at him, he said, 'Is there anything we can do?'

'You will have noticed Mr Woodend standing just behind me,' the deputy head said. 'I have no doubt we will be seeing a great deal of him and his team over the next few days, and I would like you to co-operate fully with the police, while, at the same time, sticking as closely to your normal classroom routine as possible. Any more questions?' He waited for more hands, and when there were none, he said, 'In that case, I suggest you spend as normal a lunchtime as is possible under the circumstances.'

While he'd been addressing it, the staff had been a single entity, with its whole attention focused on the deputy head-master. Now that entity was shattered, as the teachers broke up into their familiar cliques.

But not all of them followed a herd instinct, Woodend noted. The teacher with the heavy glasses who had been consulting his watch made straight for the door. And the gaunt man who had seemed consumed with grief at the news of Verity Beale's death sat alone, his head in his hands.

Woodend made his way across to the gaunt man. 'I'm sorry to intrude, Mr . . . ?' he said.

'Barnes,' the man replied, looking up. 'Simon Barnes. Do you want to talk to me?'

'If you wouldn't mind.'

'Where should we . . . I mean, there must be somewhere quiet where we can . . .'

'I'm sure Mr Hargreaves would have no objection to us using his office,' Woodend said gently.

There were already half a dozen vehicles on the Spinner's car park when Monika Paniatowski arrived, but seeing two uniformed constables standing there, the owners had all, perhaps wisely, decided to leave their cars as far away from the black Mini as possible.

Paniatowski herself parked her MGA on the road, and walked over to the two uniformed officers.

'How many of these have arrived since you got here?' she asked, indicating the other cars with a backward-pointing thumb.

One of the constables shrugged. 'Two?' he said. 'Or it may have been three.'

Paniatowski sighed. 'No more,' she said.

'Pardon, Sarge?'

'I don't want any more cars parking here until either we've established that this is a wild goose, or the lab boys have been over the entire area.'

'That won't be popular,' the constable said.

'I don't really give a bugger whether it's popular or not,' Paniatowski told him.

She walked around the front of the Mini. Between the end of the car park and the road was a flower border, which was edged with red bricks partly buried in the soil. She was not the least surprised to see that one of the bricks was missing. This was where it happened, she told herself. If it wasn't the place where Verity Beale had been murdered, it was certainly where she had been knocked unconscious.

She turned back to the constables. 'Another thing,' she said. 'To minimise contamination of the scene, I want a clear path – about a yard wide – marked out from the road to the pub door. And I want you to make sure that anybody who comes to the pub sticks to it.'

'How do we mark it out?' one of the constables asked.

'You could use chalk,' Paniatowski suggested.

'But we haven't got any chalk, Sarge. It's not somethin' we normally carry with us.'

Paniatowski sighed again. 'This is a pub. Right?'

'Right.'

59

'And pubs have dartboards. And when you play darts, you need to mark the score up. And what you mark it up with is chalk. So the chances are, the barman will have all the chalk you need.'

'I never thought of that,' the constable admitted.

'You amaze me,' Paniatowski said. 'If anybody comes looking for me, I'll be in the bar, talking to the landlord.'

She turned and headed for the pub door. The two constables followed her progress with their eyes.

'Nice arse,' the first one said.

'Nice legs, too,' the second agreed. 'But what a ball-buster that woman really is.'

'Aye, she is. That's probably why she's a sergeant an' we're still constables,' his partner said.

Though they were sitting close to each other in the deputy head's cramped office, the gaunt teacher seemed hardly aware of the big policeman's presence.

'Was Miss Beale what you might call your girlfriend, Mr Barnes?' Woodend asked softly.

The other man looked up. 'What?'

'I asked you if Miss Beale was your girlfriend.'

Barnes shook his head emphatically. 'No. No. She was nothing like that to me.'

'Then what *was* she to you?'

'She was . . . an ordinary friend. I don't mean that she was ordinary in herself. In fact, she was very special. What I mean is that—'

'I know what you mean,' Woodend told him. 'You met her in this school, did you?'

'That's right. We both teach . . . we both *taught* . . . history. But that's not what really brought us together.'

'Go on,' Woodend said encouragingly.

'I'm a member of the local Baptist church. I don't know what impression you've got of the Baptists – people often

60

do have very odd ideas about us – but the church is a very welcoming place, open to the rich and the poor alike. People travel for miles to worship there. We even have some Americans from the air-force base who—'

'If you don't mind me sayin' so, I think that you're gettin' a bit off the point, sir.'

Barnes nodded. 'Quite right,' he agreed. 'I'm always telling the boys to stick to the subject, and there I go myself, off at a complete tangent.'

'It's not always easy to think clearly when you're upset,' Woodend said. 'You were tellin' me about you an' Miss Beale.'

'It must have been the first week of term she came up to me and asked me about the church. She said she hadn't thought much about religion since well before she went to university, but she was starting to feel an aching void in her life, and she felt that God might fill it for her. Then she asked if she could come to church with me the following Sunday.'

'How did she know you attended the church?'

'She must have overheard colleagues talking about it.'

'An' why would they have done that?'

'I beg your pardon?'

'Other people's religion isn't usually a topic for conversation.'

'Mine is. For some of my colleagues, my faith serves as little more than fodder for their humour.'

'Aye, there are always a few ignorant buggers around, wherever you go,' Woodend said. 'Was Miss Beale already a Baptist?'

'No, she'd been brought up in the Church of England, but she'd found it hadn't given her what she needed.'

'Did she find what she needed in the church?'

'She'd only been attending for a few weeks, so it's difficult to say for certain what effect it was having, but she was starting to get to know some of congregation, and given time . . .'

'Did you see much of her aside from at church?'

'We'd go for a coffee afterwards. Sometimes a group of us would go somewhere for lunch.'

'But on other days? Outside school?'

'She didn't really have the time. She was working very hard. Giving classes in other institutions.'

'Aye, I've heard about that,' Woodend said. 'Why was that? Short of money, was she?'

'I don't think she was doing it for the money. She loved to teach. She loved to impart her knowledge to others.'

'Sounds like she's a great loss,' Woodend said.

'That's exactly what she is,' Barnes agreed sadly. 'A *great* loss.'

The landlord of the Spinner examined Paniatowski suspiciously. 'You don't look like a bobby to me,' he said.

Paniatowski gave him what was a pretty fair impersonation of a good-natured grin.

'I know I don't,' she said. 'For a start, my little feet would be lost in size-ten boots. But I'm the Law, all right. I can show you my warrant card if you like?'

The landlord reluctantly returned the grin. 'No, I don't think that will be necessary.'

'Tell me about the Mini,' Paniatowski said.

'People quite often leave their cars here overnight,' the landlord told her. 'They realise they've had a bit too much to drink, you see, an' they cadge a lift off one of their mates. But normally when that happens, they ring me up first thing in the mornin', to tell me they've left it an' ask if it'll be an inconvenience if it stays here until they've got time to pick it up. I was expectin' the same thing to happen with the Mini, but when it got to eleven, an' there was still no call, I thought I'd best ring the station.'

'In case it was stolen?'

'That's right,' the landlord agreed. 'I didn't *really* think it was, because the woman who drove it here looked very respectable. But it's always better to be safe than sorry, isn't it?'

'You're sure it was a *woman* who drove it here?'

'Absolutely positive. I'd just taken a couple of empty beer crates to the storeroom across the yard, an' when I was makin' my way back to the pub, she was just pullin' in.'

'And you remember when all your customers arrive, do you?' Paniatowski asked sceptically.

'No, but the reason I remember her is because she has this long red hair. Flamin' red, it is.'

'Was she alone?'

'There was nobody else in the car with her, if that's what you mean. But she'd arranged to meet somebody.'

'How do you know that?'

'A few minutes later, after she'd gone into the best room an' I was back behind the bar, a big American car arrived. The moment she saw it pull up, she ordered a drink for the driver. Bourbon was what she asked for. We don't get much call for that kind of thing round here.'

'An American car and a glass of bourbon,' Paniatowski mused. 'Do you think the man was an American?'

'I'm sure he was. He was wearin' a sports jacket like I've never seen in the shops round here. You know the kind I mean – really flashy. An' he had an accent which came straight out of *Gone with the Wind*.'

'What did he look like?'

'Tall, skinny, short hair. He wasn't in uniform, but I'd guess from the way he carried himself that he was from the base.'

'How long were the two of them here?'

'They arrived at about a quarter to ten, I'd guess. The Yank left about an hour later.'

'But not the woman?'

'No. She was here until at least half-past—' The landlord came to abrupt halt. 'What I mean to say is—'

'It wouldn't come as any startling revelation to me if I

learned you'd been serving after time,' Paniatowski said. 'Most country pubs do. Well, they've got no choice, have they? They'd never make a living if they didn't.'

The landlord nodded gratefully. 'That's true enough,' he admitted. 'What with all the taxes the government puts on drinks, and havin' to pay the bar staff a small fortune to keep them—'

'So what time *did* she leave?' Paniatowski interrupted.

'As I was sayin', it must have been at gone half-past eleven. I let her out myself.'

'How many other customers were there in the pub at that time?' Paniatowski asked.

The landlord shrugged. 'Well, you know.'

'I told you, I'm not the least bit interested in doing you for serving drinks after time.'

'There must have been around a dozen customers,' the landlord admitted. 'Most of them were regulars.'

'But the pub had been fuller when she arrived?'

'That's right. We'd had a busy evenin'.'

'How did the redheaded woman and her American friend seem to be getting along?'

An awkward expression came to the landlord's face. 'I . . . er . . . can't say I really noticed.'

Paniatowski grinned again. 'Pull the other leg – it's got bells on.'

'Pardon?'

'You noticed the two cars arrive. You noticed the way the Yank was dressed. You can remember roughly what time the man left. You're a nosy bugger, Mr Yarwood—'

'I—'

'—and there's absolutely no need to be ashamed of it, because that's part of your job, just as it's part of mine.'

'Yes, I suppose we are both paid to be nosy.'

'So how *were* they getting on?'

'The Yank was tryin' to act normal, but he kept lookin' a bit like I do when I've forgotten my weddin' anniversary again.'

'Guilty-looking?'

'Enough to leave a jury in no doubt.'

'And what about the woman?'

'If *he* looked like me, then *she* looked like my missus.'

'How do you mean?'

'Hurt – an' bloody determined that she wasn't goin' to be the only one to suffer.'

'Did the redhead talk to anybody else?'

'She did, as a matter of that.'

'Who?'

'There were these two fellers sittin' in the corner. One of them was wearin' a green corduroy jacket, I remember, an' the other had on a pair of glasses with very heavy frames. She went across an' had a quick word with them.'

'So you think she knew them?'

'I'm sure of it.'

'Why?'

'Because they all looked very uncomfortable – as if they'd much rather not have run into one another.'

'Is there anything else you could tell me about these two men?' Paniatowski asked.

'As a matter of fact, there is,' the landlord told her. 'I don't know what the man in the heavy glasses was drivin', but the one in the green corduroy jacket had an Armstrong Siddeley Sapphire – an' you don't see many of them in Lancashire, do you?'

'No,' Paniatowski said thoughtfully. 'No, you don't.'

Ten

The other kids seemed to be totally unaware that anything was wrong, Helen Dunn thought. But then, why *would* they be aware? They had their friends to distract them during the lunch break. So only she – the outsider, the one with so little else to occupy her mind – had noticed that the teachers were not their normal selves. That when they crossed the playground, they kept looking over their shoulders as if expecting an ambush. That when they spoke to each other, it was in the hushed whispers of conspirators. Yes, something had definitely happened – something dramatic – but she had no idea what it could be.

She walked to the edge of the playground. The Corporation Park lay just the other side of the street, and by raising her hands to the sides of her head, she could restrict her range of vision to the nearest clump of trees and imagine that she was in the country.

She loved the countryside, though she had had very little personal experience of it. When she'd been growing up, in a succession of camps with military – soulless – playing fields, she had devoured storybooks about children living on farms. As she'd heard the planes take off overhead, she had been listening, in her mind, to the hoot of the owls in places called Foggy Bottom and Scary Hollow. As the military bus had conveyed her to the military school, she had pretended it was a rattling old *country* bus, which only managed to struggle through another day because all the children were so fond of it. Now she lived near the *real* countryside, but she never saw it because her father was far too busy to ever give her the gift of his time.

Though there was no wind to speak of, she saw one of the bushes on the edge of the park move, and knew that someone was watching her. She was not afraid – her father had taught her that fear, like all other forms of human weakness, was to be despised. But she was curious.

Who was hiding? And *why* was he hiding – because she was sure it *was* a he. Was he watching her because she was Helen Dunn, the squadron leader's daughter, or simply because she was the only girl standing at the very edge of the playground?

She turned around to see if the teacher on yard duty was close by, but there was no sign of him. And it suddenly seemed to her as if fate was – finally! – pointing her towards an adventure. She glanced over her shoulder once more, then stepped quickly through the gate and out on to the street.

Woodend, Rutter and Paniatowski were sitting at a corner table in the crowded lunchtime public bar of the Wheatsheaf, a pub which owed its popularity more to its proximity to the police station than it did to its thin beer and cardboard-tasting Cornish pasties.

'I know it's early days yet, but I still wish I'd already started to build up a clearer picture of the victim,' Woodend said. 'What was she? A saint, or a sinner? From what Bob's said, her landlady seems to regard her as little better than a prostitute, though, to be fair, Mrs Hoddleston doesn't sound like the most open-minded of women.'

'Maybe not, but Verity Beale had had sex a couple of hours before she died,' Bob Rutter pointed out.

Monika Paniatowski's eyes flashed with anger. 'And that means she was a loose woman, does it, sir?'

'No, but it doesn't exactly qualify her for the title of Miss Purity 1962, either,' Rutter countered, stung.

'Simon Barnes sees her as a woman in search of religion

– an' as a born teacher who loved passin' her knowledge on to other people,' Woodend continued. 'Then there's the headmaster an' his deputy. What did you make of the pair of them, Monika?'

'I got the distinct impression, when we were talking to the headmaster , that there were things about Verity Beale he would much rather we didn't find out,' Paniatowski said.

'So did I,' Woodend agreed. 'Now why should that be?'

'The headmaster's main job is to protect the reputation of the school,' Bob Rutter said, rather primly. 'Grammar schools always place great store on their reputation.'

'Aye, well you'd know more about that than I would,' Woodend said. 'But what exactly do they want to protect their precious reputation *from*?' He paused to light up a Capstan Full Strength. 'Tell me about your phone call to London again, Bob.'

'The inspector I talked to seemed very willing to help us at first, then he suddenly clammed up on me.'

'Do you think that's because you somehow managed to rub him up the wrong way?'

'No. Far from it. I played it perfectly – all joviality and brother-officer, making sure we were soon on first name terms. But despite that, I obviously said something which put him on his guard.'

'Like mentionin' Verity Beale?' Woodend suggested.

'Yes, I think it had to be that. Don't you?'

Woodend took a thoughtful sip of his pint. 'We're not missin' somethin' here, are we?' he asked. 'There hasn't been some big scandal involvin' our Miss Beale which has somehow managed to slip by us?'

'None that I can think of, but I could get one of my lads to check through the back copies of the newspapers,' Rutter said.

'Aye, you do that,' Woodend agreed. 'An' check on the Armstrong Siddeley, as well. The one Mrs Hoddleston saw bringin' Miss Beale home more than once, an' which, coincidentally, was parked on the car park of the Spinner last night.'

'They could have been two completely different cars, sir,' Bob Rutter pointed out.

'They could have been,' Woodend agreed. 'But it's not really very likely, is it?'

'True,' Rutter agreed. 'So what will you be doing this afternoon, sir?'

'Oh, I thought me an' Sergeant Paniatowski might have a bash at trackin' down this Yank Verity Beale chose to spend her last night on earth with,' Woodend said.

Margaret Dunn shared both her daughter's skinniness and her slightly haunted look, the deputy head thought as he glanced at the woman who was sitting across the desk from him.

'We've only been looking for Helen for a few minutes,' he said reassuringly. 'She's bound to turn up soon.'

'She's not here,' Margaret Dunn said, biting her lower lip.

She was doing her best to contain her panic, but she was still not making a very good job of it, Hargreaves thought. If they didn't produce Helen soon, the woman would probably go into hysterics.

'If she'd tried to leave the school, the teacher on yard duty would have seen her,' he said.

But would he really? he wondered. Most of the staff had been walking round shell-shocked ever since he'd told them that Verity Beale had been murdered, and it wouldn't really have surprised him if half the school had nicked off without anybody noticing.

'She knew she had a dental appointment booked,' Margaret Dunn said. 'She knew I was going to pick her up to take her there. We've done it before. She's always waiting for me by the main gate.'

'Children sometimes forget things like that,' Hargreaves said.

But from what he'd seen of Helen Dunn it didn't seem likely, even to him, that she'd be the forgetful type. In fact, apart from that one incident in Woolworths – an incident which, at Verity Beale's insistence, her parents still hadn't been told about – Helen was a conscientious child, almost to the point of being a bit too much of a goody-goody.

There was a knock on the door, and the duty teacher entered the room. Hargreaves looked up at him expectantly, but the teacher shook his head.

'We checked everywhere,' he said. 'The playground, the classrooms, even the parts of the school which are out of bounds to the children. There's no sign of her anywhere.'

'What about the street?' Hargreaves asked. 'Have you thought to look there?'

The duty teacher nodded. 'I've had the prefects check the full length of Park Road. They've gone into the shops. Nobody's seen a girl in a King Edward's uniform.'

Margaret Dunn's sallow face turned even paler than the deputy head would ever have thought possible.

'Can we get you something, Mrs Dunn?' he asked solicitously. 'A glass of water, perhaps?'

But it was doubtful if Margaret Dunn had heard him. Her skinny hands were entwined and she seemed to be shrinking into herself.

'Oh my God!' she moaned. 'Whatever will he say? Whatever will the squadron leader *say*?'

Eleven

The duty sergeant handed the message to Woodend as soon as he returned from lunch. It was short and to the point. Deputy Chief Constable Ainsworth and Detective Chief Superintendent Whittle would like to see him in Ainsworth's office as soon as possible – if not sooner.

As Woodend walked along the corridor he found himself wondering exactly what it was that Tweedledum and Tweedledee wanted to see him about this time. If it was a progress report they were after, then they were out of luck – because there had been no progress yet.

He knocked and was told to enter. Both Whittle and Ainsworth were sitting behind the DCC's desk. They looked grim. But more than that, they looked as if they thought they were about to have a fight on their hands.

It was Ainsworth the ventriloquist – rather than Whittle his dummy – who opened the conversation.

'I know you don't like being taken off a case once you've got your teeth into it, Charlie,' he said.

'Bloody right I don't,' Woodend agreed.

'But there are sometimes circumstances which mean—'

'What's the problem here?' Woodend demanded. 'Had a call from the school, have you?'

'As a matter of fact, we have,' Whittle said.

'An' I can just guess who it was from,' Woodend said. 'That bloody headmaster! I could see from the start that I wasn't the kind of feller he'd want on the case. If you don't

71

talk like you've got a plum in your mouth an' walk as if you've a poker stuck up your backside—'

'You're pushing it, Chief Inspector, even by your outlandish standards,' Ainsworth said angrily.

'Maybe I am, but I don't like bein' buggered about just because some toffee-nosed bastard—'

'You're pushing it, and if I didn't need you so badly, I'd have you suspended immediately for insubordination.'

The words – and their implication – hit Woodend like a bucket of icy water. Ainsworth needed him badly – but not for the murder investigation.

'What's happened?' he asked.

'It seems that one of the pupils from King Edward's – a girl of thirteen called Helen Dunn – has gone missing,' Ainsworth said.

Almost without wanting to, Woodend found himself thinking of Ellie Taylor, who used to live on Lant Street in Southwark, and of her grandfather, George, who'd lost a leg fighting to maintain Queen Victoria's Empire.

'You will get Ellie back for us, won't you, Sergeant?' the old man had pleaded.

'Did you hear what I said, Chief Inspector?' Ainsworth asked.

'Aye, I heard,' Woodend said dully. 'How long has this girl been missin'?'

'Not much more than an hour, but her teachers are certain she'd never have gone off of her own free will.'

'She should have been back over an hour ago,' old George Taylor had said. *'I know it doesn't sound long, but she's a very reliable girl, an' if she was goin' to be late, she'd have let us know.'*

'Don't worry, we'll find her,' young Sergeant Woodend had promised.

'You can imagine how the press will handle this, can't you?' Ainsworth said. 'Verity Beale's murder could have been a big story, but now it won't rate more than a few inside columns. It'll be Helen Dunn's disappearance which fills the front page.'

'You're right enough about that,' Woodend agreed.

Ainsworth opened his mouth to speak again, but the words seemed to stick in his gullet, and he nodded to indicate to Whittle that he should say them instead.

'The reporters will expect you to be in charge of the inquiry,' the Chief Superintendent said. 'In fact, they'll scream blue murder if you're not, because, for some inexplicable reason, they seem to think the sun shines out of your arse.'

'Are we making ourselves clear, Chief Inspector?' Ainsworth asked. 'We want you on this case. No "buts"! No "couldn't we insteads . . . ?" You're in charge, and that's a direct order.'

'If you'd told me that as soon as I walked into the room, I could have been gettin' my team together by now,' Woodend said.

'You mean, you've no objection?' Whittle asked amazed, then, realising they'd got what they wanted without the fight they'd anticipated, he clamped his mouth tightly shut.

'Of course I've no bloody objection,' Woodend said. 'Whatever we do now, Verity Beale will stay dead, but there's still a chance we can save this kiddie.'

It was only as he reached the door that he realised there was another question he should have asked. 'Who'll be takin' over the Verity Beale investigation?' he said Ainsworth.

'We thought of using one of our own people, but in the end we decided it might be better to call in your old firm – the Yard,' the Deputy Chief Constable replied. 'You've no objection that you that, have you?'

'No, I haven't,' Woodend said, surprised to hear himself agreeing with Ainsworth for once. 'He'll need briefin', of course.'

'Yes, he will,' the DCC agreed. 'Would you be willing to lend him Sergeant Paniatowski?'

'I'd rather have Monika—' Woodend began. Then he

73

pulled himself up short. 'Aye, I could use her myself, but she'll be of more value to him,' he continued. 'But can I keep DI Rutter?'

'Yes, you can keep Rutter. And you can have the pick of anybody else you think you might be able to use. If you need to poach men from some superintendent's task force, then poach them. And don't worry about the paperwork – just take the men you need and refer the commander who you'll have pissed off directly to me.'

'Thank you, sir,' Woodend said, not only sounding humble, but actually feeling it.

'Overtime, too,' Ainsworth said. 'Authorise as much of it as you need to, because when we eventually do find this child's bo— . . . when we eventually do find this *child*, I want it to be obvious to everybody – especially the press and the Police Committee – that we've done everything we could.'

It had never been going to be easy, doing what they had to do in the park, Martin Dove thought, but it wouldn't have been as bad as it turned out if Cray hadn't been such a bag of nerves. Still, at least now the first phase was over with, and he was back in his classroom, looking as innocent as only a Latin teacher in early middle age could.

His own nerves felt a little frayed, he was forced to admit, and he was glad that instead of having to face thirty rowdy second-year pupils he would be spending the next hour with a smaller group of serious-looking sixth formers.

'Well, gentlemen, I hope that you have all done your prep and are now armed with enough quotes from Virgil to con your examiners into believing that you really understand what he was on about,' he said.

The remark was greeted with sufficient polite laughter to tell Dove that, whatever he felt inside, he at least sounded like his normal self.

'Let's start with you, Mr Cummings,' Dove said, pointing

to a youth in the front row. 'What have you got to impress us with?'

The boy closed his eyes. '*Dixit et avertens rosea cervice refulsit,*' he intoned. '*Ambrosiaeque comae divinum vertice odorem spiravere; pedes vestis defluxit as imos, et vera incessu patuit dea.*'

The snotty little bastard would choose a quote like that, Dove thought visciously.

'Very good, Mr Cummings,' he said. 'Beautifully pronounced. But do you actually know what it means?'

'She said no more and as she turned away there was a bright glimpse of the rosy glow of her neck,' Cummings translated, 'and from her ambrosial head of hair a heavenly fragrance wafted; her dress flowed down to her feet, and in her walk it showed, she was in truth a goddess.'

He could have been talking about Verity Beale apart from that last bit, Dove thought. But Verity had been no goddess. Far from it. A goddess would not have concerned herself with the doings of mere mortals like him. A goddess would not have been in the Spinner, as Verity had been the night before.

'Mr Parkinson, entertain us with your quotation,' Dove said.

'*Malo me Galatea petit, lasciva puella, et fugit ad salices et se cupit ante videri.*'

'Translation?'

'Galatea throws an apple at me, cheeky girl—'

'Cheeky girl!' Dove interrupted. 'Look at the context, boy. Whatever she's trying to be, it's certainly not cheeky.'

'Sexy girl?' Parkinson asked.

'Sexy girl,' Dove agreed.

'Galatea throws an apple at me, sexy girl, and runs away into the willows and wants to have been spotted.'

'And there you have it, gentlemen, an adage as true today as it was when it was written two thousand years ago,' Dove said. 'She might run away – but she always wants to be

75

caught. I think we'll have one more. How about you, Mr Bentley?'

'*Facilis descensus Averno: Noctes atque dies patet atri ianua Ditis*,' Bentley said. '*Sed revocare gradum superasque evadere ad auras, Hoc opus, hic labor est.*'

'Easy is the way down to the Underworld: by night and by day dark Dis's door stands open; but to withdraw one's steps and make a way out to the upper air, that's the task, that is the labour,' Dove translated rapidly in his head – and found that he had started to shake uncontrollably.

The incident room was one of the largest rooms in the entire station, but there were so many officers crammed into it that they were forced to stand shoulder to shoulder.

Woodend ran his eyes over the team. Some were from his own station. Others had been drafted in from neighbouring divisions. A few were special constables, normally only called in to help with crowd control at football matches and carnivals. There were about sixty of them altogether, he calculated.

When Ellie Taylor had disappeared, there'd only been three – himself and two constables – involved in the search.

'*And even that's probably a waste of three good men,*' Chief Inspector Brookes had said at the time.

'*But she's been missin' for two hours, sir,*' Woodend had protested. '*There's still a good chance—*'

'*Either she's nipped off for a spot of nookie with her boyfriend – in which case she'll turn up later with an excuse so thin you couldn't wrap fish in it,*' Brookes had interrupted, '*or she's been snatched by some nutter – in which case she'll be dead by now and there's not much more we can do till the corpse turns up.*'

Woodend cleared his throat. 'As you all know, a little lass has gone missin',' he said. 'Now there may be a perfectly innocent explanation for it, but it's our job to assume the worst.'

Every officer in the room nodded gravely.

'Time is our biggest enemy,' Woodend continued, 'so I'm expectin' a big initial push from you people. I want everybody who was within half a mile of the school at the time Helen disappeared questioned. I want every man in the Whitebridge area with a history of sex offences pulled in, an' given a grillin' like he's never been given before.' He paused for a second. 'Some of you have worked with me before, and know I'm very particular about suspects bein' treated strictly by the book. Isn't that right?'

Several of the officers mumbled that yes, that was right.

'Well, you can forget all about the book on this case,' Woodend continued. 'If any of the perverts you're questionin' happens to end up with a few bruises, you'll find me quite willin' to believe that they're self-inflicted wounds – an' to swear to it under oath if that's what's necessary.'

Nobody smiled, nobody who knew him saw it as typically gruff Woodend humour. They all knew that – just this once – he was being deadly serious.

'There'll be appeals for information on the wireless, the television an' in the newspapers,' Woodend told them. 'If this case runs to form, then we should get hundreds of calls jamming the switchboard. A lot of them will be from cranks with nothin' better to do with their time, but we'll treat each an' every one as if it was *the* one that we've been waitin' for.'

He lit a Capstan Full Strength. When he inhaled, he discovered that instead of the comforting harshness he was used to, it tasted like dried cow dung.

'Give up any idea you might have of gettin' any sleep, or of seein' your families an' friends, until this is all over,' he said. 'We'll be workin' round the clock. Are there any questions before Inspector Rutter hands out the assignments?'

No one said anything. What questions could there be? What – at this stage – could any of them possibly want to ask?

Woodend waited for a second, then strode rapidly to the

door. He was thankful that the men's toilets were just two doors down from the incident room, because if they'd been any further he wasn't sure he'd have made it. He entered the nearest cubicle, pulled the door closed behind him, and bent over the bowl.

Gazing down into the water, he had a terrifyingly clear vision of how Ellie Taylor had looked when they pulled her out of the Thames, then his stomach exploded and the vision was broken up by a flood of vomit.

Twelve

'Don't take this in any way personally, ma'am,' said Major Dole, 'but I'm just a tad surprised that your captain has assigned a case of this importance to a mere detective sergeant.'

And a *female* detective sergeant, to boot, Paniatowski thought. That's what's going through your mind, isn't it, Major Dole? A *female* detective sergeant! I can see it written in your eyes.

'Chief Superintendent,' she said.

'I beg your pardon?'

'We don't have captains over here in England, Major Dole. We have chief superintendents instead. And I'm not in charge of the case. I'm only doing a little of the spadework while I'm waiting for the man who's really in charge to arrive from London.'

The major nodded, as if now he was finally getting the picture. He was around thirty-five years old, Paniatowski guessed, with broad shoulders and grey eyes which, in other circumstances, she might have found rather attractive. They were sitting in his office, in the centre of the American section of the air-force base. A number of framed certificates and commendations hung on one wall, a couple of large-scale maps of different parts of Europe were pinned to another. For the second time since she'd sat down, she heard the fearsome roar of a jet plane taking off overhead.

'So how can we help you with your "spadework", Sergeant?' Major Dole asked.

79

'One of your men was out drinking with Verity Beale shortly before she met her death and—'

The major held up his hand to silence her. 'Hold it right there, ma'am,' he told her. 'You can't say with any certainty that it was one of our men who was out with her, now can you?'

'He was driving a big American car—'

'What make?'

'The landlord of the pub's not sure about that.'

'Then it might not have been an *American* car at all?'

'We don't make large cars in England, as you may have noticed. Besides, he had an American accent and—'

'There's no such thing as an American accent, any more than there's such a thing as a British accent.'

'I appreciate that, but—'

'Was he from the South? The East Coast? The Midwest? California, maybe? Or does the landlord know as little about accents as he seems to know about automobiles?'

'He couldn't pin it down that clearly, but he was absolutely sure that it was an American—'

'The man could just have easily have been a Canadian.'

'This is Lancashire, Major Dole,' Paniatowski said wearily. 'We don't get a lot of foreign visitors here. Why would a Canadian come to Whitebridge?'

'Why would anybody from *anywhere* come to Whitebridge?' Dole asked, smiling.

He wasn't making a joke, Paniatowski thought. Or if he was, it was a joke with a purpose – aimed at distracting her, either through amusement or injured local pride, from the matter in hand. Well, stuff him!

'Miss Beale gave classes here,' she said. 'So who is it more likely she was out with? A Canadian who'd come to Whitebridge to prospect for gold? Or an airman she met when she was giving her lessons?'

'Let's assume that he is one of my boys,' the major said, in a careful, measured tone. 'Where does that take us?'

'I'd like to question him.'

The major frowned. 'I'm not entirely certain what the legal and diplomatic position is in this particular situation,' he confessed.

'A very serious crime's been committed and—'

'True, it has,' Dole agreed. 'But this base is as much American territory as downtown Omaha, and the men serving on it come under the jurisdiction of the United States military authorities, not the British civil one.'

'You're saying that I can't question him?'

'I'm saying that until the position's been clarified to my complete satisfaction, I'm not convinced that I have the authority to allow you to interrogate anybody on this post.'

'That's outrageous!' Paniatowski protested.

'Wiser heads than ours have laid down the procedures,' the major said seriously. 'All we can do is to follow them.'

'Couldn't we at least narrow the list of suspects down a bit?' Paniatowski asked.

'I'm not quite clear what you mean by that,' the major told her. 'And I'm not certain I'm happy with the word "suspect" being applied to any of the men serving on this post.'

Paniatowski took a deep breath, and wondered how Woodend would have handled a situation of this kind. No, thinking like that wouldn't help at all, she decided. She already *knew* how Woodend would react, and she had neither his rank nor his physical presence to carry off that kind of eruption. Better, far better, to pretend she was the smooth-talking Detective Inspector Rutter.

'I didn't mean to suggest that any of your men was more of a suspect than anyone else in the county,' she said. 'But it would still help if we knew at least the name of the man who was with Miss Beale just before she died. And it shouldn't be too difficult to find out, should it? I don't imagine there are that many men here who drive big imported cars and were also off the base last night.'

Major Dole sighed. 'I don't know if you've been watching

the news, Sergeant,' he said, 'but if you have been, you'll know that the international situation is very tense at the moment.'

'So what?'

'So this base is not just here for decoration. We're a vital wing of the American military strike force – and Nato's as well,' the major added, almost as an afterthought. 'Ever since this crisis started to develop, we've been on a high level of alert, and while we hope it will never happen, we might be called into action at any moment. Given that, you can't really expect me to devote much of my time to investigating what is, after all, a purely local matter. I've seen you, I've explained the situation as I see it, and that should be good enough for you.'

And suddenly, Paniatowski thought she understood what was going on.

'You're worried he might turn out to be important, aren't you!' she demanded, forgetting she was pretending to be Rutter and slipping into full Woodend overdrive.

The major frowned again. 'I'm sorry?'

'You're worried that he might be one of your leading pilots, and that when you need him to drop a couple of bombs on Russia he won't be available – because he'll be in the Whitebridge nick, answering questions about the murder of Verity Beale.'

'That's the most outlandish statement that I've ever heard,' the major said coldly.

'If that's true, then all I can say is that you must have led a very sheltered life,' Paniatowski countered.

The major stood up. 'This meeting is at an end, Sergeant Paniatowski,' he said.

'Yes, I rather thought it might be,' Paniatowski replied.

Thirteen

T he Dunns' house was located a couple of streets up from the one in which Verity Beale had lodged, and had the same air of Edwardian respectability about it. As Woodend walked up the path he found himself wondering whether Helen Dunn, who had probably spent much of her life on military bases, had begun to regard the place as her home yet.

It was the squadron leader himself who answered the knock on the door. The man was in his middle-to-late thirties, Woodend estimated. He was not very tall, but he was exceptionally broad, and even though his uniform had a tailored look about it, it was still possible to detect his muscles bulging under the sleeves. An ex-rugby player, the chief inspector decided – and one who had not allowed his body to go to seed once he had given up the game.

Dunn's pale blue eyes were both emotionless and analytical, and as he ran them up and down his visitor's body, they seemed to miss nothing.

'Yes?' the squadron leader said.

'Chief Inspector Woodend, sir.'

'Are you the man in charge of the search for my daughter?'

'Yes, I am.'

'Then why the hell aren't you back at your headquarters, directing the operation?'

'The wheels have been set in motion, sir,' Woodend said. 'Everything that can be done, is being done. My not being there for an hour or so isn't goin' to make any difference one way or the other.'

83

Dunn nodded. 'You're quite right, of course,' he admitted. 'Any system that depends entirely on the presence of one man can't have been much of a system in the first place.' He ran his hand over his forehead. 'Look, I'm sorry if I seemed abrupt but I've been—'

'That's quite all right, sir,' Woodend said. 'Would you mind if I came in for a few minutes?'

'Come in?' Dunn repeated, as if he were finding it difficult to follow a normal conversation. 'I . . . yes . . . please follow me.'

He led Woodend down the hallway and into the lounge. The first word which struck Woodend as he entered the room was 'precision'. The sofa did not touch the wall, but was exactly parallel to it. The two chairs which accompanied the sofa were set at a precise ninety degrees to it, and faced each other perfectly. The pictures of vintage military aircraft on the walls hung as straight as if they were in a fastidious art gallery. There was not the slightest hint of a kink in the fireside rug. Even the ornaments on the mantelpiece and in the display cabinet seemed to have been set out according to some master plan.

It was more like a museum than a lounge, Woodend thought, except that in a museum it might be possible to find a little dust if you looked carefully, and here such a search would be futile.

'Would you like to sit down?' Dunn offered.

'No, I'd prefer to stand,' said Woodend, unwilling to disturb the symmetry of the furniture.

'Why are you here?' the squadron leader asked. 'Did you come because you felt it was your duty to offer me the conventional reassurances and platitudes? We both know that would be a waste of time. My daughter's fate is not in your hands, but in the hands of a madman. And if you find her, it won't be because you have been clever, but because he has been careless.'

'Does that mean I shouldn't try?' Woodend asked.

Dunn bowed his head. 'No, of course it doesn't mean that.'

'Well then, that's why I'm here – because I'm tryin',' Woodend said.

'I don't see how—'

'If your daughter's been kidnapped by a stranger, then I *am* wastin' my time,' Woodend told him. 'But if the kidnapper's someone who knew her – even slightly – then there's a chance that by bein' where she's been, and by seein' who she's seen, I might be able to get a lead on him.'

'It seems a long shot,' Dunn said doubtfully.

'It *is* a long shot,' Woodend agreed. 'But I'm a sniffer-out of details, a sifter of minutiae. I do that particular trick better than most, an' I sometimes find links that everybody else has overlooked. So while there's a chance that there is a link to be found that will lead me to Helen, I'll give it all I've got. Now, if you'd allow me, I'd like to look round her room.'

'Of course,' the squadron leader said. 'Please follow me.'

His daughter Annie's bedroom had always been a bit of a mess, and Woodend often chuckled at the thought of what a shock to her system it must have been when she'd moved into the student nurses' hostel and had a battleaxe of a warden inspecting her living quarters every week.

Helen Dunn would have had no such problem. Her bedroom was as neat and tidy as the living room they'd just left – her books stacked perfectly on her bookshelf, her stationery all perfectly aligned on her desk.

There were no pictures of pop singers or film stars pinned to the wall, as there had been in Annie's room. The only picture of any sort was a photograph on her bedside cabinet. There were two girls in the picture. One of them was a much younger Helen, the other a slightly older girl who was obviously a relation.

'Her sister?' Woodend guessed.

'Yes,' the squadron leader replied, his voice totally devoid of expression. 'That's Janice.'

Sally Spencer

'An' is she . . . ?'

'She died. While we were posted in Germany.'

'I'm sorry,' Woodend said. 'Was it a *sudden* illness?'

'It wasn't an illness at all,' Dunn told him. 'It was an accident. She drowned.'

It almost seemed like there was a curse hanging over the family, Woodend thought.

'Do Helen's friends come around here very often?' he asked, more to change the subject than because he was really interested in the answer.

'Helen does not have much time for friends,' Dunn answered.

'She doesn't?' Woodend asked, but he was thinking, 'What kind of kid doesn't have time for *friends*?'

'Helen wishes to study at Oxford University,' Dunn said. 'She is well aware of just how stiff competition is for places, and is striving hard to get herself into a position in which she will be one of the front runners. In addition, her sports activities take up much of her time. She's not a natural athlete, but if she works hard at it she should be able to reach a very acceptable standard eventually.'

'She sounds like a very serious girl,' Woodend said.

'She is a very *determined* girl,' the squadron leader answered.

Or was it just that she'd got a very determined father pushin' her forward? Woodend wondered.

Monika Paniatowski stood on railway station platform and watched the London train – which was bringing the chief inspector from Scotland Yard to Whitebridge – slow to a halt. She found herself wondering what he would be like, and decided that, since the Yard and Charlie Woodend had never got on, the new man would be everything that Woodend was not. The idea did not please her.

As soon as the train had finally stopped moving, the door opened and a man stepped out. He was tall, wore a black,

86

almost funereal suit, and had a hawk-like face with piercing, intolerant eyes. She could not have pictured the man from the Yard better if she'd tried.

Paniatowski walked over to the new arrival and held out her hand. 'I'm Sergeant Monika Paniatowski, sir,' she said. 'I'm here to brief you and generally show you around.'

'Brief me?' the hawk-faced man repeated. 'I'm not sure I know what you mean.'

'You are Chief Inspector Horrocks of Scotland Yard, aren't you, sir?' Paniatowski asked.

'Certainly not!' the man replied. 'My name's Porritt. I'm in haemorrhoid creams and tablets.'

'I think it's me you're looking for,' said a voice with a slight Scottish burr just behind her.

Paniatowski turned around. The man who had spoken was younger than she'd expected – not more than a few years older than she was. He was tall, broad, and had the kind of film-star good looks which would always have ensured that he played the town marshal in a white hat, rather than one of the unshaven gunslingers wearing black ones.

'Jack Horrocks,' he said, holding out a strong right hand. 'You're Sergeant Paniatowski, are you? Mind if I call you Monika?'

'No, sir, I . . .'

The Yard man smiled, revealing a set of perfectly even white teeth. 'I've never been much of a one for formality,' he said. 'Call me Jack. I could use a drink,' he glanced down at his expensive watch, 'but I don't suppose there's much chance of that at this time of day – in this kind of town. Is there anywhere we could get a cup of tea?'

'Yes . . . I . . .'

Horrocks smiled again. 'Then we'll settle for that, shall we?'

Paniatowski was feeling slightly bemused as she led the man from the Yard to the station buffet. He hadn't been what she'd been expecting at all, she thought. In fact, if she'd sat down and produced ten thumbnail sketches of Jack Horrocks, none of them would have come even close.

When they reached the buffet, Horrocks gestured that she should sit down. Monika took a seat, and watched the graceful, athletic way that the man moved across to the bar. And she was not alone, she noted – men who looked like Jack Horrocks were few and far between in Whitebridge.

'Paniatowski?' the chief inspector said reflectively, when he'd taken the seat opposite Monika. 'That's a Russian name, isn't it?'

The sergeant tried not to bridle, as she usually did when such a suggestion was made to her.

'The family probably did come from Russia originally,' she admitted grudgingly, 'but I was born in Warsaw. I consider myself a Pole – and a Lancastrian, of course.'

'Of course,' Horrocks agreed, with yet another smile. 'Chief Inspector Woodend's been in charge of this case so far, hasn't he?'

'That's right, he has,' Paniatowski agreed. 'You probably know him, don't you?'

Horrocks shook his head. 'No, I don't think so.'

'But Mr Woodend was serving at the Yard himself until a little over a year ago.'

'And I'm just coming up for the end of my first year, so we must have just missed each other,' Horrocks said. 'I understand from the minimal briefing I was given before they shoved me on the train at Euston that you've got another flap on here, apart from the murder. What is it, exactly?'

'A schoolgirl went missing at lunchtime.'

A cloud passed over the chief inspector's face. 'How old is she?'

'Thirteen.'

'You think we're finally starting to get civilised, then something like that happens to remind you that there are men walking round who are worse than animals!' Horrocks said, more to himself than to Paniatowski. 'Bastards! Hanging's too good for them. I'd roast them over a slow spit if I had my way.' He paused. 'Sorry about that little outburst, Sergeant. I've got daughters of my own, you see.'

'Understood, sir,' Paniatowski said.

Horrocks sighed. 'Well, I suppose that means we can't expect much help from the local force on our case, doesn't it?'

'I'm sure they'll do what they can for us,' Paniatowski said.

'You're probably right,' Horrocks agreed. 'But I'd feel guilty even having to ask. And I'm not sure it's necessary. We've supposedly got the best team of criminal investigators in the world back at the Yard. We'll use them for all the background inquiries. And anything that needs old-fashioned legwork, we'll do ourselves if we possibly can. Fair enough?'

'Fair enough,' Paniatowski agreed.

'Right, brief me on what we've got so far,' Horrocks said, crisply and businesslike.

'There's a couple of leads,' Paniatowski said. 'One of them is an Armstrong Siddeley Sapphire which seems to keep cropping up in our inquiries.'

'Oh yes?'

'Verity Beale's landlady saw it dropping her off at her door at least once, and though she was out with somebody else entirely last night, we believe the same car was parked outside the pub in which she drinking.'

'But you don't have the driver's name or address yet?'

'No, sir. We'd started making inquiries in that direction, but I expect they were dropped as soon as most of the team was switched to the Helen Dunn disappearance. If you like, I can—'

'The Yard should be able to come up with a list of possibles as quickly as the local boys could – if not quicker,' Horrocks said. 'Now what about the man our Miss Beale actually was out drinking with last night?'

89

'We believe he was an American from the base.'

Horrocks raised a quizzical eyebrow. 'Only *believe*?' he asked. 'I should have thought you'd have found out for sure by now. And questioned him, too, if it comes to that.'

'It's not that easy,' Paniatowski confessed. 'I've spoken to the major in charge of base security. I can't honestly say he was very co-operative. In fact, he seemed to be doing everything he could to stop me from even finding out the man's name.'

'Bloody Yanks!' Horrocks exclaimed, but without real rancour. 'You know what we used to say about them during the war, don't you?'

Paniatowski smiled. 'I wasn't in Britain myself, at the time, sir—'

'Jack.'

'Jack. But I believe they said that the trouble was they were over-paid, over-sexed and over here.'

'Spot on! Still, we'd have been lost without them. Would be even today, as a matter of fact. But that doesn't mean we can allow one of them to stand in the way of our investigation. We'd better go and have a word with this major, and tell him it's time he started playing as one of the team.'

'I don't think it'll be as easy you seem to imagine it will,' Paniatowski cautioned.

'Oh, I don't know about that. Nothing's too difficult if you approach it with the right attitude,' Horrocks replied airily.

Fourteen

T he sherries which Squadron Leader Dunn had poured for
them both once they were back in the perfectly ordered
lounge came in elegant crystal glasses which positively
sparkled.

Woodend looked down at his glass. Dunn had gauged the
amount of liquid in it to a fiftieth of an inch, he guessed, not
because he was a mean man but because he always gauged
everything with precision.

'You must have seen some action in the last show, mustn't
you?' Dunn asked.

'Aye, I was in the war – an' I did see some action,'
Woodend agreed. 'Far too bloody much of it, as far as I
was concerned.'

'Did you win any gongs?'

Woodend felt his hand unconsciously reach up to the spot
just below his breast, on which his medals had been pinned
a million years earlier. He hadn't wanted them then, and
now they languished in a drawer somewhere in his cottage,
gathering dust.

'Well, were you decorated?' Dunn demanded, with the air
of a man who was used to having his questions answered
immediately.

'Aye, I did get a couple of medals,' Woodend admitted.
'But to tell you the truth, Mr Dunn, I don't really feel very
comfortable talkin' about my experiences in the war.'

'A couple of medals,' Dunn said dreamily, missing the
tone of Woodend's comment completely. 'That must mean

you were right in the thick of it. You were lucky. Damn lucky! I was only fifteen at the time of the Battle of Britain. If I'd only have been born two or three years earlier, I could have been up there in my own Spitfire, shooting down the Huns with the rest of the chaps.'

'A lot of promisin' young lives were cut short durin' that battle,' Woodend pointed out. 'If you'd been old enough to fly in 1940, yours could have been one of them.'

'And would that really have mattered?' Dunn asked seriously. 'I love my country with all my heart, and I can think of no better way to die than fighting in its defence.'

'I've had men die in my arms, an' as far as I'm concerned, war may be necessary, but it's never glorious,' Woodend said.

But Dunn was not really listening. 'There are no great leaders left. At least, not on our side,' he said. 'The Reds need putting in their place, but both our government and the Americans seem to want to handle them with kid gloves. And what's the result of that? I'm condemned to being a peacetime pilot – a warrior in name only.'

'You might get your chance yet,' Woodend said.

'What was that?' Dunn asked, coming down off his cloud.

'I said you might get your chance yet. If the Russian government doesn't back down over this business in Cuba, you could still find out what fightin' a war's really like.'

'Yes, that *is* always a possibility,' Dunn said brightening.

Woodend took a sip of his sherry. 'Where's *Mrs* Dunn at the moment?' he wondered aloud.

'She's upstairs – in her bedroom. Why do you ask?'

'I'd like to talk to her about Helen.'

'She can't tell you anything that I haven't already told you myself,' Dunn said dismissively.

'Besides, I'll need to brief you both on how to conduct yourselves when you make your appeal on television this evenin'.'

'Tell me what we should do, and what we should say, and I'll pass the information on to her.'

'I'd prefer to talk to her myself, if she's at all in any state to see me,' Woodend said. 'I know she must be very upset an' all that—'

'She is, indeed. She's never had the self-discipline to keep her emotions under proper control.'

'—but I still think it might be helpful if I could—'

'And, naturally, she's feeling guilty, too.'

'Aye, people always do in situations like this, even when they've no reason to,' Woodend said.

'But she *does* have a reason to,' Dunn countered. 'She was supposed to pick Helen up at a quarter to one, to take her to the dentist's surgery on the base. She was five minutes late, as she *so often* is. She's admitted that to me. If she'd got there on time, Helen might never have been taken.'

'At this precise moment, we've no idea of exactly *when* Helen was kidnapped,' Woodend pointed out to him. 'It could have happened well before a quarter to one.'

'Or it could have happened in the couple of minutes *after* it,' Dunn retorted. 'But we'll never know for certain now, will we? Because my wife couldn't be on time to save her life – or anybody else's!'

'I'm afraid I'm goin' to have to insist on talkin' to her,' Woodend said firmly.

For a moment it looked as if Dunn would refuse, then he shrugged his shoulders and said, 'Very well, if you're adamant, I'll go and get her. But don't expect a lot of sense out of her – she's never been what you'd call a rational woman, even at the best of times.'

The pile of reports on Bob Rutter's desk was growing almost by the minute, but so far none of them seemed to be leading anywhere. Rutter was troubled. It was not the fact that two serious crimes had occurred less than a day apart which bothered him – for while that was rare, it was not unheard of. No, what really unsettled him was the common link of King Eddie's.

Did the fact that Verity Beale had known Helen Dunn have anything to do with her murder? he wondered.

Did the fact that Helen Dunn had known Verity Beale have anything to do with her kidnapping?

There seemed like there should be a link somewhere, but he was damned if he could see what it was.

He turned his attention to the reports spread out in front of him. With the rumours about Miss Beale's murder already starting to spread around 'Eddie's', he had sent a team up to the school to question the pupils about what might yet turn out to be an equally horrific crime.

Yes, some of the children admitted, they had seen Helen in the playground at lunchtime.

No, they hadn't talked to her – she was a strange girl, and didn't have any real friends.

Where had she been when they'd seen her? the officers had asked.

Just in the playground, some of the boys had said vaguely, though a few were willing to admit that they'd seen her near the gate, looking out at the park.

And had they seen anybody in the park itself?

No, but they hadn't really been looking.

No one saw her step through the gate and cross the road?

No, honest!

But would they have admitted it if they had? Rutter wondered.

They were only children, when all was said and done. They couldn't be expected to comprehend the seriousness of the situation. All they would really be aware of was the fact that they had seen a fellow pupil do something wrong, and had not reported it, so they could well be in trouble themselves if they didn't keep their mouths shut.

While the first team had been talking to the children in the school, a second team had been questioning the people in the park. But the officers had found no one who would admit to having also been there at the time Helen Dunn disappeared. And it was more than likely that those questioned were telling the truth – it was autumn, there was a sharp edge to the air, and while people might stroll briskly through the park, it was unlikely that anyone would choose to loiter there for any period of time.

A unit had checked the town centre, just in case Helen had nicked off school to look around the shops. But even as he was sending it out, Rutter had thought it was a waste of time – because even from what little he had learned of the girl so far, he had known she was not likely to do that.

A second unit had checked both the railway station and bus station. Patrol cars had covered the whole of the town and the outlying areas looking for a young girl in a school uniform, but with no success. Other divisions, whose territory bordered Whitebridge, had been asked to keep a lookout, but had nothing to report.

It was no longer possible to believe that the girl had simply wandered off and would soon return, shocked to find herself the centre of such a furore, Rutter told himself. She had been snatched – kidnapped by some pervert. God alone knew what was happening at that moment – what agonies she was already going through. But he held out little hope of finding her safe and sound. When they did discover her, it would be in a ditch or an abandoned building, her girlish knickers around her ankles, a scarf or a nylon stocking wrapped tightly around her throat.

He wondered if he could have done more, and knew that he couldn't. But still, as he waited for the phone to ring with good news or bad, he felt a solitary tear run down his cheek.

Monika Paniatowski negotiated her MGA round the bends on the country lanes like a racing driver who was well aware that he was already fighting a losing battle against the clock.

The speed didn't seem to bother Chief Inspector Horrocks.

Nor, for that matter, did the lack of space inside the sports car. Charlie Woodend, who was about the same size as the Yard man, always looked squashed up whenever he reluctantly agreed to be her passenger, yet somehow Horrocks managed to give the impression that there was plenty of room inside the vehicle. It was a neat trick – and Paniatowski wished she knew how he did it.

'It's not often you see a detective sergeant driving around in a car like this,' Horrocks said, as the road entered Dirty Bill's Woods. 'How do you manage it on your salary?'

Paniatowski turned towards him to see if there were any signs of insinuation on his face, but the man from the Yard looked completely guileless.

'How do I manage it?' she asked. 'It's easy. I just cut down on little luxuries like food.'

'But not booze?' Horrocks said, and once again there was no indication that he was being critical.

'When you work with Mr Woodend, you can't afford to regard booze as a luxury,' she said.

'That bad, is he?'

'No,' Paniatowski said. 'He's that *good*. Mr Woodend puts so much pressure on his team – and on himself – that if you worked for him and didn't drink, your brain would explode.'

'Interesting,' Horrocks said. 'Very interesting. I'm looking forward to meeting your Mr Woodend.'

'I'm sure the feeling's mutual,' Paniatowski replied.

Suddenly they were out of the woods, and ahead of them was a high, barbed-wire fence which stretched as far as the eye could see. Paniatowski slipped her gears through a racing change just in time to slow to a gentle glide as they reached the barrier in front of the base's main entrance.

'You still think they're just going to let us drive in, don't you?' she said to Horrocks.

'Yes, I do. I can see no reason why they shouldn't,' the chief inspector replied.

That's because you've never actually met Major-bloody-minded-Dole yourself, Paniatowski thought.

She changed down into neutral, and pressed on the brake pedal. The MGA came to a halt right beside the same unsmiling sentry who had admitted her earlier. The guard gestured commandingly to Paniatowski to wind down her window, but Horrocks signalled him to walk around to the other side of the vehicle, and – to Monika's surprise – that was exactly what he did.

'Chief Inspector Horrocks, Criminal Investigation Department,' her passenger said. 'I imagine you've already met Sergeant Paniatowski. We'd like to see your Major Dole, if that's convenient.'

'I'm gonna have to call it in before I can let you through the barrier,' the guard said.

'Of course you are,' Horrocks agreed pleasantly. 'I wouldn't have expected anything else.'

The guard walked back into his blockhouse, and picked up the wall-mounted telephone.

'Do you want to take bets on whether or not Dole will be available?' Paniatowski asked sourly.

'I never bet on sure things, Monika. It would be robbing you,' Horrocks told her confidently.

The guard hung up the phone again, and walked back to the MGA.

'All right?' Horrocks asked.

The guard nodded. 'Major Dole says that you're to go right up, sir,' he said. He turned his attention to Paniatowski. 'You know the way to his office, don't you, ma'am?'

'I do,' Paniatowski replied, easing into gear again.

She did not turn to look at Horrocks, but she was certain there would be a complacent smile on his face. She wondered how long it would take for Major Dole's stonewalling to turn that smile into a scowl.

Fifteen

Margaret Dunn sat on the sofa, twisting the almost-skeletal fingers of her right hand continually around her bony left wrist.

She was probably around the same age as her husband, Woodend thought, but even allowing for the stress she was under at that moment, it was plain that the years had not treated her anything like as kindly as they'd treated him. The woman looked a mess. Her mousy brown hair hung lifelessly over the sides of her skull, her large, frightened eyes bulged, and the skin on her right cheekbone was beginning to turn a nasty shade of purple.

'Do you have any children of your own, Mr Woodend?' the woman asked timidly.

'Aye. A daughter. A bit older than your Helen.'

'So you can imagine how I feel?'

'All too well,' Woodend told her. 'You loathe an' despise the man who's taken your daughter.'

'Yes.'

'You could watch him bein' slowly torn apart by a pack of wild dogs, an' not even be put off your dinner.'

'You're right. Does that make me a terrible person?'

'Not at all. Like I said, I'd feel exactly the same way myself.'

Had felt the same way himself!

He remembered standing in the morgue at the back of the Southwark Coroners' Court, looking down at Ellie Taylor's frail body on the cold slab. Whatever they said about kids growin' up quicker nowadays, she was still a child, with bosoms which were only just starting to develop and legs not much thicker than matchsticks.

He had forced his eyes to follow the trails of caked blood which ran down her legs from both her vagina and anus. Her front teeth had been knocked out, too, for reasons which were obvious to him but which he prayed the man standing next to him would not understand.

'You promised you'd get her back for us,' old George Taylor had said bitterly.

'I thought there was a good chance I could,' Woodend had replied.

Or rather, to be truthful, he had wanted to believe *there was a good chance.*

'Will you at least catch the monster who did this?' George Taylor had asked.

'I don't know,' Woodend had admitted.

But what he'd really meant was, 'Not unless he makes a mistake the next time he does this.'

'But however you feel about him, it's important that you don't let any of those feelin's come through when you're makin' your appeal on television tonight,' Woodend told Mrs Dunn.

'Are you saying that you want us to speak to this . . . this animal . . . as if he were no more than a slightly misguided human being?' Squadron Leader Dunn demanded.

'That's *exactly* what I'm sayin',' Woodend told him. 'An' I'll explain why. It's because if he senses any animosity from you, he'll close his mind off completely to anythin' you have to say to him. Do you understand that?'

'I suppose so,' Dunn said reluctantly.

'An' you, Mrs Dunn?'

'Yes, I understand,' the woman replied, in a voice as dry and cracked as late autumn leaves.

'Don't talk about your *daughter* – talk about *Helen*,' Woodend continued. 'Force him to see her not just as an

99

object he's snatched for his own twisted reasons, but as a real person. Tell him that you're not interested in seein' him punished. Say all you want is to get her – to get *Helen* – back. If you feel the urge to cry, don't hold in the tears.'

'Won't that make him see us as weak?' the squadron leader asked. 'Isn't that just he wants?'

'Let's get one thing straight from the start,' Woodend said, doing his best to hide his irritation. 'He's not interested in you at all.'

No, the only person the kidnapper was interested in at all was young Helen. If he wanted to see anyone crawl – anyone begging him for mercy – it would be the poor bloody girl.

'Is there anything else you want us to say?' asked Margaret Dunn, showing more self-possession than Woodend would have given her credit for a few minutes earlier.

'Talk to Helen directly,' the chief inspector said. 'Pretend she's in the room with you. If you can keep speaking to her as a person, that might help force him to see her that way too.'

'And what should I say?'

'Whatever comes naturally. That you miss her. That you want her to come home as soon as she can.'

'Should I say that we've already lost one daughter and—'

'Margaret!' the squadron leader said, his voice full of fury.

'No, you shouldn't say that,' Woodend told her, gently. 'Mention of anyone other than Helen would be a distraction – might even open an avenue of mental escape for him. He has to be focused on the girl he's kidnapped – has to be made aware of the fact that she's a human being too, with rights of her own.'

'Yes . . . yes, I can see that,' Margaret Dunn said meekly.

'Well, that's about it for now,' Woodend said. 'A police car will come an' pick you up when it's time to go to the studios in Manchester. I suggest you both get some rest before then.'

'Rest!' Dunn said, almost contemptuously. 'I've got too

many responsibilities to rest! Don't you realise we could be on the verge of World War Three?'

'Aye, I do,' Woodend replied. 'I'm just surprised that *you've* got any space left in your head to think about it.'

'What's that?' Dunn demanded. 'A joke? Or a criticism?'

Dunn was a cold bastard, Woodend thought, a *really* cold bastard! But he himself should not have allowed his personal animosity for the squadron leader get in the way of the job in hand.

'If I've offended you, Squadron Leader, then I apologise,' he said. 'I know you're under a lot of strain, an' I should have made allowances for that.'

Dunn nodded. 'Apology accepted.'

'One more thing before I go,' Woodend said. 'If the reporters have got wind about what's goin' on by the time the car comes for you, they'll be all over the street waitin' for you to come out an' talk to them. We'll keep them behind a barrier, but they'll still be close enough to start shoutin' out questions the second they see you emerge.'

'Vultures!' Dunn said bitterly. 'That's what they are – vultures hovering over other people's misery.'

'I wouldn't argue with that,' Woodend agreed.

'So what am I to do? Am I to answer their questions? Or do I just walk over to the barrier and punch their goddam heads in?'

'You're to do neither of those things,' Woodend told him. 'You'll ignore them, because if you say anythin' at all, they'll use it as an excuse to misquote you in their papers. An' that's the last thing we want. We need to reach the kidnapper through his television set, which we can control, not through the newspapers, which we can't. Understood?'

'Understood!' Dunn snapped back, crisply.

'I'll see myself out,' Woodend said. He walked over to the door, then suddenly swung around again. 'By the way, Mrs Dunn, what happened to your cheek?' he asked.

'My cheek?' the woman asked nervously.

101

'That swellin' you've got just below your eye could develop into a real beauty of a bruise.'

'Yes, I . . . I know,' Mrs Dunn stuttered.

'So how *did* it happen?'

'I . . . I walked into a door.'

'Well, when you get to the studio, make sure that the make-up girls who are lookin' after you do all they can to cover it up. If they don't . . .' Woodend continued, turning away from the woman and looking directly at her husband, '. . . if they don't, a lot of the viewers are goin' to start thinkin' that somebody's been knockin' you about, aren't they?'

Major Dole greeted Paniatowski and Horrocks at the door of his office, and waved them genially to the chairs in front of his desk. Once they were sitting down, the major returned to his own side of desk, resumed his seat and leaned back in a way which Paniatowski quickly decided was deliberately contrived to show just how relaxed he felt about the meeting.

'So just what can I do for you guys?' the major asked.

'Sergeant Paniatowski tells me that when she talked to you earlier, you indicated that you didn't feel able to bring yourself to co-operate with us over this murder investigation,' Horrocks said.

Dole frowned. '*Is* that what she said? I don't see how she could have ever gotten such an impression from what I told her.'

'What you said was that you were far from convinced we had authority of any kind on this base,' Paniatowski retorted angrily. 'You further said that with the crisis over Cuba, you didn't have time to deal with what you regarded was a purely local domestic matter.'

Dole smiled at Horrocks. 'That's a complete misreading of the situation as I presented it,' he told the man from the Yard. 'Wasn't it your George Bernard Shaw who said that the English and the Americans are two nations divided by a common language?'

'I believe it was,' Horrocks said, not returning the smile. 'But though I've only known Sergeant Paniatowski for a short time, she doesn't strike me as the sort of officer who completely misreads *any* situation.'

'Then perhaps it's all my fault,' Dole conceded, his smile melting away as quickly as it had appeared. 'And if that's the case, then I apologise. I never meant to imply that we weren't willing to help. I merely pointed out that it might take a little time.'

'No, you bloody well didn't!' Paniatowski said, with feeling.

'That will do, Sergeant,' Horrocks said, slightly sharply. 'Please carry on, sir.'

'Thank you,' Dole said. He turned to Paniatowski. 'When you were here earlier, you suggested that Miss Beale was seen having a drink with an American officer in a pub called the Spinner, didn't you?'

'No!' Paniatowski said firmly.

'No?'

'I said he was military, but I never suggested he was an officer. And I certainly didn't mention the name of the pub.'

'Perhaps you didn't,' Dole agreed amiably. 'Perhaps I got the name of the pub from the officer in question.'

'So you've identified him, have you?' Horrocks asked.

'Sure, I have. His name is Captain Wilbur Tooley, and he is fully prepared to admit that he was in the pub with Miss Beale – though not, of course, that he had anything to do with her subsequent death.'

'And we're supposed just to take his word – and yours – for that, are we?' Paniatowski demanded. 'We're expected to say that he couldn't have done it because both he and his good friend Major Dole say he didn't?'

'He's no particular friend of mine, and, no, I would not expect you just to take our word for it,' Dole replied evenly.

'So we can talk to him?'

'Yes.'

'Well, there's no time like the present,' Paniatowski said. 'Where can we find him?'

'You can talk to him – but not right now.'

'I told you he'd stall,' Paniatowski said to Horrocks. 'This is exactly the same sort of tactic he was using with me earlier. Sound reasonable – but give nothing away!'

'Is that what you're doing, Major Dole?' Horrocks asked, as if he were only mildly interested.

'No, it isn't,' Dole said. 'At the moment, we're facing a real crisis here. With President Kennedy and Mr Khrushchev in apparent deadlock, we can't afford to rule out the possibility that the Reds will decide to launch a pre-emptive strike against certain strategic targets, and in order to maintain our capability to respond effectively to such an attack, it has been deemed necessary to make sure that our capability is beyond their reach.'

'Or to put it in layman's terms, you're worried that the Russians might blow up this base before you have a chance to drop a few bombs on them?' Horrocks asked.

'Exactly.'

'And in order to make sure that doesn't happen, you're keeping your planes in the air for most of the time.'

'You got it,' Major Dole agreed.

'And one of the men who's keeping the planes out of the Communists' reach is this Captain Tooley.'

'Right again.'

'I see,' Horrocks said, stroking his chin with index finger. 'So when will Captain Tooley be landing again?'

'I'm not allowed to tell you that, Chief Inspector. Security reasons, you understand. But what I am prepared to tell you is that if you want to interview him tomorrow morning, either on base or the police station – whichever you prefer – then there should be no difficulty with that.'

'That sounds very reasonable, doesn't it, Sergeant?' Horrocks asked Paniatowski.

'Yes, that *sounds* reasonable,' Paniatowski replied, forcing the words out through her clenched teeth.

'There . . . er . . . is one other thing,' Dole continued. 'I'd be grateful if, until you've spoken to him, you didn't drop the captain's name in conversations with other people any more than is absolutely necessary.'

'Security considerations again?' Paniatowski asked sourly.

'In a way,' Dole said, reluctantly.

'In *what* way?' Paniatowski persisted.

'You're determined to have your pound of flesh, aren't you?' the major asked.

'I think I've earned it,' Paniatowski told him.

Dole sighed. 'Very well. Captain Tooley happens to be a married man. If you discover that he had anything to do with Miss Beale's death, then his little assignation with her will, of course, have to be made public. But if he's innocent – and I'm personally convinced that he is – then there really is no point in dragging his private life through the mud, is there?'

'Are you telling us he was having an affair with Verity Beale?' Paniatowski demanded.

'I think it would be better to let Captain Tooley speak for himself on that particular matter.'

'So do I,' said Horrocks. He stood up and held out his hand to Major Dole. 'Thank you for your help,' he continued. Then he looked pointedly at Monika Paniatowski.

'Yes, thank you,' Paniatowski said grudgingly.

All the way back to Whitebridge, Paniatowski kept replaying both her meetings with Dole in her head.

What had caused the change in his attitude between the first and the second encounters? What had converted him from a man apparently determined to fight her every inch of the way to one who seemed almost willing to do at least half their job for them?

Was it because she was only a detective sergeant, while Horrocks carried the weight of being a chief inspector?

It was a tempting theory, but if that had been case, why hadn't he come right out and *said* that he wasn't prepared to deal with someone so low down the chain of command? Why had he, instead, seemed to indicate that he wouldn't deal with the civilian authorities under *any* circumstances?

If she couldn't work out what had changed, she should perhaps try to isolate what *hadn't*, she told herself.

She pictured his face, and quickly came to the conclusion that there had been no real change at all. Despite his smiles and his jokes, the same, basically antagonistic Major Dole had been present at both meetings. So if he'd shifted his ground, it hadn't been because he wanted to, but because someone else – someone more important – had told him that was what he *had* to do.

Sixteen

Through the windscreen of the police car, Woodend could see the long queue of double-decker buses and taxis, vans and private cars. Occasionally one of the frustrated motorists in that queue would hoot angrily on his horn, but it was a pointless gesture, because nothing was moving. In fact, nothing had moved for a good ten minutes.

'I'm sorry about this, sir,' said his driver.

'It's not your fault, lad,' Woodend told him. 'The only people who can take any blame for this are God an' the Manchester Police. Any idea what's causin' the hold-up?'

The driver wound down his window and stuck his head out. 'Seems to be some kind of demonstration, sir,' he said. 'Yes, that's what it is, all right. There's a bunch of people in duffel coats ahead, wavin' placards about all over the place. I think I can just about make one of them out.'

'What does it say?'

'It says, "End this nuclear madness".' The driver shook his head disdainfully. 'It's probably that loony lot from the Campaign for Nuclear Disarmament. You'd think they'd have somethin' better to do with their time than to go about causin' inconvenience for other people, wouldn't you, sir?'

'I don't think they see it quite that way themselves,' Woodend said quietly. 'I think they believe that as much as it might inconvenience people to be *held* up, it'd inconvenience them even more to be *blown* up.'

The driver gave him a speculative, slightly worried, look.

'Sorry if I spoke out of turn, sir. I didn't know you looked at things that way.'

'You're entitled to your opinion, whatever I think,' Woodend replied. 'Would you like to make a guess as to how long it'll take us to get to the television studio from here?'

The driver scratched his head. 'That rather depends on them demonstrators, sir. Could be a good thirty minutes, at least.'

'Then bugger it, I'll clog it the rest of the way,' Woodend told him, reaching for the door handle. 'Pick me up at the main studio door in about an hour and half, will you?'

'Right you are, sir.'

Woodend stepped out on to the pavement and slammed the car door behind him. There were about a hundred people involved in this particular demonstration, he guessed – and his driver was right, most of them *were* wearing duffel coats. Looking at them, he was not sure whether the cause they were espousing was the height of wisdom or the very depths of folly – but he was glad that at least they *cared*.

It was a five-minute walk to the NWTV studio, and as he strode down towards Deansgate, he found himself wondering why he was in Manchester at all. His original intention had been to send Bob Rutter to supervise the Dunns' television appeal, but as it got closer to the time of the actual broadcast, he found himself wanting more and more to be there himself. He could not exactly say *why* he had the urge – there was no logical reason for it, and he was confident that Bob Rutter would cope admirably – yet he still could not shake the vague feeling that he would be *needed*.

He was about thirty yards from the studio when he saw two figures entering the building. One was a blonde woman with good legs and curvy body. The other was a man, as tall as he was himself – but infinitely more graceful. Monika Paniatowski and the detective chief inspector from the Yard – going to make their own broadcast for information about the murder of Verity Beale. He'd been actively involved in that case himself only hours earlier, but now the disappearance of Helen Dunn – and the memories that had evoked of Ellie Taylor – seemed to have turned Verity's death into no more than an ancient memory.

By the time he'd reached the studio lobby himself, there was no longer any sign of Paniatowski and Horrocks.

A large commissionaire stepped in front of him the moment he'd walked through the door. 'Can I help you, sir?' he asked in a tone which just managed to avoid being either suspicious or aggressive.

'I'm from the Whitebridge police. Chief Inspector Woodend. I believe I'm expected.'

The commissionaire nodded. 'If you'd just like to sit over there, I'll ring upstairs to say you've arrived, sir,' he said, indicating several easy chairs arranged around a low coffee table.

Woodend took a seat. There were a number of magazines scattered on the coffee table, but he felt no desire to pick one up and flick through it. Instead, as Bob Rutter had done earlier, he began to speculate as to whether the two serious cases the Whitebridge police had on their hands might not be no more than two parts of the *same* case.

It would be stretching credibility to believe that Helen Dunn had been kidnapped because she knew something about Verity Beale's murder, he thought. But what if things were the other way round? Helen's kidnapping *could* have been an impulsive act, but the fact that there had been no leads – no sightings of her at all – suggested it was more likely to have been carefully planned. And wasn't it possible that Verity Beale had learned something of that planning – and so had had to die?

'Chief Inspector Woodend?' said a voice.

Woodend looked up to find a bright, smartly dressed young woman standing over him, clipboard in hand.

'Aye, that's me,' he admitted.

'You're the one who solved the murders at our *Maddox Row* studios last year, aren't you?'

Woodend shrugged. 'If you ask me, those murders pretty much solved themselves,' he said awkwardly.

'From what I've heard from people who were there at the time, I'd say you're being far too modest,' the young woman said. 'Anyway, my name's Lynn Taylor, and I'm here to sort of look after you until the broadcast.'

'That's nice of you.'

'Just doing my job. And I'm sorry to have kept you waiting for so long, but with this Cuban missile business, everybody here's in an absolute flap, scrabbling through the archives and looking for bits of film we can use to cobble together a series of instant "specials" on the Cold War. Jolly exciting!'

'Aye, I suppose it must be,' Woodend said, thinking to himself that the world seemed to be divided up between the people who saw what was happening on the other side of the ocean as a dramatic slide into annihilation and those who saw it as a great adventure.

'Well, now you are here, what would you like to do?' Lynn Taylor asked. 'I've been told by my friends who were working at the *Madro* studio at the time of the murder that you're not averse to the odd drink or two. Shall I take you down to the bar?'

'It's temptin',' Woodend said, 'but I think I'd better go an' have a word with Mr and Mrs Dunn instead.'

Lynn Taylor frowned. 'Were you expecting *both* of them to be here?' she asked.

'Aren't they?'

'Mrs Dunn's here, but I can't say I've seen her husband. Maybe he's intending to arrive just before the broadcast.'

'So where's *Mrs* Dunn?'

'I was planning to take her down to the hospitality suite, but then I saw the state she was in, and decided it would be too much of a strain on her to see a lot of other people. So I've put her in one of the dressing rooms instead.'

'An' that's where she is now, is it?'

'I assume so.'

'Alone?'

'Well, yes.'

'Then I think you'd better take me to her right away, hadn't you?' Woodend said.

Paniatowski looked around the bar. At the table closest to hers, a couple of men in Elizabethan ruffs and tights were drinking gin and tonics. Just beyond them were two men in paint-stained overalls who could have been taken for ordinary workmen except that ordinary workmen did not wear make-up or speak with such posh accents. But it was the penguins who really caught her attention, and she watched in fascination as they waddled over to their table, lifted their beaks until they were pointing at the ceiling, and began to swig at their pints of beer.

'I take it you've never been in a television studio bar before,' DCI Horrocks said, amusement evident in his voice.

'No, sir, I haven't,' Paniatowski admitted. She opened the folder which was lying in front of her, and slid it across to Horrocks. 'All the details are in here. The last place Verity Beale was seen alive. Where her body was discovered. How many hours are unaccounted for. It might be wise to stress that any information, however obscure it might seem to the person who has it, could be of immense value to us.' She stopped, and almost blushed. 'I'm sorry,' she continued. 'I'm trying to teach my grandmother to suck eggs, aren't I? You must have made television appeals like this at least a dozen times before.'

'Probably even more than that,' Horrocks said. 'But I won't be making this one.'

'Then who . . . ?'

'Who do you think? It'll give you a chance to shine.'

'I don't think I should do it,' Paniatowski said firmly.

'What's the matter, Monika?' Horrocks asked, slightly mockingly. 'Getting stage fright at the thought of all those cameras?'

'No, sir. It's just that I think an appeal of this importance would carry more weight if it was delivered by a high-ranking officer like yourself.'

'In most cases, that's probably true,' Horrocks agreed. 'But when it's a young woman who's been murdered, what could be better than having another young woman – and such an attractive one – asking for help?'

'I'm flattered you think I could do it, but—'

'Anyway, when a man's in as much debt as I am, he can't go appearing on television. That'd be as good as giving his creditors a map to his front door.'

'I beg your pardon?' Paniatowski said.

Horrocks grinned. 'I'm joking, of course. But I still think you'd be the best person to make the appeal. I don't want to order you to do it, Monika – I never like ordering people around when I can get them to do something of their own free will – but I really would appreciate it if you'd make the broadcast.'

'All right,' Paniatowski said, still unconvinced.

Woodend knocked softly on the dressing-room door, then turned the handle and stepped inside. Mrs Dunn was sitting at the dressing table, gazing into the mirror. It was obvious that the make-up girls had already worked on her. Her hair had a little more life to it, and the bruise on her cheekbone was now almost invisible. She must have been a very attractive woman – once – Woodend thought.

'Where's your husband?' he asked. 'He's cuttin' it a bit fine, leavin' it this late, isn't he?'

'He won't be coming,' Margaret Dunn said apologetically.

'*What!*'

'He went out to the base as soon as you'd left us. He said he'd be back home in time to come down to Manchester with me. Then, about half an hour before the car arrived, he called me to say there was a real flap on, and they needed him to stay there.'

'An' doesn't the bas— . . . doesn't he realise that *you* need him, too?' Woodend said angrily.

'He's . . . he's very serious about doing what he sees as his duty,' Margaret Dunn said. 'Besides, I think I'll be better making the appeal on my own. You see, Reginald's never really had a close relationship with the girls.' She put her hand up to her mouth, as if by saying what she had, she'd shocked even herself. 'I don't mean that he doesn't love them . . . *didn't* love Janice, and *doesn't* love Helen,' she amended, 'but he doesn't find it easy to show his emotions . . . except, of course, his emotions for his country. I think he would have looked rather wooden on television, and I'm not sure that the hurt he's feeling inside would really have come across. And that's what you want, isn't it – for the hurt to come across?'

'Yes, that's what I want,' Woodend agreed.

'Then I'm right, and it'll be better if it's just me.'

'You're a very brave woman, Mrs Dunn,' Woodend said admiringly.

'Am I?' the woman replied, as if the remark had surprised her. 'I'm not sure that Reginald would agree with you.'

'Then he's never really looked at you properly,' Woodend said.

'No,' Margaret Dunn agreed sadly. 'I don't think he ever really has.'

'Where did you meet?'

Margaret Dunn laughed, though without much humour. 'At an RAF dance, of course. Where else? My father was an air commodore – a bit of a war hero, actually. I sometimes think that what really attracted Reginald to me was the hope that something of Daddy had rubbed off on his daughter.' She shook her head angrily. 'Why am I talking about me?' she demanded. 'I don't matter. Reginald doesn't matter. Only _Helen_ matters.'

There was a knock on the door, and a voice called out, 'We're ready for you now, Mrs Dunn.'

Margaret Dunn looked up at Woodend, and he could see the anxiety written in her eyes.

'Will you come with me?' she pleaded. 'Will you be sitting by my side when I try to reach out to that . . . that man?'

'Of course I will, lass,' Woodend said.

Seventeen

Woodend and Rutter sat at the corner table in the public bar of the Drum and Monkey as they had most nights for over a year. For the previous ten minutes the chief inspector had been doing most of the talking, but now he took a long slurp of his pint and waited for his subordinate to start picking holes in his theory.

'Tell me again why you think the kidnapping had to be planned in advance,' Rutter said.

'Think of other kidnappin's you've read about,' Woodend said. 'Witnesses have come forward to say they've seen vans cruisin' around, as if they were on the lookout for somethin'. Or else they've seen a kid bein' dragged along by somebody they took to be a parent at the time – but aren't so sure about any more. Neighbours have rung up to say blokes who live alone suddenly have a girl stayin' with them. An' what leads have we got this time? None at all! It just has to have been planned.'

'For Verity Beale to have learned about it, she must have come into contact with the kidnapper.'

'Or *kidnappers*! Because it wouldn't be the first time there's been more than one nutter involved in a case like this.'

'So you're saying the kidnappers must be people she knows socially?'

'Aye, they could be,' Woodend agreed. 'It could be somebody she's been out with, or the mate of somebody she's been out with. It could have been somebody she heard talkin' at the

115

next table when she was out on a date. Then again, it could be somebody she worked with – or one of them Yanks she's been teachin'. I'm not offering a blueprint for an arrest here, lad, I'm just openin' one of speculation that I don't think we can afford to ignore.'

The door opened and Monika Paniatowski entered the bar. She nodded to her two colleagues, then went over to the bar to order her customary double vodka.

'Are you going to run this theory of yours by Monika?' Rutter asked.

'No,' Woodend said.

'Why not?'

'Because she's not workin' on our team at the moment.'

'It's not like you to keep things to yourself,' Rutter said, sounding slightly reproving.

'It's not a question of keepin' things to myself,' Woodend said. 'This feller they've sent up from the Yard will have his own way of goin' about things. An' maybe since he's from the outside he might see things we'll overlook or just take for granted. So the last thing I want to do is put blinkers on him. As far as I'm concerned, the more different approaches we have to these the cases the better.'

Paniatowski, having bought her drink, came over to join them. The moment she had sat down she took a generous swig of her vodka.

'How did your very first television appearance go, Monika?' Woodend asked her.

'Fine,' the sergeant replied, noncommittally.

'Do you want to talk about it?' Woodend asked.

'About my appearance on television?'

'Nay, lass. About whatever else it is that's so obviously preyin' on your mind.'

'I'm not sure there *is* much to talk about yet,' Paniatowski confessed. 'All I've got is this feeling.'

'What kind of feelin'?'

'That there's a new set of rules in play, and nobody's

bothered to tell me what they are. That though I think I'm in control of myself, there's somebody hidden behind the curtain, pulling my strings.'

'*Who's* hidin' behind the curtain? Are we talkin' about that feller from the Yard here?'

Paniatowski shook her head. 'No. At least I don't think so. He's got his faults but . . .'

'But what?'

A slight smile came to Monika Paniatowski's face. 'Well, he's a boss, isn't he? So he's bound to have faults. And he's certainly a cocky devil, but then everybody who's ever worked at the Yard is like that.' The smile disappeared, and she became serious again. 'But I don't see him as the puppet-master. If anybody *is* pulling strings, I suspect his are being yanked as well as mine.'

'What's his name?' Woodend asked. 'Maybe I know him.'

'I don't think you do – unless it's by reputation. His name's Jack Horrocks, and he didn't start working at the Yard until after you'd left.'

'Until after I was *pushed*, you mean,' Woodend said. 'What's your general impression of him – an' you leave out that dig about all Yard men bein' cocky, because you've already scored enough points off me with that particular dig.'

'It's too early in the investigation for me to have any-thing as grand as a general impression,' Paniatowski said cautiously. 'I think I like him, but until I've seen how he handles the interview in the morning, I won't know how good a bobby he is.'

'What interview?' Woodend asked.

'We're going to talk to the American officer who was drinking with Verity Beale just before she died.'

'An' presumably also slept with her, an' all,' Woodend said.

'Presumably.'

The waiter came across to the table. 'Phone call for you, Mr Woodend,' he said.

'Who is it?'

'He wouldn't give his name. Just said it was very important he talked to you right away.'

Woodend stood up. 'Probably the Jehovah's Witnesses. I've been on their hit list for some time,' he said, forcing a grin to his face.

The phone was in the passageway which led to the toilets, next to a stack of empty beer crates.

'Woodend!' the chief inspector said, picking it up.

'I saw you on the television tonight.'

The voice at the other end of the line sounded hoarse, but Woodend suspected that was more to disguise it than because the caller had some kind of throat infection.

'So you saw me on the telly, did you?' he asked. 'What are you? A talent scout? Think you can get me a job in Hollywood, do you?'

'You're looking for the little girl.'

'If you *did* see me on the telly, you don't have to be a genius to have worked that out.'

'I've got her.'

Woodend felt the hairs on his neck prickle. The hoarse caller could be a crank, of course – they got enough of those ringing in after every major crime. But there was always the possibility that he wasn't!

'So you've got her, have you?' he asked. 'Well, why don't you hand her back before any real harm's done? You're probably a bit frightened yourself, but you don't need to be. You don't have to run any risk in returnin' her – just leave her somewhere she can be easily found, an' then call me again.'

The other man laughed. 'You'd like that, wouldn't you?'

'Yes I would. I think it'd be the best thing all round,' Woodend said earnestly.

'I'm going to be gone for a moment, but don't hang up because I've got someone I'd like you to hear.'

118

There was silence for a few seconds, then Woodend heard a girl's voice say, 'Don't hurt me! Please don't hurt me!'

'Who are you, luv? Tell me your name!' Woodend said.

'I'm . . . I'm Helen Dunn.'

The line fell silent again. Woodend began counting slowly. He had reached twelve before the man with the rasping voice came back.

'As you've just heard for yourself, she's still alive,' the rasper said. 'You *did* hear, didn't you?'

'Yes, I heard,' Woodend agreed. 'What is it you want?'

'I want to *kill* her, of course! But not yet. Killing her now wouldn't be half as much fun as waiting a while. So there's still a chance you could find us both, isn't there?'

'You don't have to go through with this, you know,' Woodend said, trying not to sound as if he were pleading.

'But I *want* to go through with it. Why don't you ask me when I intend to kill her?'

'There's no point in either of us talkin' like that.'

'Ask me!' the other man insisted. 'Ask me – or I'll do it right now.'

'When are you goin' to kill her?' Woodend said dully.

The hoarse man laughed again. 'I don't know,' he said. 'It could be three days from now, or it could be tomorrow morning. You've no way of knowing, have you? So if you want to find her, you haven't got a minute to waste.'

Then the line went silent again, and this time there was mechanical hum which told Woodend the call really was over.

'Whoever the caller was, he must have been in this pub fairly recently,' Bob Rutter said, looking round him in an attempt to remember the faces of the people who had been in the now-vacant seats.

'He could have been here,' Woodend agreed. 'On the other hand, he might know my car, an' have seen it parked outside when he drove past. Or he could just be somebody who knows me well enough to be sure that I'd be here at this time of night. The point is, was the caller the kidnapper or just a nutter?'

'You heard the girl's voice,' Paniatowski pointed out.

'I heard *a* girl's voice,' Woodend countered. 'In fact, I can't even be sure of that. I heard what *sounded* like a girl's voice choked with terror, but maybe it was just him impersonatin' a girl.' He drew heavily on his cigarette. 'But let's assume for the moment that the call was genuine,' he continued. 'Why should the kidnapper have rung me?'

'Because you're the man in charge,' Rutter said. 'Because he saw you on television.'

'I didn't mean that,' Woodend said. 'What I want to know is, why ring *anybody* connected with the case?'

'Maybe he just likes playing games,' Paniatowski suggested.

'Aye, that's not entirely unknown,' Woodend agreed. 'But if that *is* the case, the call should have come later.'

'What do you mean?' Rutter asked.

'If he is playin' a game, there's two parts to it. The first part is the one he plays with the girl, an' the second is the one he plays with me.'

'You're saying he shouldn't have rung you until there was no chance of you spoiling the first part of the game,' Rutter said.

'Or to put it another way, he shouldn't have rung you until the girl was dead,' Paniatowski added.

'Exactly,' Woodend said. 'Let's leave that question for a minute, an' move on to somethin' else. He could have rung me at the station. He could have rung me at the television studio, just after we'd made the broadcast. But he didn't do either of those things. He either ran the risk of followin' me, or took the chance that I'd be here. Why?'

'He wanted to make sure you had no possibility of either tracing the call or recording it,' Paniatowski said.

'That's what I think, an' all,' Woodend agreed. 'Which means that he's not like some of these loonies who play games with the police because what they really want to do is get caught. So I come back to my original question. Why *is* he playin' the game – an' why has he started to play it *now*?'

The waiter returned to the table. 'Another call for you, Mr Woodend. I think it might be the same man who called you last time.'

He should have rung the technical lads at the station, and had a tracer put on the pub's phone, Woodend thought as he stood up. But even if he *had* done that, it would not have been in place yet – and the caller probably knew it just as well as he did.

He reached the corridor and picked up the phone. 'Is it you again?'

'Yes, it's me again,' the hoarse-voiced caller said. 'Have you been having a nice little chat with Inspector Rutter and Sergeant Paniatowski?'

Woodend shivered. The man hadn't just driven by and seen his car, then – he'd been inside the pub. Or, at least, *watching* the pub!

'What makes you think Rutter and Paniatowski are here?' he asked, just to confirm his suspicions.

'Rutter's wearing a blue suit that makes him look more like a stockbroker than a policeman,' the caller said. 'Paniatowski's wearing a green dress which shows off quite a lot of her legs. Very tasty! If she was fifteen years younger, I might fancy her myself.'

'Would you have fancied Verity Beale if she'd been fifteen years younger?' Woodend asked.

The other man chuckled. 'So you've got there at last, have you?' he asked.

'Is that an admission that you killed her?'

'It might be.'

'Then maybe you could answer me this – why dump her body in the pigsty?'

'I don't want to talk about her any more,' the rasper

said. 'Let's get back to your team. What were you talking about?'

'What did you think? We were talkin' about *you*. We were sayin' that the smartest thing you could do – from your own point of view as well as everybody else's – is to let Helen go.'

'Liar!' the rasper said disgustedly. 'What you were really doing was trying to decide whether I was just a crank – or if I really did have the girl.'

'There was that, as well,' Woodend admitted.

'Go out to your car,' the rasper said.

'Why should I do that?'

'Go out to your car, and see what's hidden underneath it.'

'You'll like that, won't you?' Woodend demanded. 'You'll like to see me crawlin' on my hands and knees, like a dog?'

The caller laughed contemptuously. 'Considering you're an experienced policeman, you're really not very good at this, are you?'

'Not very good at what?'

'At laying verbal traps for me to fall into.'

'I'm not sure I know what you mean.'

'Yes, you do. You think that between the last call and this one, I've driven to the pub, and that when you go outside I'll be somewhere in the shadows, watching and waiting. That's why you asked if I'll enjoy it – to make sure I'll be there. But I won't be. I have been to the pub – if you'd had the sense to post men in the car park, they'd have caught me – but I'm miles away now.'

'Are you doin' this on your own?' Woodend asked. 'Or have you got helpers?'

The caller laughed again. 'Do you really think I'd share this experience with anybody else?'

'I don't know,' Woodend said.

And he didn't. Experience taught him that men like the rasper often acted alone, yet he got the distinct impression that wherever the man was calling from, there was someone else there with him.

'Perhaps you're right,' the rasper said. 'Perhaps there *are* two of us. Or even three or four. That should make things easier for you, shouldn't it Mr Woodend? If four men are involved – or maybe it's even five – then it's four or five times more likely that somebody will make a mistake and drop the vital clue which will lead you to the girl.'

'I don't want to play games any more,' Woodend said.

'But I do,' the rasper said. 'And I'm the one who's calling the tune that we both dance to. Go out to your car, Mr Woodend. Go now – before somebody else finds what I've left there for you.'

The phone went dead. Woodend made his way quickly out to the car park. His Wolseley was standing just where he had left it.

For a moment he paused to wonder if it had been booby-trapped, but then he quickly dismissed the idea. Whether the rasper was genuine or not, killing policemen was not how he got his kicks.

Woodend knelt down by the Wolseley, and ran his hand slowly under the car's chassis. Halfway between the back and front wheels, he felt his fingers brush against something. Gingerly, he explored the shape of it with the nail of his index finger. As far as he could tell, the object was a long, thin, rectangular shape.

He should call in the lads from the lab to handle the situation from there on in, he thought. But what would be the point of that? The rasper was a clever man, who had considered all the angles. Whatever he had left under the car, he would have taken great pains to ensure that there was nothing about it to connect it with him.

Taking hold of the rectangular box by one corner, Woodend lifted if from the ground, and out from under the car. He held his prize up towards the streetlight, so he could examine it

123

better. The box was covered in a green tartan material, and a zip ran around most of the top.

A pencil case!

Woodend took the zip fastener between two fingers, carefully pulled it round, and flipped the pencil case open. Inside were all the things he expected to find – ordinary pencils and coloured pencils, a sharpener, a protractor and a set of compasses. In the lid itself, someone had written a name in a careful, childlike hand. It came as no surprise to him that that name was Helen Dunn.

Eighteen

'*It is exactly eight forty-eight on the morning of Wednesday October 24th, and here are the news headlines,*' said the voice of the newsreader from the radio in Paniatowski's MGA. '*As the crisis over Cuba deepens, both the USSR and President Castro have called the American low-level flight over the island an unwarranted breach of Cuban air space. In further developments, the USA has announced the quarantine of Cuba will begin at ten o'clock Eastern Standard Time, though, for practical purposes, it is already in place.*'

Paniatowski switched the radio off, and reached, with her free hand, for the packet of cigarettes which was resting on the dashboard.

'The situation's not getting any better, is it?' DCI Horrocks asked from the passenger seat.

'No,' Paniatowski agreed. 'How do you want to handle this session with Captain Tooley?'

Horrocks grinned. 'You're a very single-minded young woman, aren't you, Monika?' he asked.

'It's the only way to do the job.'

'Did you learn that from Cloggin'-it Charlie?'

'I think I already knew it before I started working with Mr Woodend, but he's done nothing to convince me that I was wrong.'

'Do you wish you were working with him on this case, rather than with me?' Horrocks asked.

Alarm bells started to ring in Paniatowski's head.

What is this? she wondered. Some kind of test?

125

'I don't know enough about you yet to make that kind of judgement,' she said cautiously.

Horrocks chuckled. 'Not much of a one for flattering your superiors, are you, Monika?'

'Now that's one thing that Mr Woodend *did* teach me,' Paniatowski replied. 'You never did tell me how we're going to handle this session with Captain Wilbur Tooley.'

'I don't know yet. But you're a bright girl. You should be able to see where I'm going and follow my lead quickly enough.'

There were times when Horrocks sounded *just* like Charlie Woodend, Paniatowski thought. And there were times when it seemed as if he was from a completely different planet.

They got on to the base with the minimum of formalities. There was no sign of Major Dole in the office block, but the military policeman on duty knew why they were there, and took them straight to the office where Captain Tooley was already waiting for them.

Monika had never met an air-force pilot before, and – without really thinking about it – had assumed that they were all blue-eyed gods like Paul Newman. Tooley, by Newman standards, was a definite disappointment. He was tall and gangly, with floppy brown hair, earnest, bulging eyes and a highly prominent Adam's apple which bobbed up and down every time he spoke. Sitting in the chair opposite the two British police officers, he seemed more like a boy who'd been caught abusing himself behind the woodshed than a man who anyone would be happy to entrust with the control of a lethal killing machine.

'Let's get a couple of things clear before we start talking, shall we?' Horrocks said jovially to the young officer. 'This is not a formal interview in any sense of the word – though that's not to promise there won't *be* a formal interview later. Understood?'

'Understood.'

'And, that being the case, you are not actually obliged even

126

to be here, or to answer any questions which you would prefer not to answer. Is that clear, Captain Tooley?'

'Yes, sir,' Tooley said, his Adam's apple jumping like a pea which been sucked up a straw.

Horrocks smiled. 'Well, that's got the very stuffy, oh so very British, bit out the way, Wilbur. Now we can relax a little.' He glanced down at the sheet of paper which lay on the desk in front of him. 'Your full name is Wilbur Lee Tooley. You were born in Oxford, Mississippi in 1935, which makes you twenty-seven years old now, are married with two children, and have been in the US Air Force for eight years. Have I got anything wrong so far?'

'No, sir. That's all quite correct.'

'Now, as you know, we're here to investigate the death of Verity Beale. What exactly was your relationship with her?'

Tooley fixed his eyes on the corner of the room. 'She . . . she was a friend,' he said.

'That's all she was? Just a friend?'

'Yes. We met through the church.'

'That would be the Baptist Church in Whitebridge?'

'Yes.'

Horrocks frowned slightly. 'What I don't quite understand is why you went all the way to Whitebridge to worship. Wouldn't it have been more convenient to use the church on the base?'

'The Baptist Church feels more like my church back home than the base chapel does.'

Horrocks nodded. 'Of course. It's quite obvious once you've explained it. Now, when you went to the church in Whitebridge, I expect you took your wife with you.'

'Yes.'

'So *she* was a friend of Miss Beale's, as well?'

Tooley shifted his attention from the corner of the room to the surface of the desk. 'No.'

'No?'

127

'She . . . she doesn't find it easy to make friends with the Brits.'

Horrocks laughed. 'Yes, I suppose we are a pretty odd lot when you come to think of it,' he conceded. 'Let's get on to what happened the night before last, shall we? You went to the Spinner, which is a public house between Sladebury and Whitebridge?'

'That's correct.'

'But though you both went there from the base, you travelled in separate vehicles?'

'Yes.'

'Why was that?'

'Because after we'd had our drink, she was going back to Whitebridge and I planned to return to the base.'

'So Miss Beale was never actually in your car that night.'

'No,' Tooley said. 'No, she wasn't.'

Horrocks frowned again, more deeply this time. 'That's funny. I would have thought it would have been much more comfortable in your big American car than it would have been in her small British one. Still, I suppose there's no accounting for taste, is there?'

'I don't understand what you're talking about,' Tooley said – but from the troubled expression on his face, it was obvious that he was at least starting to get an inkling.

'You don't understand, Captain Tooley? Then perhaps I'd better spell it out more clearly for you,' Horrocks said, and now a hard edge had crept into his voice. 'I would have thought it would have been much more comfortable to have sexual intercourse in your car than it would have been to have it in hers. Unless, of course, you chose to make the beast with two backs out in the open air.' He grinned, though not pleasantly. 'But I can't really see you jumping on her bones *al fresco*, given how chilly it can be on an English autumn evening.'

'I never said I had sex with her!' Tooley protested.

'Didn't you?' Horrocks turned to Paniatowski. 'Then where

128

on earth did I get the idea that Miss Beale had had sexual intercourse shortly before she died, Sergeant?'

'From the police doctor, sir.'

'The police doctor,' Horrocks repeated, as if the term were unfamiliar to him. 'That would be some ancient British druid who prescribes herbs according to the phases of the moon, would it?'

'No, sir,' Paniatowski said. 'Dr Pierson studied medicine at Manchester University.'

'Quite so,' Horrocks agreed. He swung his gaze back on Tooley. 'I like you Americans. I really do. But it does annoy me a little when you seem to assume that we're all straw-sucking yokels over here on this side of the pond. The police doctor – who studied medicine at the University of Manchester – tells me in his report that Miss Beale had sexual intercourse, and I'm inclined to believe him. Now – and I hope you can follow this argument – since she was with you for most of the evening, I've drawn the conclusion that you were her partner in this little diversion. Are you telling me that you weren't?'

Tooley's skin had started to turn crimson. He glanced – but only briefly – at Paniatowski, then said, 'Does she have to be here?'

'Captain Tooley, like the true Southern gentleman he is, wants to save you from any embarrassment,' Horrocks told Paniatowski. '*Are* you embarrassed, Sergeant?'

'Not in the slightest,' Paniatowski replied.

'Then I think you may as well stay.'

'If she doesn't leave right now, I'm not saying any more,' Tooley said defiantly.

'That's entirely your choice, Captain Tooley,' Horrocks said easily. 'By the way, where is your car – or perhaps I should say where is your *automobile*, since you're one of our colonial cousins?'

'It's parked outside my house,' Tooley replied, puzzled. 'Why are you asking me that?'

'Just so the boffins I bring down here from the forensic lab will know where to find it.'

Tooley's Adam's apple went completely out of control. 'You're . . . you're going to . . .' he gasped.

'It's a messy, sticky job, sexual intercourse,' Horrocks said. 'Without going into the unpleasant biological details, it shouldn't take us long to establish whether or not anything happened in your vehicle the night before last.'

'I . . . I . . . never meant to do it that night,' Tooley said. 'I only agreed to go out with her one last time so that I could tell her I was never going to see her again. But then the Devil entered my loins and I . . .'

'And you screwed her something rotten on the back seat of your car,' Horrocks said, signs of his earlier *bonhomie* now completely absent. 'Tell me, do you make something of a habit of slaking your lust on unmarried foreign females, Captain Tooley?'

'No,' the airman said shakily. 'She . . . she was the only one I've ever been unfaithful with. But it wasn't all my fault. She led me on.'

'She led him on!' Horrocks said disbelievingly to Monika Paniatowski. 'She caught one glimpse of his magnificent masculine body,' he continued, running his eyes up and down Tooley's thin frame, 'and somehow she just couldn't control herself.'

'It's true!' Tooley protested. 'She made all the running . . . and . . . and I wasn't the only one who—'

'You're saying she had other lovers?' Horrocks demanded, swooping in like a hawk on its prey.

Tooley nodded. 'That's why I was going to break it off. As long as I thought she really loved me, I could just about bear the guilt, but when I started hearing the stories about her . . .'

'Let's get back to you, shall we?' Horrocks suggested, as if the subject of Verity Beale's sexual activities had already started to bore him. 'In September 1954, while on leave from the Air Force in your home state of Mississippi, you were arrested by Jackson City Police. Isn't that right?'

Now where the bloody hell did that piece of obscure information come from? Paniatowski wondered.

Tooley looked as amazed as Paniatowski did. 'How did you know—?' he began.

'It is true, isn't it?'

'I was arrested, but I was never charged.'

'No, you weren't,' Horrocks agreed. 'If you'd been charged, the incident would have found its way on to your service record. And it hasn't. So none of your superiors know about it – yet!'

'I demand to know—'

'In your position, I don't think I'd try *demanding* anything,' Horrocks said harshly. 'In your position, I think I'd simply tell the nice British policeman everything he wants to know, and pray that he decided to keep his mouth shut about my dubious past.'

'I . . . what do you want me to say?'

'I want you to tell me, in your own words, what you did to get yourself arrested.'

'Back in '54, the US Supreme Court ruled that racial segregation in schools was unconstitutional,' Tooley said resignedly. 'The voters of Mississippi decided that if there was no other way to keep the negroes out of white state schools, they'd abolish the school system altogether. Don't you think that's insane?'

'Insanity is sometimes a very difficult thing to define precisely,' Horrocks said.

'Well, it certainly seemed crazy to me. Not only were they going to deny the negro kids the chance they deserved, but they were going to take the opportunity away from the poor white kids, as well,' Tooley said passionately. 'It was wrong, so very, very wrong.'

'So you decided to picket the state capital,' Horrocks said, unmoved. 'Not on your own, of course.' He laughed, dryly.

131

'No, you were just a small part of quite a large group of troublemakers.'

'Troublemakers!' Tooley repeated incredulously. 'We weren't troublemakers! We were just ordinary folks protesting over something we thought was unchristian.'

'Who organised you?'

'It was mainly people from my local church.'

Horrocks laughed dismissively. 'Oh, I'm sure it was,' he agreed. 'On the surface! But who was *really* behind it? Who was pulling the strings? Was it, by any quirk of fate, the Communist Party?'

'This is crazy!' Tooley said.

'Are you a member of the Communist Party yourself, Captain Tooley?' Horrocks asked.

'No, I—'

'So you're just what they call a "fellow traveller", are you?'

'Not even that. Like I said, we were only—'

'You look like you're wilting a bit, Monika,' Horrocks said suddenly to Paniatowski. 'Go and find the American equivalent of the NAAFI, and get yourself a nice cup of tea.'

'Tea?' Paniatowski repeated.

'That's right. You know what I'm talking about, don't you? Brown leaves. Come from India. Just add hot water and they turn into a refreshing drink.'

'But I thought . . .'

'Don't think, there's a good girl – just see if you can find us some tea,' Horrocks said pleasantly.

Nineteen

Making their way up the path which led to Squadron Leader Dunn's door, Woodend and Rutter looked rough – looked, in fact, like two men who had spent most of the night involved in a heated argument. Which they had.

'Whoever took Helen's pencil case must have had access to her classroom,' Woodend had said. 'That means the kidnapper has to be one of the staff. And whoever he is, I want to be alone in an interrogation room with him. Now!'

'There must be sixty teachers at Eddie's,' Rutter protested. 'Maybe even more!'

'It won't take me more than a couple of minutes with most of them to work out whether or not they have anything to do with it,' Woodend had argued. 'That'll leave only three or four with question marks over them. An' after half an hour with each of them, I'll know which one it is who took the poor little kiddie.'

'So you're seriously expecting over sixty teachers – professional men who've never had any trouble with the law before, and can probably be really bloody-minded about their rights when they want to be – to voluntarily agree to come to the station in the middle of the night and submit to an interrogation?' Rutter had asked.

'If they won't come voluntarily, we'll arrest the buggers. Christ, they should be glad enough to be put to a little inconvenience if it means that we catch the kill— . . . the kidnapper.'

'You almost said killer,' Rutter pointed out.

'It was a slip of the tongue,' Woodend countered.

'No, it wasn't,' Rutter said firmly.

'All right, whatever that nutter said to me on the phone tonight, it's more than likely she's already dead,' Woodend agreed. 'But there's just a chance she isn't, an' I can't let that chance slip by.'

'Even if it means dozens of complaints on Ainsworth's desk in the morning?'

'Yes.'

'Even if it costs you your job?'

'Even then.'

'And what if it wasn't one of the teachers who took the pencil case at all?' Rutter had argued desperately. 'What if it was one of the cleaners? What if it was one of the lads, doing it on the instructions of an older brother? Do you know if there were any problems with the plumbing at the school that morning? I don't. But maybe there were – and maybe one of the plumbers took the pencil case!'

Woodend had finally bowed his head in defeat. 'All right, how do you want to handle it?' he asked.

'We go and see the Dunns tomorrow morning and ask them if there was any teacher who showed a special interest in Helen. Or if there was any teacher she talked about more than she talked about the others. Then we get them alone, produce the pencil case, and see how they react.'

'It's not a great plan, is it?' Woodend had asked.

'No, but it's a lot less insane than yours,' Rutter had countered.

They reached the front door, and Bob Rutter knocked. It was Dunn himself who answered. His appearance shocked them both – but not for the reasons that either of them might have anticipated.

They looked like wrecks. He did not.

There was no evidence written on Dunn's face that the man had started to go to pieces, as most fathers would have in his situation. His eyes were not red through lack of sleep or excess of alcohol. He had shaved – probably no more than an hour earlier. And his shoulders had not acquired the slump of defeat which the shoulders of so many men who had lost their children naturally adopted.

It was probably his military training which was carrying him through the dreadful experience, Woodend thought. The squadron leader was maintaining a stiff upper lip on the surface, but underneath the poor bugger was probably all churned up.

'Has there been a development in the investigation?' Dunn asked abruptly.

'We're not sure, sir,' Woodend admitted. 'Would you mind if we came inside for a couple of minutes?'

Dunn shifted his weight slightly, effectively blocking the doorway to the two policemen.

'Can't you say what you have to say out here?' he asked.

'It might be easier if—'

'I don't want to seem inhospitable, but my wife's inside, and I don't want her any more upset than she already is.'

'We have something that we think you'd both better look at,' Bob Rutter said.

'Whatever it is, there's probably no need for Margaret to see it as well as me, and I'm perfectly capable of examining it here,' Dunn replied firmly.

Rutter looked at Woodend for guidance, and when the chief inspector nodded he reached into the evidence bag he was carrying, and produced the green tartan pencil case.

'Yes, that's Helen's,' Dunn said dully. 'Where did you find it?'

'You're sure it's hers?' Woodend asked. 'You haven't even looked inside it yet.'

'Don't you think I know my own daughter's equipment when I see it?' Dunn snapped.

'Hand it over to the squadron leader, anyway,' Woodend told Rutter. 'It won't do any harm for him to give it a closer inspection.'

Rutter passed the pencil case to Dunn. The squadron leader flipped it open, and gave the inside a cursory glance.

'As I said, it's Helen's,' he said. 'I should have thought that would have been obvious to you, since her name's written inside it. Are you going to tell me how it came into your hands?'

'We believe the kidnapper left it for us to find,' Woodend said. 'What I don't quite understand is how he got hold of it in the first place – and we think that's where you might be able to help us.'

'I'm afraid I'm not following you,' the squadron leader said, sounding genuinely puzzled.

'We know from the people we've talked to at the school that the last place Helen was seen was in the playground,' Woodend explained. 'Now since the pencil case was, presumably, in her desk—'

'Why should you presume that?' Dunn demanded.

'Why *shouldn't* I presume it?'

'I've always taught my daughters . . . I've always taught *Helen* . . . to take care of her own property. I've always made it clear to her that if she lost something, I would consider it to be more a result of her own carelessness than the dishonesty of others – because others simply *can't* be dishonest if you don't give them the chance to be.'

'That seems rather harsh,' Woodend said.

'Life is harsh,' Dunn told him. 'Most of Helen's education has been at service schools – I wanted to send her away to a private school as a boarder, but her mother wouldn't hear of it – and many of the children she's been forced to rub shoulders with have not always been the most trustworthy.'

'You mean, a lot of them were the children of "other ranks",' Woodend said, disapprovingly.

'If you wish to put it like that, then yes, I suppose that is what I mean,' Dunn said unapologetically. 'Though the RAF fares a little better in this respect than the other services, there are still only two classes of men in the armed forces – those

136

who give the orders and those who would be completely
lost without firm discipline being imposed on them. Can
you really expect the children to behave any differently to
their parents?'

'Nice view of human nature, you have,' Woodend said.
'So you're sayin' that Helen probably had her pencil case
with her in the playground?'

'I would be very surprised indeed if she hadn't.'

'Tell me about your other daughter, Squadron Leader,'
Woodend said. 'The one who died.'

'I know which one you mean without any amplification,'
Dunn said coldly. 'And I completely fail see what her death
could possibly have to do with Helen's disappearance.'

'You wouldn't see, not bein' a trained policeman,' Woodend told him, equally frostily.

'If you could just explain—'

'All right,' Woodend agreed. 'I'm under no obligation to,
but I will. I'm not interested in your other daughter's death in
itself, only for the effect it might have on Helen. I'm tryin' to
get inside her head, you see – tryin' to understand what might
have motivated her to act as she did.'

'I don't see why that is necessary,' Dunn said. 'It's not as
if Helen asked to be kidnapped, is it?'

'No, but it's highly unlikely that the kidnapper snatched
her from the playground,' Woodend said. 'The other kids
would have noticed if he had. So she played at least a small
part in the process – she went to him, rather than him comin'
to her – an' I'm tryin' to work out what made her do that.'

'And you think my elder daughter's death—?'

'I don't know,' Woodend admitted. 'I'm just gropin'
around here, tryin' to find somethin' which might help me.
An' your elder daughter's death is as good a place to start
as any. Now, normally, I wouldn't be as blunt with people as
I'm bein' with you, but you seem to me to be the kind of feller
whose shoulders are broad enough to take the pressure.'

Dunn nodded. 'Very well,' he said. 'Helen was naturally

shocked when Janice was drowned – more than shocked. But she pulled herself out of it very quickly – just I would have expected her to – because she saw her duty as clearly as I saw mine.'

'Her *duty*?'

'Helen's mother has never been a strong woman. Normal life is hard enough for her to get through, without her burden being increased by a family tragedy. She would have gone completely to pieces after Janice died if it hadn't been for the support that Helen and I gave her. And I have to admit that Helen has been magnificent throughout the whole affair. She has tried her utmost not only to be the best daughter she can be, but also to fill the space left by Janice as well. Does that answer your question?'

'Yes,' Woodend said pensively. 'I think it does.'

'Do you have any more questions?'

'Just the one,' Woodend said.

'And what might that be?'

'When you answered the door just now, the first thing I expected you to ask me was whether I'd found your daughter. But you didn't do that – an' I'm wonderin' why.'

'You'd have been happier if I'd chosen to behave completely irrationally, would you?' Dunn asked.

'Come again?'

'I'm a pilot. I'm trained to assess crisis situations, and to react instantly. When I saw you at the door, I could tell immediately that you didn't have good news to bring me – or any tragic news, either – so what would have been the point in wasting time by asking you if you did?'

'No point at all,' Woodend agreed. 'But most men would have done, anyway.'

'I'm not most men.'

'No,' Woodend said pensively. 'You're not, are you?'

'What was the name of that German inspector who helped

us out on the Westbury Park case?' Woodend asked Rutter as they drove back to police headquarters.

'Kohl. Hans Kohl.'

'You got on well with him, didn't you?'

'Very well. He's a good bobby.'

'An' do you still keep in touch with him?'

Rutter shrugged. 'Sort of. We exchange Christmas cards, and he sent Maria some flowers when Lindie was born. Why do you ask?'

'Get in touch with him,' Woodend said. 'Ask him to see what he can find out about Janice Dunn's death.'

'Any particular reason?' Rutter asked.

'Not *that* particular,' Woodend admitted. 'I'm just tryin' to build a better picture of the whole situation. With any other case, I'd probably have relied on whatever the parents told me, but tryin' to get any information out of Squadron Leader Dunn is like tryin' to squeeze blood from a stone.'

'A *cold* stone,' Rutter said.

'A very cold stone indeed,' Woodend agreed.

Twenty

It was as Monika Paniatowski's MGA overtook a lorry in a way which could have only been called reckless – even by her own high-speed standards – that DCI Horrocks finally spoke.

'Is there something on your mind, Monika?' he asked. 'Because if there is, I rather think I'd like to hear about it – before you kill us both.'

Paniatowski slowed down almost to a crawl, infuriating the driver of the lorry she'd so recently shot past. 'Are you any more comfortable with this speed, sir?' she asked.

'Out with it, Monika,' Horrocks said.

Why not? Paniatowski asked herself. Why not tell the bastard exactly what was going through her head?

'What the hell sort of stunt do you think you were pulling back there at the base, sir?' she demanded.

'Stunt?' Horrocks repeated. 'I'm not sure I know what you mean. If you remember, I asked you if it would embarrass you to stay in the room while Tooley told me more about his adulterous activities. I certainly wanted you to, because I knew that would make him uncomfortable – and men who are not at their ease often let slip more than they intended to. So when you said you didn't mind staying, I took you at your word. If I'd realised how much it would upset you—'

'It didn't upset me,' Paniatowski said. 'I'm a detective sergeant, not a nun. If he'd pulled out his John Thomas, slapped it on the desk, and asked us both to sign it for him,

140

I wouldn't have got upset – I'd just have asked him if he wanted my full name or only my initials.'

'So if that didn't bother you . . . ?'

'It's what happened later that I'm angry about.'

'You mean the fact that I *did* eventually ask you to leave?'

'You know bloody well that's what I mean.' Paniatowski said, pressing down harder on the accelerator again and picking up speed as she approached a sharp bend. 'Listen, sir, can't we make a deal?'

'What kind of deal?'

'If you don't treat me like a complete bloody idiot, I won't treat you like one.'

Horrocks nodded. 'All right.'

'Why did you throw me out?'

'The reason I asked you to leave when I did was because I could see that the rest of the interview would have nothing to do with the particular investigation you were involved in.'

'Then what *did* it have to do with, sir?'

'I thought I told you to call me Jack.'

'I've tried that, and I don't feel comfortable with it. Chief Inspector Woodend's a friend of mine – I trust him – and I don't even call *him* by his first name.'

Horrocks smiled. 'Which is another way of saying, I suppose, that you *don't* trust me.'

'You haven't given me much reason to so far, have you?'

'Perhaps not,' Horrocks replied. 'All right, let's start again, shall we? Your interest in talking to Captain Tooley was to see how he squared up as a murder suspect. Having heard him for yourself, do you think it's likely that he's Verity Beale's murderer?'

'No, not really,' Paniatowski admitted.

'Neither do I. His brain might be residing somewhere in his underpants, but that doesn't make him a killer. He's a worried man – we both saw that – but I think he's far more worried his wife will find out about his little fling than he is about being charged with the murder. Do you agree with me on that?'

'Yes, I do.'

'So, having put him fairly low down on our list of suspects, I took the opportunity to do a favour for a colleague.'

'A colleague? From the Yard?'

'No, not from the Yard. From the Federal Bureau of Investigation in Washington DC.'

'You seem to have some long-distance friends,' Paniatowski said.

'His name's Sam Goldsmith, not that that will mean anything to you. I met him at one of these international conferences which senior officers have to attend from time to time, and we seemed to hit it off right from the start.'

'How very cosy for the pair of you,' Paniatowski said, still refusing to be mollified.

'You're getting what you told me you wanted, Monika – just don't push it too far,' Horrocks said, with a hint of reproach in his voice.

'Sorry, sir. Carry on.'

'As you may, or may not, know, the FBI has a records and files system that we could only dream of possessing here in England,' Horrocks continued, 'and so, last night I gave old Sam a ring to see if there was anything useful he could tell me about Tooley. Or anyone else on the base, for that matter.'

'Go on.'

That's where I got the information about Tooley being something of a Red sympathiser – from Sam. Frankly, I didn't think that would be of much use to us in the Verity Beale case, and it hasn't been. On the other hand, since Sam had tried his best to help us, I thought I'd return the compliment by finding out whether there was anything Captain Tooley has done since he's been here in England which could be added to his FBI dossier.'

'And was there?'

'Not on the surface. Frankly, I think the Americans in

general – and the FBI in particular – are a little too obsessed with "Reds under the bed". Still, I suppose you can't blame them at the moment, what with all this palaver blowing up over Cuba. And it never does any harm to have the Yanks on your side, does it?'

'I suppose not.'

'So have I explained my actions to your satisfaction?'

'It might have helped if you'd briefed me about what you were going to do before we ever saw Tooley,' Paniatowski said.

'Yes, you're right. Now I've got to know you better, I won't make the same mistake again,' Horrocks said, perhaps just a little ambiguously.

'Any word yet on the Armstrong Siddeley which was parked outside the pub where Miss Beale had her last drink?' Paniatowski asked.

'The Yard's still working on it,' Horrocks said brusquely.

'What about Verity Beale's personal history before she came up to Lancashire?'

'They're still working on that, too.'

'The forensics from the Spinner car park?'

'I'm waiting for that report, as well.'

'With all due respect, sir, it doesn't seem as if the Yard's doing very much at all,' Paniatowski said.

'And with all due consideration for your feelings of impatience, Sergeant, it's the officer in charge, *not his bagman*, who decides whether or not the case is moving at a satisfactory pace,' Horrocks replied, with an edge to his voice.

Paniatowski swallowed – hard! 'Sorry, sir,' she said. 'So given that we haven't got much information to work on, where *do* we go from here?'

'Well, as you've been at such pains to point out, there's not really much we *can* do until we hear from London,' Horrocks said. 'Why don't we go for a drive?'

'A drive?'

'Yes. I thought you could show me a bit of the countryside, and then we could stop off at a pleasant pub for lunch.'

'We're in the middle of a murder investigation, sir,' Paniatowski pointed out.

'True. But it's unlikely the murderer's going to go away just because we take a few hours off, now is it? Besides, I'm a new boy here. I think it might be useful to get the lay of the land – develop a feeling for the area. Isn't that the way your beloved Chief Inspector Woodend – Cloggin'-it Charlie – usually works?'

'Yes, sir, it is,' Paniatowski said. 'But how did *you* know that?'

Twenty-One

Only the previous morning, Park Road had been no more than a quiet street which ran past Whitebridge's oldest school. The murder – and the kidnapping which followed it – had changed all that. The modest sign which announced the name of the school was now flanked by two hastily painted notices which screamed that the public were not admitted under any circumstances. The playground, empty the last time Woodend visited the school, was being patrolled by three uniformed men from a private security firm. And on the fringes of the park itself stood at least a couple of dozen people, gazing with morbid curiosity at the school buildings, as if they expected them to be the backdrop for some sudden, dramatic incident.

Nor was that all, Woodend noted as he slowed down and indicated that he was pulling in. Standing at the gate, and obviously arguing with one of the security men, was a young woman who had long black hair and was dressed in one of the trench coats which had almost become *de rigueur* for crime reporters.

The chief inspector sighed heavily. He was not surprised that Elizabeth Driver had chosen this particular story as the material from which to spin a piece of creative fiction she would then pass off as hard news, but she was certainly a complication he really didn't need on a case which mattered as much to him as this one did.

Ignoring the double yellow lines on the road, he parked his car just beyond the school gate. By the time he had opened the door to step out, Elizabeth Driver, notebook in hand, was standing directly in front of him.

'Those bloody idiots on the gate won't let me go into the school,' she complained.

'How amazin',' Woodend replied.

'I could really help them with this one.'

'Maybe you could if you wanted to,' Woodend agreed, 'but let's face it, Miss Driver, helpin' other people has never really been one of your priorities, now has it?'

'So you won't give me a quote on the murder?'

'The murder investigation has nothin' to do with me,' Woodend said, thinking to himself: Unless it's connected to the kidnapping.

And if it *was* connected, Elizabeth Driver was the *last* person he'd tell!

The reporter smiled. 'I know the murder investigation hasn't got anything to do with you. That's rather what I hoped for a quote on.'

'Come again?' Woodend said.

'I've covered enough murders now to know the way the police run things, and I've never come across anything like this investigation.'

'What do you mean by that?' Woodend asked, becoming curious, despite himself.

'There's normally a big team assigned to a murder. This time, in case you haven't noticed, the team consists solely of your mate, Sergeant Monika Paniatowski, and a chief inspector from London.'

'An' in case *you* haven't noticed, we've got a missin' girl who's takin' up most of our manpower,' Woodend countered.

'So you're saying that Miss Beale's horrific murder is being largely ignored?' Elizabeth Driver prompted.

'No, I'm not sayin' that at all – as you well know. What I *am* sayin' is that it's bein' mostly handled by people outside this force – mainly from the Yard – which is somethin' you should already know if you were doin' your job properly.'

'Another thing,' Elizabeth Driver said, undeterred, as always, by the implied rebuke. 'Why is this copper from London doing his level best to keep away from the spotlight? He wasn't part of the television appeal last night, and he hasn't called any press conferences yet.'

'Maybe somebody's warned him about people like you,' Woodend suggested.

'If you'd just put aside your personal dislike for me for a moment, and listen to what I have to say, you might learn something very interesting,' Elizabeth Driver told him.

'All right,' Woodend agreed. 'You've got two minutes.'

'Despite the fact you've worked in Scotland Yard yourself, you don't actually know this Chief Inspector Horrocks, do you?'

'You were supposed to be tellin' me somethin' I didn't know, not interrogatin' me.'

'That's just what I thought,' Elizabeth Driver said, reading her own meaning into his words. 'You've never actually heard of the man, have you? And do you know why?'

'Because I left the Yard before he joined it?'

'Exactly!'

'So we don't know each other because we've never met. Now there's a scoop for your front page if I ever heard one.'

'Why don't you ask me *when* he joined the Yard?'

Woodend sighed. 'All right, if that will keep you happy. When did he join the Yard?'

'I don't know.'

'Well, that's another highly instructive piece of information.'

'But I *should* know, shouldn't I? It should be a matter of public record.'

'What exactly are you sayin' here?' Woodend asked.

'I got one of my colleagues in London to ring the Yard and

ask how long Horrocks has been working there. The man in Personnel he talked to said there was no such DCI.'

'So whoever was answerin' the inquiry couldn't read the records properly. That's nothin' new.'

'Half an hour later, the same man rang my colleague back. He was very apologetic. He said that, of course, there was a DCI Horrocks. He couldn't think what had ever made him say there wasn't.'

'Well, there you are, then.'

'So my colleague asked when Horrocks had joined the Yard, and the man suddenly went all vague again – said he'd have to check up on the exact details, and he'd get back to him on it.'

'An' he probably will.'

'Then,' Elizabeth Driver said, with a hint of triumph creeping into her voice, 'my colleague asked where Horrocks had been working before he was transferred to the Yard, and the man said he believed it had been in "B" Department, which, as I'm sure you know, is the Traffic and Transport Division.'

'Aye, by some quirk of fate I do happen to know that,' Woodend replied dryly.

'But there's no record of any DCI called Horrocks working in "B" Department.'

'So maybe he's been recently promoted,' Woodend suggested.

'There's no record of a *DI* Horrocks working there, either.'

'Then perhaps the man from Personnel was wrong about where he'd been posted last.'

'And there's no record of a DI *or* DCI Horrocks working in "A", "C" or "D" Department, either,' Elizabeth Driver said, as if she were playing her trump card. 'Don't you think that's just a little strange?'

'I think your mate in London has probably got the whole thing round his neck,' Woodend said. 'I think that if he goes back an' checks over his facts again – carefully, this time –

he'll soon find out exactly where Mr Horrocks was workin' before he moved to the Yard.'

'You might be pushing out the official line to me, but you don't sound at all convinced yourself,' Elizabeth Driver told him.

No, I probably don't, Woodend thought. An' that just might be because I'm *not*.

Bob Rutter sat as his desk at the top of the horseshoe in the incident centre, looking through tired eyes at the rest of the team. Apart from a lull in the middle of the night, every one of them had been almost constantly on the phone since Cloggin'-it Charlie and Helen Dunn's mother had made their appeal for information the night before.

Some of the calls had come from cranks, eager to implicate their neighbours or advance some insane pet conspiracy theory. Others had come from well-meaning people who desperately wanted to help, but who, in fact, had nothing to contribute. There had even been a few calls which had sounded promising, but had led the follow-up teams to quite another young girl than the one who had gone missing.

It was possible – even probable – that this whole exercise would turn out to be a complete waste of effort, he thought. Yet every time he heard a telephone ring, Rutter experienced a tiny flicker of hope that this call might be the one which would prove to be a breakthrough.

He turned to the large stack of statements and reports which had been building up on his desk since the previous afternoon. Each of the reports had been thoroughly checked through by at least two officers, and anything which might be of even the slightest importance reported to the collator, who had logged it for future cross-reference. That should have been the end of the process. Rutter was under no obligation to go through the pile himself, yet, feeling almost as driven as his boss was, he found himself reaching towards the stack.

The first file he opened was a report on the search of the

park which had been carried out the previous afternoon. There had been no rain for some time, the report pointed out, and thus, though crushed grass around the bushes opposite the school would indicate that someone had been standing there at some point in the day, there was no possibility of lifting any footprints. Nor were there any other clues, such as cigarette ends or personal objects which had been accidentally dropped.

Rutter put the file to one side and reached for the next, which listed objects recovered from other parts of the park. He ran his eyes quickly down the list. Coins amounting to a grand total of one shilling and threepence ha'penny. A penknife. A scarf. A left glove. Four contraceptive sheaths (used) and one still in its packet. A pencil case. A set of house keys. An empty whisky bottle. A pornographic magazine. A Serbo-Croat phrase book . . .

A Serbo-Croat phrase book! Who the bloody hell could have any possible use for a Serbo-Croat phrase book in Whitebridge? Rutter wondered.

He reached for a third file – this one a report of people and vehicles spotted in the vicinity at the time of the disappearance – and the name of one vehicle leapt off the page at him!

Rage was a rare experience for Rutter, but it blazed through him now.

'Which incompetent half-wit's in charge of checking car registrations against owners?' he screamed.

His team looked up, startled.

'That . . . that would be me, sir,' Sergeant Cowgill said.

'And did you happen to notice that there was an Armstrong Siddeley Sapphire parked on the road at the bottom of the Corporation Park around the time Helen Dunn disappeared?' Rutter demanded.

'Yes, sir, I did.'

'Then why the bloody hell haven't you found out who it belongs to?'

'I'm workin' my way down the list as fast as I can, sir,' Cowgill said defensively.

'Working your way down the list! It should have been the first bloody vehicle you checked on. It was spotted outside the Spinner, for Christ's sake. Verity Beale's landlady saw—'

He stopped, suddenly. He and Woodend had discussed the possibility of the murder and the kidnapping being connected, but as far as all the men in this room were concerned, they were two completely separate cases.

Of course Cowgill would have attached no special significance to the Armstrong Siddeley. Knowing as little as he did about the Verity Beale case, why should he have?

Rutter took a deep breath. 'Sorry about that outburst, Sergeant,' he said. 'Would you do me a big favour and move the Armstrong Siddeley to the top of your list? I'd like to know who it belongs to as soon as possible.'

'I'll get on to it right away, sir,' Cowgill promised.

If she'd been out drinking with Woodend, Monika Paniatowski would probably have ordered a vodka. But she wasn't with Woodend in this country pub a few miles outside Lancaster – she was with Detective Chief Inspector Jack Horrocks of Scotland Yard. And caution told her to stick to fruit juice.

Horrocks took a sip of the gin and tonic he'd ordered for himself, then said, 'You've got to learn to play the game, Monika.'

'I beg your pardon, sir?'

'The game – you've got to learn how to play it properly, or you'll end up like your boss, Cloggin'-it Charlie.'

'There are a lot of worse ways that I *could* end up,' Monika Paniatowski said tartly.

Horrocks shook his head. 'No, there aren't – as you'd soon realise if you really thought about it. Charlie Woodend's got as far as he's ever going to go. He's a dinosaur. A throwback. But you, Monika – you could be the first female chief constable in the country.'

'Do you think so?'

'Yes, I do, but as I said, you'll have to learn how to play it skilfully – learn how to create the right impression. You think we've wasted our time this morning, now don't you?'

'Honestly, yes,' Paniatowski replied.

'I admire honesty in a person – as long as it's used in moderation,' Horrocks said. 'But the fact is, we haven't been wasting time at all. We've merely been letting it *pass by*. And do you know why?'

'No.'

'Because if we'd solved the case immediately, our superiors would have assumed it must have been open and shut from the start. Whereas, if we wait a while, they'll draw the conclusion that it was probably quite complicated and, but for our brilliant detective work, it might have gone unsolved for ever.'

'But by letting the trail go cold, aren't we running the risk that we *won't* get a result?' Paniatowski asked.

'Not at all.'

'You sound as if you know something that I don't know.'

'I probably know a great many things you don't know.'

'I meant about this case.'

'Yes, I know you did,' Horrocks admitted. 'And you're quite right, I do know things you don't.'

'How can you, when I've been working on it for longer than you have, and you haven't seen anything that I haven't seen myself?'

Horrocks tapped the side of his nose with his index finger. 'Ways and means, Monika,' he said. 'Ways and means.'

'I don't understand.'

'And sometimes it's *better* not to understand. Let me just assure you that the case *will* be solved, and though you might not see exactly *how* it's done, I'll make sure that you get most of the credit for it.'

'Why should you do that?'

'Because I don't want the credit for myself – and even if

152

I did, my superiors would not be very pleased if I accepted it.'

'You're not making a lot of sense,' Paniatowski said.

'I'm sure I'm not, but if you want this investigation to be a real step up for you, that's something you're just going to have to get used to. And there's one other thing I should probably make clear, while I'm about it.'

'And that is?'

'Once this case is over, and I'm back in London, I'll want you to continue to work for me. The work won't be acknowledged directly. Your chief constable will probably pretend he knows nothing about it – but it will *only* be a pretence, and if you carry out the tasks I set you satisfactorily, you could find yourself promoted to inspector before very much longer.'

'I don't see why you should need me to continue to work for you once this case is over,' Paniatowski said.

'Of course you don't,' Horrocks agreed. 'But, in time, you will. And if you're anything like as ambitious as I think you are, you'll be very glad I picked you rather than Inspector Rutter.'

'So you know about Mr Rutter as well as Mr Woodend, do you?' Paniatowski asked.

Horrocks smiled. 'As I said earlier, I know about a lot of things.'

Twenty-Two

Walter Hargreaves did not look a happy man, Woodend thought. The deputy head's hands seemed to have taken on a life of their own, and fiddled relentlessly with the paper clips on his desk. His moustache, always pencil-thin, seemed to have shrunk even further since the last time they had met. All the confidence and competence the man had exuded at their previous meeting – and which Woodend was sure had been developed through a lifetime of achievement – seemed to have evaporated. If ever a man could truly be called a shadow of his former self, then that man was Walter Hargreaves.

'This is a very difficult time for all of us at King Edward's,' the deputy head lamented.

'I imagine it is,' the chief inspector agreed. 'But you'd be wrong to blame yourselves for that poor little lass's disappearance, you know. It could have happened in any school.'

'King Edward's has always had its enemies,' Hargreaves continued, talking more to himself than to Woodend. 'Centres of excellence will always draw the envy of those who are excluded from them. And, over the years, it has had its share of crises, too. In the late eighteenth century, things were so bad that the school shrunk in size to no more than one teacher and a single room in the back of a church. Did you know that?'

'No, I didn't,' Woodend said.

'Yet it survived, because, whatever else happened to it, it

managed to keep its shining reputation intact. Now, in the course of a single day, we have received two blows which threaten to destroy several centuries of work by hundreds of dedicated men like myself. There are journalists at our very gate, you know.'

'Well, one journalist, anyway,' Woodend amended.

'Leeches – that's what they are. They sense our temporary weakness and are just waiting for their opportunity to fasten themselves on the body of the school and suck the precious life-blood out of it.' He sighed. 'If only the board of governors, in its wisdom, had appointed one of our own to guide the progress of the school. If only they had seen that it needed someone at the helm who loved the school – and who would put its interests first.'

'An' you're sayin' that this headmaster you've got now doesn't do that?' Woodend asked, his curiosity aroused.

'What?' Hargreaves asked, as if he had only just remembered that there was someone else in the room.

'You were sayin' that this headmaster seems not to be puttin' the interests of the school first,' Woodend prompted.

'If that's the impression you gained from what I've said, then I'm afraid you've misunderstood me,' Hargreaves said hastily. 'The headmaster is doing an excellent job – a *really* excellent job.'

'What did he do in the war?'

'Why do you ask that?'

'Why does anybody ask anythin'? I asked because I'm interested in the answer.'

'The headmaster was with General Wingate in Burma – organising the Chindits in their guerrilla war against the Japanese in the jungle. He was decorated for bravery in the field. Several times, in fact. Perhaps that was the deciding factor when the governors were making their decision on who to appoint.'

'You were a candidate for the job yourself?' Woodend guessed.

'I applied,' Hargreaves admitted.

'An' what did *you* do durin' the war? Did you see action?'

Hargreaves shook his head regretfully. 'I had flat feet. They wouldn't take me. I spent my war in England – working for the Pay Corps. *I* was never given the chance to be a hero.' He paused, as if he had suddenly realised that Woodend was leading him somewhere he would rather not go. 'What has any of this got to do with Helen Dunn's disappearance?' he asked.

'Not a lot,' Woodend admitted. 'So let's get *back* to Helen, shall we? What's she like as a pupil?'

'Academically, very successful. Athletically, more than adequate,' Hargeaves said evasively.

'But she doesn't seem to have many friends in the school?'

'None at all. She was by nature a rather solitary individual. Some children are.'

'You do know you're talkin' about her in the past tense, don't you?' Woodend asked. 'Does that mean you think she's already dead?'

Hargreaves ran his hand agitatedly through his silver-grey hair. 'No . . . I . . . No, of course not. It was a slip of the tongue, that's all.'

'If we *are* to have any chance of findin' her alive, we need everybody who knew her to be open an' frank with us,' Woodend told him.

'Naturally,' Hargreaves agreed.

'Which means you need to tell me a hell of a lot more about her than I could have read off her report card. Is she a disruptive kid?'

'Not in school, no.'

'But *outside* it?'

One of the paper clips Hargreaves had been fiddling compulsively with snapped in two. The deputy headmaster looked down at it, as if surprised that his hands were capable of even such minor destruction. 'This is all very difficult,' he said.

'A girl's life is at stake!' Woodend reminded him.

The deputy head sighed. 'One of the staff took Helen's class into Whitebridge to see an exhibition in the Town Hall,' he said reluctantly. 'When it was over, the teacher gave the class permission to go to a nearby tea shop. Helen slipped away from the group. She went into Wilkinson's Department Store. Just as she was leaving, the store detective challenged her, and asked her to open her briefcase. Inside were several things that – not to put too fine a point on it – she'd been attempting to steal.'

'What kinds of things?'

'I forget the details now, but they were all trivial items which she could have bought out of her pocket money if she'd wanted to.'

'Did the store call in the police?'

Hargreaves shook his head. 'Helen was in uniform.'

'What's that got to do with it?'

The deputy head looked at him, almost pityingly. 'The *King Edward's* school uniform,' he amplified.

'I still don't get it.'

'Both David Wilkinson, who manages the shop, and his father, who is chairman, are old boys of the school. They would never have done anything to damage King Edward's reputation.'

'So nobody called the police. What did Helen's father have to say about the incident?'

'He . . . er . . . wasn't told.'

'Why the hell not? Didn't he have a *right* to know? Wouldn't you *normally* have informed the parents?'

'Normally, yes,' Hargreaves agreed.

'So what was different about this particular case?'

'The teacher who was tutoring Helen privately after school interceded on her behalf and promised there would be no repetition of the incident.'

'I'll need to speak to this teacher. What's his name?'

'As a matter of fact, it was Miss Beale.'

'I see,' Woodend said heavily. 'So Miss Beale – a new teacher to the school, a teacher who can't have had more than a few years' experience – asks you to go against normal practice, and you agree? Just like that!'

'Not just like that,' Hargreaves said. 'I would have told her it wasn't possible, but unfortunately . . .'

'Yes?'

'Unfortunately, she had the headmaster's backing.'

'Did she? An' why was that?'

'Perhaps he was seeking to protect the school.'

'An' did nobody give any thought to protectin' the kid?'

'I'm afraid I'm not following you,' Hargeaves said unconvincingly.

'Well, you bloody well should be,' Woodend told him. 'The girl goes into a department store. In the middle of the school day! Dressed in a clearly identifiable uniform! An' what does she do once she's inside? She steals some things that she doesn't even really want. Didn't you even bother to ask yourself why?'

'I *know* why!' Hargreaves said. His voice sounded angry – but Woodend did not think the anger was directed against the man who had forced him to make the admission. 'She stole with the sole intention of getting caught. She wanted to do something to make her father notice her – to see her as an individual, rather than just a project he was developing.'

'Aye, that's what I think, an' all,' Woodend said. 'It was a call for help. So why did you ignore it?'

'Because I had no choice in the matter. Because I was merely obeying instructions.'

'That's what all those Nazi bastards used as their defence at the Nuremberg Trials,' Woodend said. 'But that made no difference to the judges – they still strung the buggers up.'

Twenty-Three

Rutter glanced quickly up and down the neat suburban street, saw there was no sign of an Armstrong Siddeley Sapphire anywhere, and signalled to the two teams of DCs in their strategically parked cars that they were to make no move unless he called for assistance. That done, he walked up the path of 33 Lime Grove.

The woman who answered the door was in her middle thirties, he guessed, though there was still something of a childlike quality to her open, trusting face. She was wearing a floral apron and rubber kitchen gloves, and seemed quite surprised that anyone should be calling at that time of day.

'Mrs Cray?' Rutter asked.

'Yes?'

'I'm Inspector Rutter, from the Whitebridge Police. I was wondering if I could speak to your husband.'

'He's not in,' the woman said, starting to look a little concerned. 'What's this all about?'

'Nothing you should get worried over,' Rutter said, not yet *quite* sure he was lying. 'We're just conducting a few routine inquiries, and we thought your husband might be able to help us with one of them. Where is he, by the way? At work?'

'That's right.'

'And his place of work is the BAI factory?'

'Yes. He's a quality control engineer. This hasn't got anything to do with the murder – or the missing girl – has it?'

'What makes you ask that?' Rutter said. 'You don't happen to know Verity Beale or Helen Dunn, do you?'

'Not as far as I'm aware,' Mrs Cray said. 'But since they're the ones who've been in all the papers . . .'

'Those cases are both being handled by more experienced officers than me,' Rutter said, flashing one of his famous boyish grins. 'I'm dealing with a much less important matter. You don't happen to remember whether or not your husband was at home the night before last, do you?'

'The night of the murder, you mean?'

'Yes, it was the night of the murder, now I come to think of it. *Was* he at home? Or, to put it another way, were you together? Did you go out for a meal or something?'

'We rarely go out as a couple. The children aren't really old enough to be left in the house alone, and reliable babysitters are very hard to find.'

'So you both stayed in, did you?'

'No, *I* stayed in. Roger had to attend a meeting.'

'What kind of meeting?'

Mrs Cray shrugged. 'I don't know. I assumed it had something to do with his work.'

'You sound like you don't get much time alone together,' Rutter said, sympathetically.

'Oh, it's not that bad,' Mrs Cray said. 'With the kids at school all day, we can sometimes manage to meet for lunch in Whitebridge.'

'Did you have lunch together yesterday?'

'No, Roger couldn't. He had another meeting and . . . and why are you asking me all these questions about my husband's whereabouts?'

Rutter turned and waved to one of parked cars, then swung round to face Mrs Cray again. 'I've just called a policewoman over,' he explained. 'I'd like her to stay with you for a while.'

'What for?'

'She won't be any trouble. You can carry on with your housework. She'll even help you with it if you want her to.'

'I'm not an idiot,' Mrs Cray said angrily. 'Why will she be here?'

'She'll be here to make sure that you can't call your husband,' Rutter admitted.

'So he is in trouble?'

'I don't know. And I certainly don't want to alarm you unnecessarily.' Rutter hesitated for a second, then added, 'But in all fairness, I think you should be prepared for a shock.'

Roger Cray walked through the main hangar-workshop where the fuselage of the TSR2 – the golden future of Britain's air defences, so some thought – was being constructed.

Everything was going wrong, he told himself worriedly. Everything was going terribly, tragically wrong.

Martin Dove had made it all so simple when he'd explained it during their clandestine meetings.

'I'm a teacher at the *grammar* school, for God's sake!' Dove had said. 'A pillar of the local establishment! Somebody you can trust your children with. Nobody's going to suspect me, not even for a moment.'

'And what about me?' Cray had asked worriedly.

'Why should they suspect you?'

'Because of who I am!'

'Let's think about who you are, if that's what's concerning you,' Dove had said, irritatingly calmly and logically. 'You're a highly qualified man, holding down a highly respectable job. You've no criminal record – you don't even have any outstanding parking tickets. You're paying off a mortgage you can easily afford, and you have a wife and two children. Now isn't that all true?'

'Yes, it's all true.'

'You're Mr Middle Britain – so conventional you're almost boring. It's never going to cross anybody's mind that you'd risk all that to do something which could mean you'd end up behind bars for the rest of your life. That's what makes it so safe, you see – we're both totally above suspicion.'

Oh, he had a way with words, did Martin Dove, Cray thought bitterly. He could talk anybody into anything. But his words didn't seem to mean so much when they came up against stark reality.

'You all right, Mr Cray?' one of the welders called to him from the scaffolding.

'I'm fine,' Cray shouted back.

But he was thinking, Is it *so* obvious I'm in a state that even a man standing so far away from me can see it?

They should have called it off the moment Verity Beale had seen them together in the Spinner, he thought.

Verity Beale!

What a cunning, scheming bitch she had been! The first time they'd met, he'd thought the encounter had been accidental. But it hadn't been at all! Nothing Verity Beale did – or, rather, *had* ever done – had been accidental. She had played him like a violin. He could see that now. She had pretended to be interested in him, whereas all she'd really had an interest in was what he stood *for*.

Yes, once they'd seen Verity in the pub, they should have realised the game was up, and cut their losses. And if it had been left up to him, that was just what he *would* have done. But bloody Martin Dove had persuaded him – once again – that if they took the necessary precautions they could still get away with it.

He wondered if anybody had seen them together in the park the previous lunchtime – wondered if, even now, some policeman was matching up a series of reports which would eventually lead to his arrest.

He couldn't bear the thought of a trial. He would never be able to stand the shame. If it looked as if an arrest was imminent, he promised himself, he would take his own life without a second's hesitation.

As a distraction from his problems, he looked up at the shiny metal body which was gradually taking shape under the hangar roof.

The TSR-bloody-2! He had to laugh when he heard the politicians talking so confidently about it on the television.

He remembered the joke he had once heard.

Question: What's the definition of a camel?

Answer: A camel is a horse designed by a committee!

That was what this plane was – a horse designed by a committee. Everybody involved wanted something different from it, and because of that, what had originally been intended as a small, fast, strike-fighter had become a monster forced to incorporate a larger crew, a higher speed, longer range, higher altitude and a shorter take-off. And it simply could not be done! As a direct result of all the interested parties – the Army, the Navy *and* the Air Force – insisting on keeping what *they* wanted, the end product was bound to be something that *nobody* wanted.

Cray lowered his eyes from the fuselage to ground level. He had not been expecting to see the two men standing in the workshop doorway, looking around as if they weren't quite certain where to go next – but when he did, he felt his heart start to beat faster.

He was being irrational, he told himself. The men, whoever they were, probably had a perfectly legitimate reason for being there which had nothing to do with him. But even as his brain argued the case for their innocuousness, his heartbeats were accelerating from a canter to a gallop.

One of the foremen approached the men, and when they had exchanged a few words with him, he pointed towards the plane.

'Nothing to do with me,' a frightened voice somewhere in Cray's brain screamed. 'Nothing to do with me! Nothing to do with *me*!'

They were walking towards him now. One of them was tall, almost totally bald, and had one of those drooping moustaches that the villains always sported in cowboy films. The other was shorter but broader, and had on glasses with metal frames. They were both wearing suits, but they were not the muted conservative suits that men from the Ministry of Aviation favoured. Nor was the grim set of their features anything like the expressions of mild boredom he was used to seeing on the faces of the bureaucrats he was accustomed to dealing with.

The shame of it, he thought again.

And he found himself wondering how his mother would feel when the newspapers arrived at the nursing home where she lived, with his story splashed all over the front pages.

The men drew level with him, and came to a halt.

'Mr Cray?' asked the taller one with the drooping moustache. 'Mr Roger Cray?'

'That's . . . that's me,' Cray stuttered.

'And that's your Armstrong Siddeley Sapphire out there in the middle of the staff car park, is it, Mr Cray?'

'Yes.'

'In that case, if you don't mind, sir, we'd like you to come along with us.'

'And if I do mind?'

The man with the bald head and the moustache smiled, but it wasn't a pleasant smile – not by any stretch of the imagination. 'We'd like you to come along with us anyway.'

'You're policemen, are you?'

'That's right.'

'I think I'd like to see your warrant cards,' Cray said, trying to sound braver than he actually felt.

The bald man looked at his shorter companion. 'He wants to see our warrant cards,' he said.

'Then it's a great pity that we've left them at home, isn't it?' the shorter man replied.

The bald man shrugged. 'Sorry, sir, we don't seem to be able to oblige you there.'

'I want to call my solicitor,' Cray said.

'Perhaps later,' the shorter man told him.

'I want to call him now,' Cray insisted.

The bald man bowed his head and bent forward until his face was almost touching Cray's.

'Solicitors are for normal people,' he said in a low, menacing voice. 'People who have rights.'

'I . . . I have rights,' Cray protested.

The shorter man shook his head. 'No, you don't, Mr Cray,' he said. 'Not any more.'

'Even criminals have the right to—' Cray began.

'But then you're not even that – not even a *normal* criminal,' the shorter man interrupted him. 'You're scum! I've seen better things than you crawl from under a rock.'

'Maybe we shouldn't take him away, after all,' the bald man said his partner. 'Maybe we should just leave our-selves.'

'Thank you!' Cray gasped, before he could stop himself.

'Of course, before we do go, it'd only be fair to have a word with the other people who are working here, and tell them exactly what he's done, don't you think?' the bald man said.

'You wouldn't do that!' Cray said, almost fainting with fear.

'That's exactly what we'll do, if necessary,' the shorter man said. 'But it won't *be* necessary, will it? Because now you've had time to think about it, you realise that the best thing you can do is come with us voluntarily.'

'Where will you take me?' Cray asked. 'To Whitebridge Police Headquarters?'

'You'd like that, wouldn't you?' asked the bald man. 'You'd feel safe in Whitebridge Police Headquarters. But no, we're not going there. We've got a special place for people like you.'

Twenty-Four

Woodend surveyed the teaching staff of King Edward's Grammar School, who were sitting in a half circle around him. Some were still in a state of shock over what had happened, others seemed to have come to terms with it. Some looked like men driven into teaching by a sacred mission to impart their knowledge, others had expressions which stated clearly that they would have taken any job which guaranteed them a reasonable rate of pay and longish holidays. They were, in other words, as diverse as any other bunch of professionals he might find gathered together in one place, he thought.

'The last time I talked to you, it was about Miss Beale's murder, but that's not my direct concern any more,' he said. 'I'm investigatin' Helen Dunn's disappearance now, an' I'd be grateful for anythin' you could tell me that might help me find her.'

One of the teachers, a middle-aged man with a haircut which looked as if it had been performed with wire cutters, raised a hand.

'Yes, Mr . . .' Woodend said.

'We've already had your lads—'

'Could each of you give me your names before you speak?' Woodend asked. 'It'll make it easier for me to remember who said what.'

'Lewis Etheridge, Head of Craft,' the man with the wire-cutter haircut said, as if by announcing his position, his words would carry more weight. 'We've already had your

166

lads swarming all over the place. Isn't it a waste of time to repeat what we've already put down in our statements?'

'That's possibly true,' Woodend agreed. 'But it's also possible that by talking to you all together, rather than to each one separately, I might spark off a memory which might otherwise have stayed hidden. An' if there's a chance that might help Helen, shouldn't we give it a try?'

The majority of the teachers nodded, and even Etheridge shrugged his shoulders in resigned acceptance.

'Right, for starters, did any of you notice anythin' odd about Helen yesterday?' Woodend asked.

A teacher with a short beard put his hand up. 'Martin Dove,' he said. 'I'm not trying to sound flippant here, but Helen Dunn was odd *most* of the time. It was very hard to draw her out in class discussion—'

'You're talking about her like you know she's already dead,' said a voice from the edge of the group.

'She *is* very hard to draw out in class discussion,' Dove corrected himself. 'Most of the time she seems to live in a world of her own – except that when you mark her work, you realise she's been listening to – and remembering perfectly – every word that's been said. So I can't say I did notice anything *particularly* strange about her yesterday.'

Other teachers nodded in agreement, but none of them seemed to feel they had anything more to contribute.

'Right, let's move on to lunchtime,' Woodend suggested. 'Who was on yard duty yesterday?'

'I was,' said a middle-aged man with an ample stomach covered with a green suede waistcoat. 'Dennis Padlow, Head of Languages.'

'An' did you notice Helen, Mr Padlow?'

'Yes. She was standing by the railings near the gate. It's not the first time I've seen her there. She always seems to want to get as far away from the other pupils as possible.'

'What time would that have been, Mr Padlow?'

167

'In the earlier part of the lunch hour, I would say,' the head of languages said. 'Probably about half past twelve.'

'Did you stay in the playground for the whole of the lunch hour?'

'In the playground, yes, but not necessarily in that *part* of the playground. I also had to patrol the lower and back playgrounds.'

'So you couldn't say with any certainty when she stopped bein' by the railin's?'

'I'm afraid not.'

'Was she carryin' anythin' in her hand?' Woodend asked.

'I'm not sure I know what you mean,' Padlow said.

'The pencil case, you idiot,' someone muttered.

'Oh, of course, the pencil case,' Padlow agreed. 'Helen always carried – carries – her pencil case around with her, almost as if she's afraid that some other pupil will steal it if she leaves it in her desk.'

So it really was true! Woodend thought. That cold bastard Dunn had his daughter so intimidated that she actually carried her pencil case around with her.

'Are you sure she had it with her yesterday?' he asked.

'I couldn't swear to it,' Padlow replied. 'You know what it's like when you take something for granted – you tend to see it even if it's not there. But I'm almost certain she did.'

'Could you describe it to me, sir?'

Padlow frowned in concentration. 'It's just a fairly typical pencil case, I suppose,' he said. 'Long and thin, with rounded edges. Covered in a plastic with . . . I think . . . a green tartan design on it.'

'Nearly right, Dennis,' said another teacher, 'but it's a red case, not a green one.'

'No, it *is* green,' a third teacher said.

'Maybe she has two,' Padlow said, as if he were the chairman of a committee, doing his best to seek a reasonable compromise between warring factions.

It didn't really matter which colour it was, did it? Woodend

thought despondently. If the girl had had the pencil case on her, then any leads which might come from checking who had access to her classroom had just disappeared in a puff of smoke.

'Is there anythin' else anybody can tell me that might be useful?' he asked. 'Think hard.'

All the teachers made a show of searching their minds, but none of them seemed able to offer anything new.

'Right, thank you for your time,' Woodend said. He focused his gaze on the gangly man sitting at the edge of the semi-circle. 'Could I have a few words with you on your own, Mr Barnes?'

'Of course,' the history teacher said.

Any attempts at conversation that Paniatowski had made on the journey back from Preston were ignored by the man sitting next to her in the MGA. Well, Charlie Woodend sometimes went like that when he was thinking through a case, she told herself, and though Horrocks was as different from Woodend as chalk was to cheese, maybe that was what he was doing too.

It was not until they passed the sign which announced that they were entering Whitebridge that Paniatowski spoke to her passenger again.

'I'm sorry to disturb you, sir,' she said, 'but I really do need to know where we're going.'

'What's this road we're on now?' Horrocks asked.

'Preston New Road, sir.'

'Then that will do fine. Slow down, and drop me off at the next red traffic light.'

'I beg your pardon, sir?'

'Next red traffic light. Drop me off. What is it about that you don't understand?'

'The dropping you off bit. Don't you want me to come with you, wherever it is you're going?'

'I've no objection in principle to you tagging along while

I continue to orientate myself,' Horrocks said easily, 'but I've got another task I'd rather you devoted yourself to, if you don't mind.'

'What task?'

'That light's turning red. Pull in to the curb.'

Paniatowski did as she'd been instructed, and Horrocks stepped out of the car.

'What I want you to do,' he said from the curb, 'is to go to the library and check through the back copies of the local newspapers for any references to Verity Beale. Shouldn't take you more than three hours to do that, should it? I'll meet you back at the station when you've finished.'

'You're not serious, are you?' Paniatowski asked.

'About it taking you three hours?'

'About me going through the local newspapers.'

'Why wouldn't I be serious about that?'

'Because it's not the kind of job that you ask an experienced DS to do. If anybody has to do it – and I don't really see the value of the exercise myself – it should given to the greenest DC available.'

'But we don't *have* any DCs available, green or otherwise,' Horrocks pointed out. 'They've all been drafted into this kidnapping case. That's why I need *you* to go to the library.'

'If you're just looking for something to keep me occupied for the next couple of hours, why don't you just come right out and say it?' Paniatowski demanded, barely controlling her anger.

Horrocks smiled. 'I'm just looking for something to keep you occupied for the next couple of hours,' he told her. 'But remember what I said, Monika. However much – or however little – you contribute to solving this case, I'll personally see to it that you don't come out the loser. Years from now, you'll look back on this as your real break.'

'I want to *earn* my break when it comes,' Paniatowski said.

'And so you will,' Horrocks replied. '"They also serve who only stand and wait." One more thing, Monika.'

'Yes, sir?'

'If you should happen to run into Chief Inspector Woodend before we meet again, I want you to remember that, for once, you're not working on the same case as your boss is. You *will* remember that, won't you?'

'I'll do my best, sir,' Paniatowski said noncommittally.

'And that means that you shouldn't discuss the case you *are* working on with him – neither any of the details nor any of the specifics,' Horrocks continued, ignoring her tone. 'Treat him as if he were a journalist. Say you have no comment.'

'I wish you'd tell me what's going on, sir,' Paniatowski said. 'I wish I knew why—'

'The light's changed to green again, Monika,' Horrocks said. 'Better pull off again before some keen young copper gives you a ticket for obstruction.'

Then he smiled again, turned away from her, and strode off purposefully up the street.

The fence which surrounded the British Aircraft Industries' plant at Blackhill was as high as the one surrounding the air base just up the road from it. And it needed to be, Bob Rutter thought, because protecting the secrets of the planes they were still building was just as important as protecting the secrets of those which were already flying.

He slowed down as he approached the gate, and reached in his jacket for his warrant card. He could see a guard sitting in the blockhouse, and expected him to come out immediately. But the man gave no indication of getting up, and after waiting for close to a minute, Rutter hooted his horn.

The guard rose reluctantly to his feet, stepped out of his cosy cabin, and made his way to Rutter's car.

'Can I help you, sir?' he asked.

Rutter showed him the warrant card. 'DI Rutter, Whitebridge CID.'

'Yes?' the guard said, as if he regarded the information as far from fascinating.

'I'd like you to open the gate for me,' Rutter said, starting to feel exasperated.

'Have you got a search warrant, sir?'

'A search warrant? What do I need a search warrant for? I only want to question one of your workers.'

'It's like this, sir,' the guard explained. 'In my office, I've got a list of the people I'm allowed to admit into the complex, and if you're not on that list, you don't go through.'

'What the hell is this?' Rutter demanded.

'The rules, sir,' the guard said, his face devoid of all emotion.

'What if I were to go straight back to Whitebridge and get a bloody search warrant?'

'I think you'd find that more difficult than you seem to imagine, sir,' the guard said. 'But if you *did* get a search warrant, then, of course, I'd have to let you in, because even a sensitive quasi-military establishment of this nature is not above the law.'

He didn't talk like the average security guard, Rutter thought. And under closer inspection, he didn't *look* like the average guard, either. He was far too confident, and his eyes far too aware, for him ever to have settled for such a humble position.

'I want to speak to somebody in authority,' Rutter said.

'I'm afraid I really couldn't disturb anybody just at the moment,' the guard said.

'Then let me phone them from your office.'

The guard shook his head. 'Wouldn't do any good, sir. I've had very strict instructions, not an hour ago, from the head of security. I'm not to admit anybody who isn't on the list.'

'He can't have meant that to include the police.'

'But he did, sir. He mentioned the police specifically.'

'Could you at least bring the man I need to question to the gate?'

'I suppose so, if he's willing to come. What's his name?'

'Roger Cray. He works in—'

172

'Quality control. I know. But he isn't here. He left the plant half an hour ago.'

Had the bastard done a runner? Rutter wondered frantically. Or even worse, had he gone to wherever he was keeping Helen Dunn a prisoner?

'Did he say why he was leaving, or where he was going?' he asked.

'No, he didn't. But I imagine he was going wherever the two policemen with him were taking him.'

This was insane! Rutter thought. This was completely bloody insane!

'What two policemen?' he asked.

'Can't say I caught their names.'

'And how did *they* get in to the plant? Did *they* have a search warrant?'

'Couldn't say that either. I wasn't on duty when they arrived,' the guard lied.

Twenty-Five

Woodend and Simon Barnes walked to the edge of the playground, and came to a halt at the spot where Helen Dunn had last been seen.

'I didn't know Verity Beale had been givin' Helen Dunn private lessons,' Woodend said.

'Didn't you?' Barnes asked. 'I would have mentioned it myself, the last time we spoke, but it didn't seem very relevant then. After all, at that point none of us had any idea that Helen would go missing.'

'I suppose you're right,' Woodend agreed. He offered his packet of Capstan Full Strength to Barnes and, when the teacher shook his head, lit one up for himself. 'Miss Beale did seem to have rather a lot to do with the military, didn't she?' he continued.

'I haven't really thought about it,' Barnes admitted, 'but it's certainly true that Helen's father is in the Air Force.'

'But it's not just that, is it?' Woodend persisted. 'There were the classes on British culture that she gave at the American base.'

'Ah yes, *those* classes,' Barnes agreed. 'I rather think she must have regretted ever taking them on.'

'What makes you say that?'

'It caused resentment among certain members of staff.'

'Because she was doin' so many extra classes that she kept getting' sick an' missin' school?'

'That may have been part of it,' Barnes conceded.

'An' what's the other part?'

'There's an unwritten rule operating in this school that the senior teachers get first refusal on whatever extra classes are available.'

'An' that didn't happen in this case?'

'No, when the base job first came up, several of my colleagues said that they wanted it, but it was given to Verity without anyone else being asked if they were interested.'

'Yes, I can see how that might cause resentment,' Woodend said. 'An' as a friend of hers, you can't have liked that resentment very much, can you? In fact, I would imagine it made you right angry.'

'As a Christian, I try to take a charitable view of all my colleagues,' Barnes said evasively.

'*Try?*' Woodend prodded.

'We are all of us too often critical of others,' Barnes said philosophically. 'I'm as guilty of that as anyone, but on such occasions I always try to remember what it says in the Bible: "Why beholdest thou the mote that is in thy brother's eye, but considerest not the beam that is in thine own eye?"'

'Still, it's not always easy, is it?' Woodend asked. 'What was it that Alexander Pope said? "To err is human; to forgive, divine."'

'I've never thought Pope had it quite right, you know,' Barnes said earnestly.

'Because he was a secular writer?'

'No, not just because of that. Because, I think, he was overlooking a fundamental truth. If we ascribe the power of forgiveness only to the deity, then aren't we denying that part of God which resides inside each and every one us? And how can we *not* forgive others when we all act, at one time or another, as if we were "the jewel of gold in the swine's snout"?' Barnes laughed, suddenly and self-deprecatingly. 'I'm sorry, Chief Inspector.'

'What for?' Woodend asked.

'For preaching. My religion is the driving force in my life, but I don't see why I should inflict it on others.'

'I've had worse things inflicted on me in my time,' Wood-end said. 'But tell me, Mr Barnes, how did this resentment that some of the other teachers felt manifest itself?'

'I know that at least one member of my department went to complain about it to the deputy head.'

'An' what did Hargreaves have to say?'

'He said that his hands were tied. There was nothing he could do about it, because that commander at the base had specifically requested that Verity be given the job.'

'Hang about!' Woodend said. 'Miss Beale was new to the school – an' new to the area – yet the commander at the base asked *specifically* for her?'

'That's what Walter Hargeaves said. Of course, he may not have been telling the complete truth.'

'Or to put it another way, he may have been lyin'.'

Barnes smiled. 'Walter is famous for both his verbal footwork and his wry sense of humour. It's often said of him that he speaks with a forked tongue – and with one fork firmly in each cheek.'

Woodend laughed. 'Let's get back to Miss Beale an' Helen Dunn,' he said, becoming serious again. 'Did you know that Helen had been caught shopliftin' in Whitebridge?'

'Yes.'

'An' that Miss Beale had fought to have it kept from her parents?'

'Yes, again. Verity said she felt that the poor girl should be given a second chance.'

'An' she seemed to have enough clout to make her wishes become reality, despite normal school policy.'

Simon Barnes seemed to have stopped listening and, instead, was gazing thoughtfully into the park.

'I said, she seemed to have enough clout to make her wishes become reality,' Woodend repeated.

Barnes turned, as if he was just snapping out of a trance. 'There's been something that's been weighing on my mind since yesterday,' he said. 'I've been debating with myself

176

whether or not to tell you about it, and, to be honest, I'm still not sure I've come up with an answer.'

'If there's even the remotest chance it might help us to find Helen, you *have* to tell me.'

Barnes nodded. 'All right,' he agreed. 'But before I do, you must understand that I personally cannot believe that the person I'm going to mention had anything to do with Helen's disappearance.'

'Noted,' Woodend said. 'Who is it?'

'And it wouldn't be the first time I've seen him going into the park, either. In fact, it's become quite a habit of his.'

'The name!' Woodend said. 'Give me his name, Mr Barnes.'

'I was in the staff room yesterday lunchtime, at around twenty-five to one, and I just happened to look out of the window,' Barnes said. 'I saw one of the staff cross the road and disappear into the park.'

'His name!' Woodend repeated.

'It was Martin Dove,' Barnes said.

'The Latin teacher?'

'Yes.'

The one who had been glancing at his watch all the time Woodend had been asking questions about Verity Beale! The one who seemed as if he had much more important matters on his mind than the murder of one of his colleagues!

'There's Martin now!' Barnes said. 'But I don't know who those people with him are.'

Woodend turned to follow Barnes's gaze. The Latin teacher was walking across the playground, flanked by a bald man with a droopy moustache on one side of him and a short, broader man on the other. He looked far from happy with the situation.

The chief inspector stepped into the three men's path. 'Could I just have a quick word, Mr Dove?' he asked.

The prisoner and escort – because that was what they looked like – came to a halt.

'I'm awfully sorry, but I afraid Mr Dove can't spare the time to talk to anybody at the moment,' the bald man said, his tone in no way matching the regret expressed in his words.

'Who are hell are you?' Woodend demanded.

'Who the hell are *you*?' the bald man countered.

Woodend reached into his jacket pocket, and pulled out his warrant card. 'Chief Inspector Woodend. Central Lancs police.'

'Then we're all in the same game,' the bald man said. 'But we got here first, didn't we?'

'I'd like to see some identification,' Woodend told him.

'I'm sure you would,' the bald man responded. 'But I'm not going to produce any, am I?'

'In that case—' Woodend began.

'Mr Dove is coming with us,' the bald man said. 'You can try to stop us if you like, but I really wouldn't recommend it.'

'Wouldn't you?' Woodend asked. 'And why's that?'

The bald man grinned. 'Because if it came to violence there's two of us against you and that streak of piss and wind you've got standing next to you.'

For the first time in his life, Woodend knew what it meant when people said they needed to pinch themselves to make sure they weren't dreaming.

These two strangers might have refused to show him their warrant cards, yet his instincts told him that, despite their refusal, they really were policemen of *some* sort. And yet policeman just didn't act like they were acting.

It wasn't that he thought all bobbies were paragons of virtue. Far from it! He'd had to deal with some real nasty buggers in his time, men who'd been willing to stab him in the back at the first opportunity – Christ, he was working for a couple of them at that moment – but even bastards like Ainsworth at least followed the protocol when they were face-to-face with him!

'What kind of lunatic game do you think you're playin',

comin' on to my patch an' actin' like it was your own?' he demanded.

'I thought we'd made it perfectly plain what the game was,' the bald man said. 'The rules, as well. We're taking Mr Dove away with us, and if you try to stand in the way, you'll only get hurt.'

'I'll have your bollocks served up on a plate for this,' Woodend snarled. 'Who's your boss?'

The bald man smirked. 'Names don't matter,' he said. 'Just take it from me that my boss is bigger than your boss. Now step out of the way.'

It was very tempting to have a pop at him, if only to see the smirk disappear as the nose flattened. But Baldy was right – Woodend couldn't take on both of them – and, seeing no other option, he stepped to the side and let them pass.

The two 'policemen' and their prisoner crossed the road. They stopped in front of a parked Ford Zephyr, and while the bald man was bundling Martin Dove into the back seat, his partner opened the driver's door and climbed behind the wheel. And then they were gone, driving off down Park Road.

Woodend reached into the voluminous pocket of his hairy sports jacket and pulled out the radio which he – and the rest of the Central Lancs Police – had only recently been issued with.

'There's a black Ford Zephyr just reachin' the bottom of Park Road,' he told the controller. 'I want it intercepted as soon as possible.'

'Do you have the number, sir?' the controller asked, and when Woodend had recited it to him, he said, 'I'm afraid there's nothing we can do about that particular vehicle, sir.'

'What do you mean, there's nothin' you can do?' Woodend demanded. 'I've just *told* you what to do.'

'Yes, sir,' the controller said awkwardly. 'But I've also received a strict instruction from DCC Ainsworth that a car with that registration is not to be impeded in any way.'

Twenty-Six

I will not be intimidated, DCC Ainsworth told himself.
I'm in charge here, I'm perfectly capable of being a
hard, ruthless bastard when necessary, and I will *not* be
intimidated!

Yet it was hard not to be intimidated by Woodend at that
moment. He was a big man under normal circumstances, but
now, swollen with rage, he seemed to fill half the room.

'Why don't you sit down, so we can discuss this calmly
over a couple of glasses of Scotch?' the DCC suggested.

'With respect, *sir*, it's answers I want right now, not
Scotch!' Woodend replied.

'Then you'd better ask your questions, hadn't you, Chief
Inspector?' Ainsworth suggested.

'I've just seen Martin Dove – a teacher who may be
involved in both Helen Dunn's kidnappin' and Verity Beale's
murder – arrested by two bobbies who wouldn't even show
me their identification,' Woodend said. 'Then I ring up my
inspector an' find that the same thing's happened to him when
he tried to question an engineer called Roger Cray. So what
I want to know is this – who are these fellers and what the
bloody hell are they doin' on my patch?'

'They're from the West Riding Police. Both Cray and
Dove come within the scope of an investigation they've
been conducting for some time – an investigation which has
nothing to do with any cases we're handling.'

'What kind of investigation?'

'I'm afraid I'm not at liberty to reveal that at the moment.'

'So the two fellers who I saw arrestin' Martin Dove at Eddie's were from Yorkshire?'

'That's correct.'

'Then why did they have London accents?'

'I have a Kent accent, yet I still work for the Central Lancs Police,' Ainsworth said. 'What's the point you're trying to make, Chief Inspector?'

'That I don't believe a bloody word of any of this!'

'I'd think carefully before you called me a liar again, Charlie,' the DCC said, his voice suddenly as cold as an outside lavatory in February. 'You're not dealing with a soft touch like DCS Whittle here. One more word out of place, and I'll have you on suspension for insubordination.'

He meant it, Woodend thought. Whatever flack he had to take from the Police Federation later, Ainsworth was clearly willing to make good his threat now. And suspension was something Woodend dared not risk, because, with him out of the picture, who would there be to look out for poor little Helen Dunn?

The chief inspector took a deep breath. 'I'm sorry, sir, I was completely out of line just now,' he forced himself to say.

'So you accept the fact that the two detectives you saw in the playground were from Yorkshire?'

'If that's what you tell me, sir, then of course I have no alternative but to believe you.'

Ainsworth nodded. 'I really think you *should* sit down, Charlie,' he said, opening his drawer and taking out two glasses and a bottle of Bell's.

Woodend sat, and watched as the DCC poured out two shots of Scotch. 'How long have you known about this Yorkshire Police operation, sir?' he asked, trying as hard as he was able to sound reasonable.

'I can't go into specifics, you understand,' Ainsworth replied, 'so let's just say that I've known about it for quite some time.'

'It must be an important operation.'

'It is.'

'Important enough to mean that while these two bobbies from Yorkshire were allowed into the BAI factory, my lad Bob Rutter – investigatin' a case that really matters locally – couldn't get past the gate.'

'I understand and sympathise with your concerns, Chief Inspector,' Ainsworth said.

'That's as may be, sir – but you're still not prepared to tell me what I need to know.'

Ainsworth shook his head. 'I'm really sorry, but I can't.'

'Why wouldn't these two fellers from Yorkshire show me some identification, even though they were operatin' on our patch?'

'They were instructed not to show their warrant cards to anyone below the rank of DCC.'

'Who by?'

'What's your next question?' Ainsworth asked.

'You do know they threatened to beat the shit out of me if I got in their way, don't you?'

'I'm sure that was just a joke in poor taste.'

'They weren't jokin',' Woodend said firmly.

'Then I'll put in a complaint about their behaviour through the proper channels.'

'An' which channels might they be?'

'Next question,' Ainsworth said.

'When can I see Cray and Dove?'

'You can't.'

'I can't? But they're vital to my investigation.'

'You're wrong about that.'

'Cray's car – which is an Armstrong Siddeley Sapphire, an' so is practically bloody unmistakeable – was seen parked outside the Spinner the night Verity Beale was murdered. It was spotted again on the edge of the park, just before Helen Dunn disappeared. This mornin' I've learned that Dove was also observed goin' into the park just before Helen was kidnapped. Is all that coincidence? I don't think so for a minute – an' I'd be willin' to bet you that if I showed

Martin Dove's photograph to the landlord of the Spinner, he'd recognise him as Cray's drinkin' companion.'

'You'd win your bet,' Ainsworth said. 'Dove *was* with Cray in the Spinner the night before last. And the two *were* meeting in the park at the time Helen Dunn disappeared. But what they were up to has nothing whatsoever to do with either the kidnapping or the murder. I can assure you of that.'

You lyin' toe-rag! Woodend thought. But aloud, all he said was, 'An' what if your assurance just isn't good enough?'

'It'll have to be.'

'You're askin' me to investigate this kidnappin' not only with my hands tied behind my back, but blindfolded as well,' Woodend protested.

'And I'm very sorry to have to do so, as I've already been at pains to point out. But that's the way it has to be.' Ainsworth took a sip of his Scotch. 'If I were in your shoes, Charlie, I'd forget Dove and Cray altogether. Why not concentrate on your other leads instead?'

'Because we don't *have* any other leads,' Woodend said.

'Then find some,' the DCC told him.

The moment Woodend had left his office, Ainsworth picked up the telephone and asked to be connected to a number which he had already called several times previously that day.

'Yes?' said the cool voice on the other end of the line.

'What the bloody hell do you think you're playing at there?' Ainsworth demanded.

'I take it that you've just had a visit from Cloggin'-it Charlie?' the other man said.

'Too right I've just had a visit from Woodend. He ran into your men at the school. They threatened him with violence.'

'And what else did you expect them to do?'

'I would have expected them to use a little tact, for God's sake!' Ainsworth said, exasperatedly.

'You may not realise it, but we're fighting a war here,' the other man said. 'It might not involve soldiers in uniform or pitched battles, but it's still a war for all that. We don't have time to go pussyfooting around, so even though we never set out to hurt Chief Inspector Woodend's delicate feelings, you can't expect me to shed any tears over the fact that we have.'

'Woodend's only one part of the picture,' Ainsworth said. 'I'm doing my very best to keep a lid on a bubbling pot here, and what you're doing isn't helping me at all.'

'You won't have to hold that lid down for much longer,' the other man promised him. 'By tomorrow morning it should be all over.'

Then, without waiting for Ainsworth to reply, he hung up.

Roger Cray looked around the room into which the bald policeman and his partner had thrust him. There was not much to see. It was a small room, and from the teddy bear pattern on the tattering and peeling wallpaper, he guessed that it had once been a child's bedroom. And it was somewhere in Whitebridge – he was sure of that – because though he had been blindfolded for most of his time in the car, the journey had not long been long enough for them to have gone far beyond the city centre.

He wished he could look out of the window, but the place it had once occupied had been so efficiently bricked-up that not a single ray of light from the outside penetrated it.

For a moment, he contemplated escape, then quickly dismissed the idea. He had no tools to smash his way through the brickwork – the room was bare except for a single rickety chair, and that would soon splinter if he tried to use it as an implement. Nor could he see a way of getting through the door, because though the rest of the room was in a state of dilapidation, the door was new, and seemed to be made of solid steel. Besides, he admitted to himself, even if he had had a hammer and chisel, he would not have dared to use them, because the two men who brought him there might hear him – and he was more frightened of those two men than he had ever been of anything or anyone before.

He heard footsteps in the corridor outside, then the sound of a key turning in the lock. The door creaked open, and he found himself praying that he could at least keep control of his bladder.

The man who entered the room was tall, with film-star good looks, and was a complete stranger to Cray. He smiled, and said, 'Sorry to have kept you waiting for so long.'

'I . . . I want you to let me go,' Cray stuttered.

'I'm afraid that isn't going to happen,' the smiling man told him. 'At least, not until you've given us what we want.'

'And what *do* you want?' Cray asked, tremulously.

'Tell me about Verity Beale.'

'I don't know . . . I'm not sure how to . . .'

'Start at the beginning, go on to the end, and then stop. When and where did you meet her?'

'I . . . I met her at the plant where I work about six weeks ago.'

'And what was she doing in an aircraft factory?'

'She . . . she said she wanted to organise an educational trip to it for some of her pupils. We got talking and . . .'

'And you arranged to see each other socially?'

'Yes.'

'I'd really be very interested to know why she picked *you* to start socialising with.'

'I don't know.'

The other man's expression hardened. 'Don't lie to me, Mr Cray,' he warned. 'You'll never get out of here if you lie to me.'

Never!

Never?

The word bounced around Cray's brain like an exploding bomb. 'I . . . I thought at first she was attracted to me,' he admitted.

'Did you sleep with her?'

'No, but she let me . . . she let me . . .'

'Feel her up?'

'I suppose so.'

'You said you thought *at first* that she was attracted to you. What were your *second* thoughts on the matter.'

'That she was more interested in me because of the friends I had.'

'Specifically, she was interested in your friend Martin Dove.'

'Yes.'

'But he's not really your friend at all, is he?' the other man asked. 'He's really no more than someone you share an interest with.'

'You could put it like that.'

'I *do* put it like that. You're two pieces of shit who naturally found yourselves sticking together. But I digress. What made you start to suspect that Verity Beale was more interested in your associates than she was in you?'

'The questions she asked. She tried to make them sound casual, but I could tell there was something more behind them.'

'So it must have come as quite a shock to you when you saw her enter the Spinner the night before last?'

'Yes . . . I . . . yes.'

'It threw a real spanner into the works, didn't it? You saw weeks of careful planning going down the drain.'

'Martin said it didn't really matter. He said we could still go ahead as planned.'

'But you weren't convinced, were you? So you came up with another plan, and Dove reluctantly accepted it. The two of you pretended that you were leaving the pub. But you didn't go far. You waited on the edge of the car park. You saw the American, who Verity Beale had been drinking with, leave on his own. That was a lucky break for you, wasn't it?'

'No . . . I . . .'

'Then, when she came out herself – alone and helpless – about half an hour after closing time, you grabbed her.'

'I didn't . . . I couldn't . . . !' Cray gasped.

'Perhaps you knocked her unconscious right at the start, or

perhaps that came later. The details don't really matter. You bundled her into your car, and drove out towards Preston. Then one of you strangled her. Which one of you was it, Mr Cray? You? Or Dove?'

'Neither of us! We didn't . . . we never even thought of—'

'There's really no point in you taking the blame for something Martin Dove did. Maybe you didn't even know he was going to do it. Perhaps he told you to take a walk, and when you came back she was already dead.'

'This is crazy!' Cray protested. 'We're not killers. All we were trying to do was—'

'You could hang, you know,' the other man interrupted.

'But we didn't kill her!'

'Not for that. For the other thing. You'll find when you go on trial – if we ever allow you to get that far – that the judge and jury will have absolutely no pity for you.'

'If you ever allow us to get that far!' Cray almost screamed.

'But it doesn't have to happen that way,' the other man said, his voice suddenly soothing and reassuring. 'If you co-operate with us, I'll make sure that you get an easier time of it than Martin Dove does.'

'We didn't mean any harm,' Cray sobbed. 'We knew what we were doing was wrong in the eyes of most people, but we still felt driven to it.'

The other man looked at his watch. 'I have to be going, but I'll be back,' he said. 'Use the time between now and my next visit to really think about what you can do to get out of this mess you've landed yourself in.'

He turned and walked to the door.

'Who are you?' Cray asked anguishedly. 'Who are you working for?'

The other man smiled. 'I'm working for justice, decency and the British way of life,' he said. 'And if you feel the need to put a name to me, then I suppose you could call me Horrocks.'

Twenty-Seven

Woodend paced Rutter's office with all the anger of a caged and taunted lion.

'How could I ever have brought myself to apologise to that lyin' bastard Ainsworth?' he demanded for the fifth or sixth time. 'How could I have allowed rank to stand in the way of me tellin' him what a loathsome shit he is? An' even more to the point, how I could I have let myself leave his office without first beatin' the truth out of him?'

'It wouldn't have helped the investigation to have you locked up, sir,' Rutter pointed out.

'But then what *will* help the investigation?' Woodend asked. 'Find some new leads, Ainsworth said. But we don't need any new leads, because Dove and Cray are our men! They have to be! An' we don't even know where they're bein' held.'

'Perhaps if we went over Ainsworth's head . . .' Rutter suggested.

'To who? Chief Constable Henry-bloody-Marlowe? He's a bigger twat than Ainsworth. I'm almost tempted to go the papers with this – let Elizabeth Driver loose on it.'

'That'd ruin you,' Rutter said.

'Aye,' Woodend agreed. 'But it might just save Helen Dunn's life!'

There was a knock on the door, and a uniformed sergeant holding an evidence envelope in his hand entered the room.

'Sorry to disturb you, sir,' he said to Rutter, 'but one of

my lads found somethin' rather puzzlin' under a bush in the park.'

'What is it?' Rutter asked.

'This, sir.'

The sergeant placed the envelope on the desk, and Rutter carefully extracted the contents. It was a child's pencil case – a long, oval one, with a red plastic cover in a tartan design.

'Open it up, Bob,' Woodend said.

Rutter pulled on the zip, and flipped the case open. Inside the top, written in ball pen in a handwriting which looked remarkably like her sister's, was the name 'Janice Dunn'.

'Oh Sweet Jesus,' Woodend said, striking his forehead with the palm of his hand. 'So Ainsworth was tellin' the truth after all – at least about the kidnappin'.'

'I don't quite see . . .' Rutter said.

'It never crossed my mind,' Woodend moaned. 'I never suspected, even for a minute, that . . . that . . .'

'That what, sir?'

'Don't you *know*?' Woodend asked exasperatedly. 'Isn't it bloody obvious, lad?'

One of the bastards he had in detention would crack soon, the man who sometimes called himself Jack Horrocks thought as he walked through the main door of Whitebridge Police Headquarters. Oh yes, either Cray or Dove – or possibly both of them – would cave in and give him all the grisly details he needed. And why? How could be so sure? Because he saw them for what they were – nothing but a pair of amateurs!

How he despised them for that – for being dilettantes, for having the temerity to ever believe that they could play in the Big Boys' league.

Yet at the same time, he acknowledged the fact that for a man like himself – a man in a hurry, a man who wished to rise to the top of his particular ladder with the greatest possible speed – pathetic wretches like Cray and Dove were just the kind of fodder he needed to feed off.

Horrocks came to a smart, almost military halt in front of the duty sergeant's desk. 'Where can I find DS Paniatowski?' he asked.

The sergeant looked up from his ledger. 'Are you Mr Horrocks, sir?' he asked.

'That's right.'

'Sergeant Paniatowski called in a couple of hours ago. Said she was at the library.'

'Which is just where she was supposed to be.'

'Said she'd had a sudden attack of gastro-enteritis. Well, to be honest, what she actually said was that she was shittin' and pukin' all over the place. Said I should apologise to you for her, but that she was goin' to have to go home. Hopes she'll be fit enough to be back at work in the mornin'.'

'Could you call her for me?' Horrocks asked.

'Certainly, sir.'

But all the sergeant got for his trouble was the engaged tone.

'Probably taken the phone off the hook so she can get a decent sleep,' he said, replacing the receiver on its cradle.

'Yes, that's probably exactly what she's done,' Horrocks agreed.

Actually, he was not at all displeased about Paniatowski's sudden illness, he told himself. He had needed her at the start of this investigation, because she was the one who knew about the initial spadework. And very valuable that knowledge had been, too. She had mentioned the Armstrong Siddeley Sapphire to him, and that had set him off on Cray's trail. But he'd got Cray now, and so Paniatowski had really become superfluous to requirements.

Besides, he was starting to have serious doubts about her as a possible recruit for his network. True, she was both intelligent and ambitious, but she seemed to lack the degree of compliance he demanded from an agent. So perhaps it was best all round that she had suddenly become indisposed. Her attack of gastro-enteritis should keep her out of the way for at least twenty-four hours, and by the time she was up on her feet again he could be well away from this provincial backwater and back in London, where really important things were happening.

Woodend had been prepared to deal with Squadron Leader Dunn if that was what was necessary, but it certainly smoothed his path for him that it was Mrs Dunn who answered the front door instead.

'Have you found her?' the woman gasped.

'Not yet,' Woodend replied, allowing his voice to express more optimism than he was actually feeling.

Margaret Dunn nodded fatalistically, as if she expected no other answer – as if, in her mind, she had already selected the clothes which she would wear for her daughter's funeral.

'If you want to speak to my husband, I'm afraid he's out,' she said. 'He didn't want to go, of course – he'd much rather had stayed here with me, waiting for news – but there's a big flap on at the base.'

A big flap, Woodend repeated silently.

The words did not come naturally from Margaret Dunn's mouth. They were certainly her husband's words – and possibly also her father's – but they were not hers. She should never have married someone in the services.

'I'm sure you can help me just as much as he could,' Woodend said.

'Me?' Margaret Dunn asked, as if she were surprised that anyone could consider her to be of any use for anything.

'Aye,' Woodend agreed. 'I wanted to ask you about Helen's pencil case – or rather, Helen's pencil *cases*. She does have two, doesn't she, although one of them didn't originally belong to her?'

'I bought a green one for Helen, and a red one for Janice,' Mrs Dunn said. 'After . . . after Janice's accident, Helen asked if she could have her sister's pencil case. I think she wanted it because it would remind her of Janice.'

'An' which one does Helen actually use?' Woodend asked.
'Both of them.'

'Not at the same time?'

'No, of course not. I think that she uses her own mostly, but when she's . . . when she's feeling particularly lonely, she uses Janice's.'

'An' which one was she usin' yesterday?'

'I didn't see it, because it was in her briefcase. Is it important? I can go upstairs and check which one is there now, if you want me to.'

'No, it doesn't really matter,' Woodend lied. 'An' I wouldn't go mentionin' any of this to your husband, if I was you.'

'No?'

'No. What with havin' to deal with both the distress he must be feelin' over your daughter's disappearance *an'* the flap at the base, he's got enough on his plate at the moment.'

Monika Paniatowski made good time on the first stretch of her journey, thanks mainly to using the recently opened M6 motorway. But the going was considerably slower after she left it, and by the time she was clear of central Birmingham she was already well behind the schedule she had set herself.

Not that it really mattered, she thought, as she cut across country to join the busy A6. A schedule only had real significance when it was leading towards a definite aim, and she had no more than the vaguest idea of what she would do once she reached London.

Perhaps the whole idea of travelling down to the capital was crazy, she pondered, as her foot pressed down more heavily on the accelerator pedal and her eyes scanned the near distance for signs of police traffic vehicles waiting in ambush for drivers like her.

But what other choice did she have than to go down to

London? None at all! Because she was tired of playing by the rules that no one had bothered to explain to her, in a game where she did not even know what the prize was.

She had learned a great deal from working with Cloggin'-it Charlie Woodend, and one of the most important lessons had been that to look at the present without also examining the past was like treating a photograph as if it were a living person.

Nobody came without a personal history. And it was that history which made them the kind of people they were, and determined how they would react in any particular situation. Which was why it was pointless to pretend, as Horrocks seemed to be doing, that Verity Beale simply had no past – that she had suddenly appeared in Lancashire, a few months earlier, already fully-formed.

Or perhaps he didn't really think that at all, she told herself. Perhaps he only wanted *her* to think that – was trying to con her into believing that one snapshot in the life of Verity Beale was the whole picture.

Well, if that *was* the way his mind was working, he was in for a shock. Because she was not the kind of detective to spend her time feeding her brain with dusty library files while there was a chance to sink her teeth into the juicy meat of real evidence.

Twenty-Eight

The air in Bob Rutter's office was thick with the smell of cigarette smoke and desperation.

'Why would he do it?' Woodend asked anguishedly. 'Has all the pressure he's been under tipped him over the edge? Has he gone completely insane? Because if he hasn't, I just can't see what the hell he thinks he'll get out of it.'

'You're certain you're right about him?' Rutter asked cautiously. 'You're absolutely sure that there couldn't be some other rational explanation for the pencil case?'

'I'd like there to be,' Woodend confessed. 'Honest to God, I would. But I can't think of one. Can you?'

'No,' Rutter answered. 'No, I can't.'

'So he has to be the one, doesn't he?'

The sound of the phone ringing made both of them jump like frightened rabbits. Rutter reached for it. 'Yes?' he said. 'Oh, hello, Hans. How are you?' He covered the mouthpiece with his hand. 'Inspector Kohl,' he told Woodend. 'He says he's got something interesting for us.'

The chief inspector nodded, and found himself wishing that the British police could be half as efficient as the Germans seemed to be.

'Yes?' Rutter said into the phone. 'Yes, I see . . . You're sure of that? . . . What? . . . You've seen the reports yourself?'

The conversation lasted for three or four minutes, and when Rutter finally put the phone down, his face was grim.

'Even before the base commander reported Janice Dunn's

194

death to them, the German police *already* had a file on her,' he said.

'A file? On a kid? What, in God's name, for?'

'She'd made friends with some German lads who were just a bit older than she was. One of them stole a car, and they all went off for a joyride. Naturally, Germany being Germany, they were caught before they'd gone more than a couple of miles.'

'An' what did the German police do about it?'

'Very little. It was a first offence for the boy who'd stolen the car, and anyway, from what Hans hinted, his father was somebody quite important in local government. As for the rest of them, it was never clearly established that they even knew the car was stolen, so they all got off with a slap on the wrist.'

'An' a file on them.'

'And a file on them,' Rutter agreed.

'But did Reginald Dunn find out about it?'

'Oh, yes. All the parents were informed.'

It was all starting to make sense, Woodend thought – though the sense it was making was sickening him deep down in the pit of his stomach. 'Did Kohl tell you the details of Janice's death?' he asked.

'Yes, he did. She was quite a strong swimmer, apparently. She'd won some local competitions, and was in training for a regional contest. She did her training at the indoor pool on the base, but, of course, she could only do that when there was somebody qualified on duty to supervise her.'

'Naturally.'

'The story is that she felt she needed more practice than she was getting, and so, one night, she went to the pool alone.'

'Why wasn't it locked up?'

'The man in charge swears that it was.'

'Then how did she get in?'

'That's never been satisfactorily established. Anyway, the point is that when she failed to go home at the time she was supposed to, the Dunns raised the alarm. They searched everywhere, including the town outside the base. But, of course, nobody thought to check the swimming pool. They found her the next morning, when they opened up for business. The general opinion seems to be that she got cramp when she was halfway across the pool.'

'The man's a monster!' Woodend groaned.

'You really think he killed his own daughter?'

'I don't want to, but look at the facts. Reginald Dunn's just about the most ambitious man I've ever met in my life. Worse than that – he's convinced himself that it's not a personal ambition which is drivin' him – that he only wants to do well for the good of his country. He went into marriage like a medieval prince—'

'What do you mean by that, sir?'

'He married into the right kind of family – an RAF family. An' I don't think that's done him any harm. He's already a squadron leader, an' is all set to move up to wing commander, especially if the war he's been praying for actually comes to pass. Probably havin' a family was part of the plan, too. It gives him stability – makes him look like the kind of man you can rely on. But that's where things started to go wrong for him. He wanted his daughters to shine, because the credit would be bound to reflect on him. But then Janice went off the rails. It was only joyriding in a stolen car the first time, but who was to say where it would lead from there? And would you trust a man to control a squadron of very expensive planes flown by highly trained men when he couldn't even seem to control his own daughter?'

'So he decided to kill her before she could do his reputation any more damage?'

'That's how it seems to me.'

'But wouldn't there be physical evidence of that. Bruising? The signs of a struggle?'

'Not if he drugged her first. An' even if there *were* some bruises, so what? Athletes are always gettin' bruised. For a

196

doctor to detect foul play, he'd probably have to be lookin' for it – an' what doctor on a carefully guarded air-force base is ever likely to think that he's got a murder on his hands?'

'But to murder his own child . . .'

'He won't see it in those terms. He probably justified his actions by convincin' himself that the RAF needs him more than it realises, an' if sacrificin' his daughter was the price of makin' sure that he continued to rise in the Air Force, then it was a price well worth payin'.'

'And then, once they were back in England, Helen started to go off the rails as well,' Rutter said.

'Exactly. She was caught shop-liftin'. The school doesn't think her parents know about it, but I'm willing to bet that Dunn does. So he finds himself faced with the same problem again. There's no tellin' what she might do next – what disgrace she might bring on him. But it's even more complicated to deal with this time, because it'll look very suspicious if he stages another drownin' accident. In fact, it'll look suspicious if he stages *any* kind of accident. So he comes up with the idea of pretendin' that some nutter has snatched the poor bloody kid. Nobody can blame *him* for that, can they? If it's anybody's fault, it's the school's for not takin' care of her properly, and the police's for not findin' her in time. Don't you see how all that makes sense?'

'The other night, when we got the call, we couldn't work out why he was ringing,' Rutter said. 'It didn't seem to conform to any known pattern.'

'That's because it *doesn't*,' Woodend said. 'He wants to be above suspicion himself, so he has to create the very clear impression that there really is a nutter out there. An' what better way to do it than by ringin' the bobby in charge of the investigation?'

'And that's where the pencil case comes in.'

'Exactly. He had to have some proof that the nutter who he was pretendin' to be had actually got the girl. The pencil case gave him that proof. He'd been plannin' to send it to me long before he actually snatched the girl.'

'So what happened?' Rutter asked. 'How did it come to end up under a bush in the park?'

'I don't know,' Woodend admitted. 'Maybe Helen lost it in a struggle – though I can see no reason why she *would* have struggled with her own father. So maybe, instead, she started to sense that somethin' was wrong, an' threw the pencil case under the bush as a means of tippin' us off. But the details don't really matter. What *is* important is that when Dunn got her to wherever he was takin' her, he discovered that she didn't have the pencil case with her anymore. So what was he to do?'

'He could have sent us something else,' Rutter suggested. 'Like what?'

Rutter shrugged. 'Her skirt? One of her socks?'

'I'm sure he thought of it,' Woodend agreed. 'An' then he probably realised that anybody could lay his hands on a bit of school uniform, an' even her mother probably couldn't say that it was definitely Helen's. No, the pencil case was better. The pencil case was personal and unique. The problem was, he didn't have it. But he knew where he could lay his hands on another one – in Helen's bedroom.'

'But if what you're saying is true – if the kidnapper really is her father – then keeping her alive would be a huge risk.'

'I know,' Woodend agreed gravely.

'So you think he's probably killed her already?'

'What I'm *prayin'* is that he's not yet been able to steel himself to murderin' her. But if he *has* already killed one of his daughters, then I don't really see what's holdin' him back from killin' the other.'

Rutter put his head in his hands. 'So what do we do now?' he asked. 'We can't just pull Dunn in and beat the truth out of him, can we?'

'If I thought it would help us find Helen alive, that's precisely what I'd do – even if it meant me goin' to prison myself,' Woodend said. 'But it wouldn't do any good. However much we hurt him, Dunn wouldn't come clean, because if he did he'd have lost everything.'

'So what *are* we going to do?'

'The only thing we *can* do is keep him under round-the-clock surveillance, an' hope that he leads us to her.'

'That's not *much* of a hope, is it?' Rutter asked.

'No,' Woodend agreed. 'It isn't.'

Twenty-Nine

M onika Paniatowski walked up to the pleasant Edwardian terraced house which was listed as Verity Beale's
address on her driving licence, and knocked confidently.
There was the sound of two sets of footsteps – one plodding,
the other scuffling – in the hallway, then the front door
opened to reveal a woman in late middle age and a small
boy. The woman was holding firmly on to the boy's reluctant
hand, and from the identical sulky expressions on their faces,
it was obvious that they were related.

Paniatowski smiled. 'You must be Verity's mum,' she
said. 'What a pleasure to meet you at long last. I'm Elaine.
Elaine Pardoe.'

The woman frowned. 'Elaine who?'

'Elaine Pardoe,' Paniatowski said brightly. 'Surely Verity's mentioned me to you? I shall be very offended if she
hasn't.'

'I don't know who you are – and I don't know who this
Verity is, either,' the woman said.

Paniatowski laughed, then stepped back to examine the
number on the door. 'But there must be some mistake,' she said.
'This is the address Verity gave me, and she's always answered
my letters, so she must have received them, mustn't she?'

'Nanna!' the small boy cried.

'Shut up, Cedric!' the woman said, glancing briefly down
at him, then turning her attention back to Paniatowski. 'I've
lived here ever since I got married, which is nearly thirty
years ago now and—'

'Nanna!' the small boy insisted.

'The bogeyman comes and gets little boys who can't be quiet when they should be,' the woman said. 'I've brought all my children up here,' she continued, addressing Paniatowski again. 'I've never had anybody living here but my own family, not even during the war.'

'Perhaps I have got the number wrong, after all,' Paniatowski said dubiously. 'Maybe Verity lives somewhere else down this street.'

'I've told you, there's nobody called Verity lives around here,' the woman said, with growing impatience.

'But you must have seen her,' Paniatowski persisted. 'She's in her mid-twenties. A very attractive girl. She's got flaming red hair, all the way down to her shoulders.'

The woman sniffed. 'I go up to the Artillery Arms once in a while,' she said. 'Just for a glass of port, you understand. It's on doctor's orders.'

'And you've seen her in there?'

'Up until a few months ago, there was a young woman with long red hair in the pub nearly every night. But there's no point in asking me her name, because I don't know it.'

'You never heard anyone else call her anything?'

'I never got close enough to her for that. I'm particular who I rub shoulders with.'

'Was there something wrong with her?' Paniatowski asked.

The woman turned to her grandchild again. 'Cover both your ears, Cedric,' she said.

'I can't when you're holdin' my hand,' the boy pointed out.

'Then cover the one that you can cover,' his grandmother told him. She waited until the boy had done as instructed, then said to Paniatowski, 'We get a lot of soldiers drinking in the Artillery Arms.'

'I suppose you must, with being so close to the barracks,' Paniatowski said.

'I'm pleasant enough to them myself – they're protecting Queen and country, when all's said and done – but I've always been careful never to let myself get *too* familiar with them.'

'And this woman with the red hair did?'

'It's not my place to say, especially if she's a friend of yours,' the woman said. 'You're not listening, are you, Cedric?'

'No, Nanna.'

'But if you leave the pub with a different man every night, then you're bound to get yourself talked about, aren't you?'

'You're probably right,' Paniatowski agreed. 'You said she was there every night until a few months ago. Do you happen to remember exactly when it was she stopped going?'

'Not exactly, no. But I'd say it was somewhere towards the end of the summer.'

Or to put it another way, just before Verity Beale first appeared in Whitebridge, Paniatowski thought.

'Well, it's obvious to me now that my old friend Verity never actually lived here at all,' she said, 'which is strange because I could have sworn that she said it was Raglan Road.'

'Raglan Road!' the woman repeated. 'This is *Ruskin* Road. Raglan Road's five or six streets away from here.'

Paniatowski gave an embarrassed giggle. 'I am a dizzy thing, aren't I?' she said. 'Fancy getting the names mixed up like that. Sorry to have bothered you unnecessarily.'

'It's no trouble,' the other woman said, without much conviction. 'You can unplug your ears now, Cyril.'

Squadron Leader Dunn lowered himself on to his living-room sofa and took a measured sip of the whisky and soda he held in his right hand. He had never much cared for alcohol, but he had noticed early in his career that men who did not drink at all tended to be viewed with suspicion by their fellow officers. And now drinking had become so much a part of the persona he'd created for himself that he indulged even when he was not being observed by others.

He found his mind – unbidden and unwilled – turning to thoughts of Woodend. When they'd first met, he'd seen the chief inspector as no problem at all. Even the way the man dressed – in that ridiculous hairy sports coat of his – had seemed to indicate that he had neither the discipline nor the self-respect to pose much of a threat. But that feeling of security had not lasted long. Woodend had asked questions about Janice – questions which a small-town policeman should never have thought to ask – and as loath as he was to admit it, Dunn was forced to accept the fact that the man was not a run-of-the-mill policeman.

That wouldn't have mattered if everything had gone strictly according to plan, because even a smart cop, as it now appeared Woodend was, would not have seen through the smokescreen that should have been thrown up. But everything *hadn't* gone according to plan. The pencil case, which had been a cornerstone of the whole operation, had somehow gone missing, forcing him to improvise by using the one he'd found in Helen's bedroom. And that had been a big mistake, he realised now.

He should have used a piece of her clothing instead, he told himself, because while that would have been less immediately convincing, it would also have been far less risky. But he *had* used the pencil case, and, as a result, had opened a breach through which a clever man like Woodend just might be able to glimpse the truth.

Dunn took another sip of his whisky, and, as the alcohol massaged his nerves, began to understand – perhaps for the first time in his life – why other men set so much store by drink. He wondered what Woodend was up to at that very moment – wondered how much he already knew, and how much more he could imagine.

Dunn raised his glass to his lips again, and was surprised to find that it was already empty. He never had a second drink, but perhaps that night he would break his own rule, he thought, getting to his feet and walking to the kitchen. Yes, perhaps, just this once, a second drink was a good idea.

The whisky bottle was standing by the sink. He unscrewed it and, without making any attempt to gauge the amount, half-filled the glass. It was then that he noticed that his hand had developed a slight tremble.

He had not thought about God for years – to him, the Air Vice-Marshal was far more powerful and awesome than any deity – but now he discovered himself repeating a silent prayer over and over again.

'Please don't let Woodend find out what I've done with Helen. Please . . . *please* – don't let him find out.'

Monika Paniatowski crossed her legs with slow deliberation, and looked around the best room of the Artillery Arms. Most of the customers, standing or sitting in small groups, were men with short haircuts and a military bearing.

As she sipped at her vodka, she caught the odd snatch of conversation drifting her way from the group closest to her.

'Won't be our kind of war at all,' said one of the men. 'All the fighting – if that's what you want to call it – will be done by button-pushing boffins in concrete shelters.'

'Tosh, Rodney. Absolute balderdash,' said a second. 'Nobody's going to go nuclear over this.'

'Oh? And what makes you say that?'

'They won't because they *daren't*. They'll fight a limited war because that's the only way the world can survive – and that means they'll need us, just like they always do.'

'Maybe there won't be a war at all,' suggested a third member of the party.

The other two men looked at him with something akin to pity.

'Do you really think Khrushchev can afford to back down at this stage?' asked the one called Rodney. 'Do you really think he's going to call his ships back? And if he doesn't, could Kennedy afford the loss of face that would go with letting those ships through the blockade?'

From their accents and general demeanour, they were obviously all officers, Paniatowski thought, whereas most of the soldiers in the public bar, where she'd had her first drink, had equally obviously been enlisted men. She smiled to herself at the thought that, though there was no sign on the door of the best room prohibiting the squaddies from mixing with their betters, there might as well have been.

'I do like girls who have nice smiles,' said a drawling voice just above her head.

She looked up. The man standing over her was tall, blond, and – from the gleam in his eyes – obviously fancied himself as something of a lady-killer.

'And I do like men who know how to give women compliments,' Monika told him.

The soldier beamed with pleasure. 'Would you mind if I sat down?' he asked. 'Or are you waiting for someone?'

'No, I'm all alone,' Paniatowski replied.

The soldier slid quickly into the seat opposite her, and signalled to the waiter for another round of drinks. 'Name's Sebastian,' he said.

'Elaine,' Monika replied. 'Do you live round here?'

'Not exactly *live*. I'm a captain in the Royal Artillery. Our barracks are just around the corner.'

'Oh, I see!' Monika said. 'That would explain the name of the pub.'

Sebastian chuckled, as if she'd just said something incredibly witty. 'I take it you *don't* live round here,' he said.

'You're right,' Monika agreed. 'I'm down here visiting my uncle. It's the first time I've ever been in the area.' She gave him a slightly puzzled frown. 'It seems a very strange place to have an army barracks.'

Sebastian chuckled again. '*Really* don't know the area, do

you?' he asked. 'Do you mean to say you've never heard of the Woolwich Arsenal?'

'I thought they were a football team,' Paniatowski said innocently.

'You *are* amusing,' Sebastian told her. 'The Arsenal's one of the places where the Ministry of Defence develops its weaponry. That's the main reason we're here.'

'To test the weapons?'

'Oh much, much more than that. The boffins may be able to design the things, you see – do all the clever calculations and so forth – but without experienced soldiers like me to advise them, they'd be bound to make all kinds of ghastly mistakes.'

'So you're really quite important,' Paniatowski said.

'Just a part of the team,' Sebastian said, self-deprecatingly. 'So tell me, Elaine, what do you do?'

'I'm a nurse.'

'That must be interesting,' Sebastian said, doing his best to hide his I've-heard-what-nurses-are-like-when-they've-got-a-few-drinks-inside-them expression. 'I say, Elaine, you wouldn't like to move on to somewhere a little less crowded, would you?'

'Well no, I wouldn't mind, but I was rather hoping to see a friend of mine,' Paniatowski said.

Sebastian's mouth drooped slightly. 'Oh, I see,' he said, sounding disappointed.

Monika laughed. 'A *girl*friend, silly,' she said. 'Maybe, if she turns up, you could get one of your friends to join us and we could make a foursome.'

'That would be jolly,' Sebastian agreed. 'Do you think she *will* turn up?'

'She told me this was her local, so I think it's more than likely. Perhaps you know her by sight. She's a very pretty girl with long red hair.'

Suspicion instantly flooded into Sebastian's eyes. 'You don't mean Vanessa Barker, do you?' he asked.

Vanessa Barker? VB?

'That's her,' Monika agreed. 'Do you mean to say you *do* know her?'

'Know her – and know *all about her*,' Sebastian said harshly. 'Now if you'll excuse me, it's time I rejoined my friends.'

He stood up, and walked quickly across to join the three officers whose conversation Monika had been listening to earlier. As Sebastian spoke earnestly to them, they each gave Monika several furtive – and hostile – glances. Then the four of them split up and joined other groups. By the time five minutes had passed, all the soldiers were crammed together in a bunch near the door, and Monika, still sitting at her table, had most of the room to herself.

Interesting, she thought. What had just happened didn't answer all the questions she had in her mind – but at least it was a start.

It was time for her to leave, she decided. She made her way towards the door and the officers moved quickly to the left or to the right, creating a passageway for her like the parting of the Red Sea. As she left the room, she was conscious of a couple of dozen pairs of hostile eyes focusing on the back of her head.

The public phone was in the passage. Monika picked up the receiver, and asked to be connected to a Whitebridge number.

The phone at the other end had just started to ring when she heard a voice behind her say, 'I suppose you think you're very clever!'

She turned, and was not surprised to find herself facing one of the officers. He was a short, darkish man, and seemed to have had rather more to drink than most of companions.

'I said, I suppose you think you're very clever,' the man repeated.

'I don't know what you're talking about,' Paniatowski replied.

'Coming down here to spy on us,' the man said drunkenly. 'Well, let me tell you one thing – if you can't trust us, you can't trust anybody.'

A second officer, looking rather less the worse for wear, appeared in the doorway of the best room.

'Leave it, Toby,' he advised.

'I *won't* leave it,' the drunken man said. 'It's time these people realised that we're . . . that we're . . . that we're something-or-other.'

'Loyal,' his friend said. 'The word you're looking for is "loyal".' He took the drunk firmly by the arm and began to manoeuvre him back into the best room. 'But he's got a point,' he said, as a parting shot to Paniatowski. 'Sending people like you down here is nothing less than an insult.'

The phone had stopped ringing, and now a voice said, 'The Drum and Monkey. Can I help you?'

'I'd like to speak to Chief Inspector Woodend, please,' Paniatowski said. 'He's usually at the corner table by this time of night.'

The next morning there were many people in Whitebridge who looked out of their bedroom windows on to a familiar view, but with fresh eyes. How could anything so ordinary – so commonplace – manage to seem so precious? they asked themselves. But they already knew the answer to that question. It was precious because it was still there – and when they had gone to bed the previous night they had not been sure that it would be.

The fact that the world had survived the night brought them fresh hope. Perhaps, while they had been sleeping, Khrushchev or Kennedy – or even both of them – had understood the lunacy of what was happening, and had pulled back from the brink of destruction. Perhaps, when they turned their wirelesses on, they would be told that the world had survived the crisis, and there was still a chance, after all, that they would live to see their children grow up.

It did not take long for such hopes to be shattered. The American blockade was still holding firm, the newsreader announced, and the Russian ships were showing no signs of intending to turn back.

So this was it! There would be no summer holidays in Blackpool next year. There would be no need to worry about the effect of slugs on the tomato plants, because there would be no slugs and no tomatoes. Maybe it would be the Russians who launched the first missiles, or perhaps it would be the Americans. It didn't really matter, one way or the other. Civilisation, which had taken countless generations to develop to its current level, would come to an abrupt end on an overcast day in October 1962.

They went through the motions of washing, shaving, getting dressed and giving their shoes a quick polish. They drank their first cups of tea and smoked their first cigarettes of the day. And, when the time came, they opened their front doors and set out for the bus stop.

But there didn't seem to be much point in any of it, any more.

Thirty

It was just after nine o'clock in the morning when Woodend entered through the main door of King Edward's Grammar School. On his first visit, there had still been a little of the young Charlie Woodend about him – just a trace of the short-trousered boy who had looked up at the school with something like awe. Then, he had waited in the foyer, examining the photographs of smiling schoolboys, until he had been summoned. Now, he strode purposefully over to the office where lurked Mrs Green – the dragon-lady whose main job it was to protect the headmaster's inner sanctum from unwanted intruders. Once there he raised his arm, knocked sharply on the door, and immediately turned the handle.

Mrs Green glanced up from her desk with the look of disdain on her face which a lady's maid would have worn had she been told she must share her carriage with her under-gardener.

'Can I help you?' she asked, most unhelpfully.

'I doubt it very much,' Woodend replied. 'I'm here to see your boss. Is he in?'

The secretary frowned disapprovingly. 'As a matter of fact, he's not,' she said sternly. 'But even if he were, you couldn't see him without having first made an appoint—'

'So he's not here,' Woodend interrupted. 'An' why's that, I wonder? Could it be that he's suddenly got the call to go down to the big city?'

'I can't imagine how you would know that,' Mrs Green said, her disapproval deepening by the second, 'but yes, the

210

headmaster *has* been called away to London. There are some urgent family matters that he needs to attend to – not that that's any business of yours.'

Woodend shook his head slowly from side to side. 'They never cease to amaze me, these people,' he said. 'They're so bloody arrogant – so sure of their own position – they can't even be bothered to think up a convincin' excuse to cover their tracks.'

'I can assure you—' Mrs Green said, disapproval rapidly sliding into outrage.

'No, you can't,' Woodend told her. 'You can assure me of nothin', because you haven't any more idea of what's really goin' on around here now than I had myself a couple of days ago. Well, if I can't speak to the engineer, I'll have to make do with the rubbin' rag.'

'I do beg your pardon!'

'If anybody wants me, I'll be with the deputy head.'

Mrs Green glanced up at the timetable on the wall. 'But Mr Hargreaves has a class in five minutes,' she protested.

'Aye, well he'll just have to cancel it, then, won't he?' Woodend said. 'Have you got a telephone number you can reach the headmaster at?'

'No, I—'

'I didn't think you would have. They don't hand out numbers like that to mere civilians like you.'

Mrs Green was swelling with rage. 'I have the headmaster's complete confidence,' she said. 'I know everything—'

'Not this time, you don't. Because this has nothin' at all to do with runnin' a school.' Woodend's expression suddenly softened. 'Listen, Mrs Green, don't feel too bad about it, because you're not the only one who's been kept in the dark – by a long chalk. I tell you what. Why don't you draft the letter? You know that'll make you feel better.'

'Which letter?'

'The letter of complaint about my behaviour that your

boss will be sure to want to send to the chief constable the moment he gets back from conductin' his "family business" in London,' Woodend said.

Roger Cray shifted his weight slightly in an attempt to find a more comfortable position on the straight-backed chair.

They couldn't do this to him, he told himself for the hundredth time. This was England, not Russia. In England there were solicitors and barristers, trial by jury and writs of habeas corpus. Citizens couldn't be detained without being charged. That simply didn't happen!

But it *had* happened. He had spent an almost sleepless night in this room with the bricked-up window. All he had been given to eat were sandwiches so old that their ends had started to curl up. And when he had wanted to use the toilet, he had been forced to use a bucket – a bucket! – in the corner of the room.

He heard the key turning in the lock of the steel door, then the door itself swung open and the man who called himself Horrocks was standing there.

'Are you feeling a little more co-operative this morning, Mr Cray?' Horrocks asked, somehow managing to sound both solicitous *and* contemptuous.

'I . . . I want to see my lawyer,' Cray croaked, realising how dry his mouth felt.

'Your friend Dove's been singing like a bird all night,' Horrocks lied. He laughed. 'That's rather good, isn't it? Dove? Singing like a bird? But it's *what* he's been singing about that's important. From what he's already told us, we've got enough evidence to lock you up and throw away the key. And that's exactly what we're going to do, unless . . .'

Unless what?'

'Unless you decide you'll give us some of the details that Mr Dove's holding back on – in which case I'll do my best to see that you get off with a lighter sentence.'

Cray ran his tongue nervously over lips which felt like they were made from sandpaper. 'What . . . what do you want to know?'

'That's better,' Horrocks told him. 'What I'd really like to know is exactly what information was in the secret papers you handed over to your little friend in the park the day before yesterday.'

'Hasn't he given them to you?'

Horrocks frowned. 'Unfortunately, he's already passed them on – and we can only speculate as to where they ended up.'

'But you *know* where they'll have ended up,' Cray protested. 'They'll be in London.'

'Possibly they will. But we both know that is only the first stage on their long journey.'

'No, it's—'

'What was in them?' Horrocks demanded. 'Drawings of the fuselage? Plans for the engine?'

'No. It was nothing like that at all. It was mainly costing estimates.'

Horrocks shook his head mournfully. 'Now why should the Russians be interested in costing estimates?' he asked.

'The Russians?' Cray exclaimed, amazed. 'What are you talking about? They were never intended for the Russians. They were supposed to go to the newspapers.'

'You must think I was born yesterday,' Horrocks said.

'Look, this is how it happened,' Cray said desperately. 'I'd already started to have some sympathy for the Campaign for Nuclear Disarmament before Martin Dove ever approached me, and when he told me how, given my position, I could help, it all made sense.'

'How you could help!' Horrocks repeated. 'That's just another way of saying, how you could betray your country, isn't it?'

'No,' Cray protested. 'We didn't want to betray *anybody*. We just wanted to show the British public that not only are nuclear arms morally wrong, they also eat up money which could be much better used elsewhere. The TSR2 is costing a fortune – and it's all for nothing, because it'll never fly. It's the biggest white elephant we've ever built, and we thought the British people had a right to know.'

'So that's what your masters in Moscow instructed you to do, is it?' Horrocks asked.

'Oh, for God's sake, you're talking like a schoolboy,' Cray said exasperatedly. 'When are you people ever going to grow up?'

Walter Hargreaves sat at the opposite side of his desk from Woodend, nervously twisting another paper clip in his hands.

'I don't quite understand why you're here, Chief Inspector,' the deputy head said. 'As I understood it, you're now working on the kidnapping rather than the murder.'

'So I am,' Woodend replied, 'but since there's not much I can do in that direction at the moment, I thought I might as well give my sergeant a bit of a helping hand on the Verity Beale case.'

Besides, he added mentally, if I'd just sat there at my desk, waitin' for Reginald Dunn to make his move, I'd have stood a very good chance of losin' what's left of my sanity.

'I don't really see what I can tell you now that I haven't already said before,' Hargreaves told him.

'You probably don't,' Woodend agreed. 'But that's because you think you can still get away with feedin' me the same load of old bollocks you've been dishin' out since this investigation started. Well, you can't. I'm sick of bein' buggered about an' chasin' my own shadow.'

'I beg your pardon?'

Woodend sighed. 'Don't make it any more difficult than you have to, Mr Hargreaves.'

'I'm still not sure what you want me—'

'Last night, Sergeant Paniatowski was down in Woolwich, which, since it's where the Arsenal is, makes it a very

214

sensitive place in some ways. She went to the local pub, an' got talkin' to some of the people who drink there regularly. An' it turns out that until last summer, one of them regulars was a redheaded woman called Vanessa Barker. Tell me, does anythin' strike you as particularly significant about that name, Mr Hargreaves?'

'No, I don't think so.'

'You're an educated man with a quick brain, Mr Hargreaves. You can do better than that.'

'I suppose you mean that she has the same initials as Verity Beale,' the deputy head said resignedly.

'Aye, that's exactly what I mean,' Woodend agreed. 'I've come across that kind of thing quite a lot durin' my time on the force.'

'What kind of thing?'

'Criminals changin' their names but keepin' their proper initials. Not that I'm sayin' Miss Beale, or Miss Barker – or whatever else her bloody name really happened to be – was a criminal. But it doesn't surprise you to learn that she was involved in somethin' which was not – how shall I put it? – exactly on the level. Now does it?'

'No,' Hargreaves said. 'It doesn't.'

'So why don't you tell me about it?'

'I knew something was not quite right from the start. When the headmaster interviews potential new staff, he always does it here at the school. That's a common enough practice in all schools. It gives the interviewees the opportunity to see the place they'll be working in if they take the job, so they can decide for themselves if they're going to be happy there.'

'But that didn't happen in this case?'

'No. The headmaster went down to London for a couple of days, and when he came back he simply announced that he'd hired a new history teacher. We hadn't even advertised the post.'

'An' there's more, isn't there?'

'Yes, there's more. Shortly before Miss Beale started

215

working in the school, the headmaster called me down to his study and said that there were special conditions attached to her employment. If she didn't appear at school in the morning, I was not to ring her up to find out what had happened, as I would do with other staff. And however many days she had off work, I was not to ask her for a doctor's note when she eventually appeared again. If her head of department complained to me about her teaching, I was told to assuage him as best I could. If parents complained, I was to deal with them, too.'

'An' what conclusions did you draw from that?'

'Isn't that obvious?'

'Maybe. But I'd still prefer you to spell it out for me.'

'All right,' Hargreaves agreed. 'Given the headmaster's wartime background in intelligence work, and given the sensitive nature of some of the installations in the area – the base and the aircraft factory – I was reluctantly forced to come to the conclusion that she was a government agent.'

'You mean, you think she was a spy?'

'I suppose so.'

'Then say it!'

'I think she was a spy.'

'Which is why you weren't entirely surprised when you were told that she'd ended up murdered?'

'I don't think I'd actively thought she'd be killed – we never really imagine there's ever going to be such drama in our own lives – but when I *was* informed, it certainly didn't come as the shock it would have been if any other member of staff had been murdered.'

The phone rang on the desk. Hargreaves picked it up, listened for a second, then handed the receiver over to Woodend.

'Is that you, sir?' Bob Rutter asked.

'It's me. Has somethin' started to happen?'

'We think so. Dunn's just left his house.'

'Maybe he's goin' to the base.'

216

'That's not the direction he's heading in.'

Woodend felt his grip on the receiver tightening. 'Where are you now?'

'I'm just leaving the town centre. I can be outside the school in three minutes.'

'Make that *two* minutes,' Woodend ordered him.

Thirty-One

T he worrying and self-doubt began to assail Woodend again the moment he climbed into the passenger seat next to Bob Rutter.

Had he been right when he'd said there was no point in pulling Dunn in for questioning? he asked himself. Wasn't it just possible that even a hard bastard like the squadron leader could have been made to feel remorse under the pressure of a skilful interrogation team?

If Helen had already been dead when he had made his decision, then the decision itself made no difference one way or the other. But what if she hadn't been? What if Dunn had decided to kill her, but had botched the job, so that while the team had been doing nothing more than *watch* Dunn, she had been lying alone and terrified, while her life slowly slipped away? And even if Dunn had done nothing yet, wouldn't the strain of an extra night's captivity, which this waiting approach had imposed on her, end up scarring her for life?

I should have pulled the bastard in, Woodend told himself. I should have taken the chance and pulled him in.

The chief inspector reached into his pocket for his Capstan Full Strengths, and realised that his hands were shaking so much he would never be able to extract a cigarette from the packet.

'How many vehicles have you got on this job, Bob?' he asked, wishing he'd organised it himself even as he acknowledged the fact that Rutter would have done it at least as well as he could.

218

'We're using four vehicles in all,' Rutter replied, slipping into gear and pulling away from the curb. 'Two cars and two vans.'

'What sort of vans?' Woodend said, knowing, even as he spoke, that there was absolutely no need for him to get bogged down in such operational details.

'One of them's a painter-and-decorator's van which belongs to Sergeant Cowgill's brother-in-law,' Rutter said. 'I borrowed the other from the Post Office. It took a little arm-twisting, but it was worth it. Nobody notices postmen driving around town.'

'Where's Dunn now?' Woodend asked.

'Out on the ring road.'

'Headin' in which direction?'

'Heading in no direction at all. For the last few minutes, he's simply been going back and forth between the round-about at Green Gates and the one where you turn off for Feltwick. I think he might be doing it just to make sure that he isn't being followed.'

'Then let's hope to Christ that he doesn't decide that he is.'

'He won't,' Rutter said confidently. 'Only an expert would spot a tailing operation which is using four vehicles.'

'There could be another reason why he's not goin' straight to his destination,' Woodend said sombrely.

'I know there could,' Rutter replied. 'The same thoughts have been going through my mind.'

'One of us should put that thought into words,' Woodend said. 'Do you want to do it?'

Rutter nodded. 'Helen isn't dead. Yet! But he knows he's got to kill her now, and he's just getting up the nerve.'

'Your lads have been told not to lose sight of him, haven't they?' Woodend asked, the panic evident in his voice. 'They do know that the moment he enters a buildin', they're to go in after him?'

'They know.'

219

'An' I mean *the very moment*,' Woodend said urgently. 'Not a minute later. Not even half a minute. Because it doesn't take very long to choke the life out of a little kid.'

'They know that as well,' Rutter said.

The radio crackled into life. 'This is Unit Three. Target has left the ring road, and is heading back into town, in the direction of the Caxton area. Over!'

Woodend picked up the microphone. 'This is Unit One,' he said. 'Don't lose him. Whatever happens, for God's sake don't lose him.'

Martin Dove looked even worse than his partner in crime, Horrocks thought, gazing down at the man sitting on the chair in front of him. And given what a state Cray was in, that really was no mean feat.

'I've been just talking to your mate, Roger,' he told the bearded Latin teacher. 'He's very sensibly decided to come clean and confess that you've been dealing with the Russians.'

'But that's just not true!' Martin Dove protested weakly. 'I'm not a communist. I'm nothing more than a liberal with a social conscience. That's why I joined CND in the first place.'

'How did you feel when you saw Verity Beale in the Spinner, the other night?' Horrocks asked, abruptly changing the subject.

'We were a little concerned,' Dove admitted.

'A little concerned! We've got a stack of witnesses to say you were shitting yourselves,' Horrocks lied. 'But even if you're telling the truth, and you were only a "little concerned", why be concerned at all?'

'Because we knew she wasn't what she seemed.'

'So you were suspicious of her?'

'I should have thought that was obvious.'

'Why?'

'I wondered why she was interested in Roger Cray in the

first place,' Dove said. 'She was a very attractive young woman, and he's just an ordinary, run-of-the-mill middle-aged man. I couldn't see the appeal.'

'And could *he*?'

'Not really, but like most men who find themselves in that position, he thanked his lucky stars that it had happened – and tried not to think too much about *why*.'

'But eventually he did start to get suspicious, didn't he?'

'Yes. Because she started asking him questions about himself and his activities – questions which simply wouldn't have come up in any normal conversation. And a couple of times she let slip that she knew things about him she couldn't possibly have known if she'd been who she really said she was.'

'So he told her the game was up?'

'Of course not. That would have been the same as admitting that he really did have something to hide.'

'So what did he do instead?'

'He just started seeing a lot less of her. And when he *did* see her, he dropped oblique hints that he'd given up any interest in politics or protest movements.'

'Let's go back to that night in the Spinner,' Horrocks suggested. 'You saw her there, and you panicked.'

'I told you, we didn't panic. We were just—'

'Mildly concerned. Yes, I know. So mildly concerned that you waited for her in the car park, and then killed her.'

'No! It's not true! Why should we have done that?'

'Because you were afraid she'd ruin your plans if you didn't.'

'The difficult part was already over,' Dove babbled. 'Roger had collected most of the information together. The only thing left to do was to hand it over. And she wasn't following us. We could see that.'

'Could you really?'

'Yes. For God's sake, she was out on a date! It was just

221

coincidence that she and the Yank chose the same pub as we did. You *have* to believe that!'

'There's one thing I still haven't been quite been able to work out,' Horrocks mused.

'What is it?'

'Who actually strangled her. Was it you? Or was it Cray?'

'Unit Four, Constable Duckworth speakin',' said the voice from the radio. 'Suspect has turned on to Jepson Avenue, an' appears to be slowin' down. He's just goin' past my house now, an'—'

'Your house!' Woodend said. 'You mean you live on Jepson Avenue yourself?'

'Yes, sir. Sorry, sir. What I meant to say was that he's just passin' Number Fifty-Six. An' he's indicatin' he's about to pull in.'

'All units proceed towards Jepson Avenue with all possible speed,' Woodend said. 'But slow down when you're gettin' close, and don't enter the avenue yourselves until I give the word.'

'He's stopped in front of Number Twenty-Eight,' Duckworth said.

'Who lives there?' Woodend asked.

'Nobody at the moment, sir. The last people moved out over a year ago. I did hear that it was bought by a property company in London soon afterwards, but they haven't put it up for sale yet.'

Why would a property company in London want to buy a modest house in Whitebridge? Woodend wondered. And even if they did, why would they keep it empty?

'Where are you now, Unit Four?' he asked.

'We've pulled up a few doors beyond the target's vehicle, sir. We're in the decorator's van, an' my partner's just about to open the back doors an' take out some cans of paint so Dunn doesn't get suspicious.'

'Good thinkin',' Woodend said. 'What's he doin' now?'

'He's got out of his vehicle, an' he's got his hand in his pocket. I think he's lookin' for keys. Yes, that's what he was doin'. He's pulled a set of keys out, an' he's selectin' one.'

'Get ready to move, Duckworth!' Woodend said. 'I don't want you more than four or five seconds behind him.'

'We won't be, sir,' the constable promised. 'The target's at the front door now. He's reachin' up to the lock . . . an' . . . an' somebody's openin' the door from inside.'

'A man or a woman?' Woodend demanded.

'It's a man, sir. He's about five eleven, an' he's got a bald head an' a droopy moustache.'

'Bloody hell fire!' Woodend said.

'They're both goin' inside, sir!' Duckworth said, almost shouting with the tension. 'They're closin' the door. We're about to move.'

'Stay where you are!' Woodend ordered him.

'Sorry, sir? I don't think I heard you right.'

'Stay exactly where you are,' Woodend repeated slowly. 'Don't do anythin' until we get there. Over an' out.'

'Have you lost your mind, sir?' Rutter demanded, as Woodend replaced the microphone in its holder.

'No, I haven't,' Woodend replied, sounding much calmer than he had earlier – but very, very much angrier. 'I just don't want Duckworth an' his partner rushin' in there – because there's no hurry any more.'

'I don't understand,' Rutter confessed. 'A couple of minutes ago, you were saying that every second was vital.'

'That was before I knew the bald man with the droopy moustache was involved,' Woodend told him.

'I don't see what difference that makes to anything,' Rutter said frantically. 'Even if Dunn has got help – even if there are *two* of them involved in the kidnapping—'

'Kidnappin'?' Woodend said. '*What* kidnappin'?'

Thirty-Two

T he decorator's van was parked a few yards up the street
from Dunn's car, and the two DCs dressed in painters'
overalls were doing their best to try and look as if they were
busy getting ready to start work.

Woodend climbed out of Rutter's vehicle and strode across
the road towards Number 28 Jepson Avenue. Despite the fact
that the house was supposed to be empty, there were still
curtains up at the windows, and it was possible that someone
was watching him from behind one of them. But at this stage
in the investigation, he didn't really give a damn whether they
could see him coming or not.

He had almost reached the front door when Bob Rutter
caught up with him. 'Don't do anything hasty, sir,' the
inspector cautioned.

'Hasty?' Woodend replied. 'Me? I never do anythin' hasty.
I think you must be confusin' me with some other DCI
Woodend, Bob.'

'Look, sir, if you're so sure that there's no immediate
danger to Helen Dunn—'

'There isn't.'

'—then shouldn't we go back to the station and get a search
warrant before we go in there?'

'Sod that for a game of soldiers!' Woodend said angrily. 'I'm
tired of bein' given the run-around on this case. I just want to
get this whole bloody business over with as soon as possible.'

'I know you do,' Rutter agreed. 'But without a warrant, any
charges we might bring later will be thrown out of court.'

'You don't seriously believe we're *ever* goin' to be allowed to charge somebody for any of this, do you?' Woodend asked.

Rutter shrugged, said, 'No, we probably won't be,' then reached up to press the doorbell.

'An' sod that for a game of soldiers as well,' Woodend told him. 'Kick the bloody door in.'

'Are you sure that's wise, sir?'

'Of course it's not wise! It's probably very bloody stupid. But it's the way I feel like doin' it.'

Rutter hesitated for a second, then stepped back, raised his right leg, and hit the door just below the lock with the heel of his shoe. The door creaked in protest, but swung shakily open.

'Nice job,' Woodend said approvingly. 'I always knew you had the makings of a good bobby in you.'

The kitchen door was flung open, and the bald man with the drooping moustache appeared in the passage. When he saw Woodend standing in the doorway, he came to an abrupt halt and bunched his fists.

'Well, well, if it isn't Bulldog Drummond himself,' Woodend said mockingly. 'Fancy you lettin' us catch you on the hop. I thought your mob were supposed to be professionals.'

The bald man's face flushed bright red with rage. 'I'll have your balls for this!' he said.

'No, you won't,' Woodend told him. 'These were your rules we've been playin' by – an' your rules that have made you lose. It's not my fault that you seem to be as bad at this particular game as you are at everythin' else, now is it?'

'You've no business being here,' the bald man said. 'I want you to leave right now.'

'I'm sure you do,' Woodend agreed. 'But that's not goin' to happen.' He stepped into the hallway. 'Where are they? Upstairs?'

The bald man took two steps forward, blocking off Wood-end's access to the stairs.

'I'm trained to look after myself – and you're not,' he warned. 'Don't make me hurt you.'

'Oh, piss off!' Woodend said contemptuously.

He took another step forward. The bald man transferred his weight to the balls of his feet. His arm cut through the air, the open palm at an angle to the floor, the heel aimed at the chief inspector's throat. Woodend swung his left arm, deflecting the blow, while at the same time his fist made contact with his opponent's jaw. The bald man's head snapped back, and he would probably have toppled over if Woodend hadn't followed through the punch with another one to his stomach. The bald man made a whooshing sound and bent forward, his nose connecting with Woodend's knee as he did so. The bald man's body swayed, as if undecided which of the blows to react to. Then his knees buckled and he crumpled to the floor.

Woodend rubbed his bruised knuckles, and turned to Rutter. 'I'm not generally in favour of settlin' a dispute with physical violence,' he said, 'but I have to admit I really did enjoy that.'

Squadron Leader Dunn was already standing on the upstairs landing by the time Woodend reached the top of the stairs. His normally decisive air had deserted him, and he seemed like a man with no idea what to do next.

'Is Helen in there?' Woodend asked, pointing to the bedroom behind Dunn's shoulder.

'Yes, she is,' the squadron leader admitted.

'Then you bugger off, so that I can have a quiet little chat with her,' Woodend said.

Reginald Dunn shook his head. 'I'm staying. I want to be there when you talk to her.'

'No chance,' Woodend said.

'I'm her father. I have the right—'

'You forfeited any rights you might have had when you

agreed to let her be used as a pawn in somebody else's game,' Woodend cut in.

'Possibly you're right,' Dunn agreed. 'Yes, perhaps you are. But I only did it for the good of—'

'I know! You only did it for the good of your country,' Woodend said contemptuously.

'I realise that might not mean much to you—'

'It means *a lot* to me, you bastard!' Woodend said hotly. 'But unlike you, I don't believe in abstractions. *My* country's made up of individuals – people like your daughter – an' the problem with sacrificin' a few of them for the greater good of the rest is that once you get started, it's difficult to know where to draw the line. Now bugger off before I do somethin' we both might regret.'

Dunn nodded, then, head bowed, edged past Woodend and made his way down the stairs.

The chief inspector knocked on the bedroom door, turned the handle, and stepped inside. Helen Dunn, still dressed in her school uniform, was sitting on the bed, her head buried in her hands.

'It's all right, love,' Woodend said softly. 'There's absolutely nothin' to be afraid of.'

Helen dropped her arms, and looked at him with deep, worried eyes. 'Are you a policeman?' she asked.

'That's right, I am. But I wouldn't let the fact bother me at all, if I was in your shoes.'

'Will I . . . will I get into trouble?'

'Of course you won't, lass,' Woodend said, sitting down on the bed next to her.

'Will my *dad* get into trouble?'

'No,' Woodend said. 'I believe he should, but I don't think he's goin' to. Do you want to tell me what happened?'

'I don't . . . I'm not quite sure.'

'Then let's talk about somethin' else,' Woodend suggested.

'Like what?'

227

'Anythin' you like. Why don't you play at bein' the bobby for a while, an' ask *me* the questions.'

A slight, uncertain smile came to Helen's lips. 'Where do you live?' she asked, testing the waters.

'Me an' the missus have got this little stone cottage out on the edge of the moors.'

'So you live in the countryside?'

'Yes.'

'That must be wonderful. Do you have any children?'

'Aye. I've got a daughter. Annie, her name is. She's trainin' to be a nurse in Manchester.'

'And does that make you proud of her? That she's going to be a nurse?'

'Yes, it does,' Woodend said. 'But I've have been proud of her whatever she'd chosen to do.'

'Really?'

'Really! She's a lovin' sweet girl, an' that's more than any parent has the right to expect.'

'But you didn't have any more children?'

Woodend shrugged awkwardly. 'No . . . I . . . After Annie was born, my wife had to have this operation. I don't really think it's somethin' that we need to go into now.'

'I had a sister,' Helen said.

'I know you did.'

'She died.'

'I know that, too. Do you want to talk about it?'

'We both tried so hard to please Dad – Janice even more than me – but somehow we never came up to his standards,' Helen said sadly. 'Janice got into trouble with the police when we were in Germany. It wasn't really her fault, but Dad was furious. He said she'd ruined her life – and his as well. She . . . she wanted to make it up to him. There was this swimming championship coming up, and she thought that if she could just win it . . .'

'So what did she do?' Woodend asked. 'Steal a key to the swimmin' pool, an' have a copy made?'

Helen nodded. 'She thought that if she could get in more practice than the others, she'd have more chance. She went there one night on her own and . . .'

'An' she drowned.'

'Yes.'

'Why did you start shop-liftin'?' Woodend asked.

'I'm not sure,' Helen confessed. 'I suppose it might have been because at least I was doing something wrong that I *knew* was wrong.'

'Rather than all the things you'd done that your dad told you were wrong *after* you'd done them?'

'That's right.'

'You wanted him to find out about it, didn't you?'

'Yes.'

'You wanted him to know you were guilty of one big thing, so all the little things wouldn't matter?'

'I suppose so.'

'But when it came to the crunch, you panicked.'

'I thought I could face him, but then I realised that I couldn't.'

'An' so you asked Miss Beale to help you?'

'She was the only one I could think of who I could turn to. She said she'd talk to the headmaster about it.'

And the headmaster, knowing who Miss Beale really was, would have done anything she'd asked him to, Woodend thought.

'She wanted you to do somethin' in return for her help, didn't she?' he guessed.

Helen nodded again. 'She asked if I'd do her a favour.'

'An' what favour was that?'

'She wanted me to write down the names of all the people who came to our house.'

The bitch! Woodend thought angrily. The bloody, scheming, insensitive bitch!

'Do you want to tell me what happened to you the day before yesterday?' he asked.

'I was in the playground. I noticed that someone was watching me from across the road. I went to see who it was.' Her mouth turned down at the edges. 'I was a bit disappointed when I found out it was only my dad.'

'What did he say to you?'

'He said that something serious had happened, and my country needed my help.'

'Your country!' Woodend repeated. 'Not him? Your country!'

'That's right. He said that the people he was working for needed a red . . . a red something-or-other.'

'A red herrin'?'

'That's right. And he said that I was the best they could come up with at short notice. He wanted me to pretend that I'd been kidnapped.'

'And what did you say?'

'I asked if Mum knew about it, and he said, no, she didn't, because she couldn't be trusted. I said if he didn't tell her, then I wasn't going to do it, and he said I had to, because it was my duty.'

He had allowed his wife to go through the hell of thinking their daughter really had been kidnapped, Woodend reminded himself. He had even hit her for arriving late at the school, because that would help allay any suspicion that he had been involved in the kidnapping.

'When did you lose Janice's pencil case?' he asked.

The girl's eyes widened. 'You seem to know everything,' she said.

Woodend grinned. 'Not everythin'. Far from it. But I do know that you lost the pencil case. How did it happen?'

'Dad said his car was at the other side of the park. He said we had to get to it quickly, before anybody spotted us together. I wasn't looking where I was going – I think I was upset about Mum not knowing what was going on – and I tripped over. I must have lost the pencil case then, but I didn't notice I hadn't got it any more until we arrived here.

230

Dad was very angry. He said the pencil case had been part of the plan.'

So he had gone back and taken the spare one from her bedroom, without really understanding that that would create the trail which would lead the police to this house.

'Was it you on the phone the other night?' he asked. 'The girl who said she was Helen Dunn, an' asked me to help her?'

Helen nodded. 'Yes.'

'An' the other voice was your dad's?'

The girl shook her head. 'It was this other man. Dad said I was to trust him and do what he told me to do.'

'And what he told you to do was act scared?'

'That's right. He said we had to keep up the pressure on you. He said we had to make sure that you were so busy looking for me, you wouldn't have time to do anything else.' Her voice cracked slightly. 'I didn't want to lie, but . . .'

'It's all right, lass. Don't upset yourself,' Woodend said soothingly. 'I'll tell you what. When all this fuss has died down, you must come out to visit me in my cottage.'

'Do you really mean that?'

'Aye, I do. My missus will make us some afternoon tea, then we'll go out for a walk. There's a little wood near our house, an' if you sit in the middle of it, hardly breathin', you can watch the rabbits play.'

'I'd like that,' Helen said, and sounded as if she meant it.

'How very cosy you make it all sound!' said a sneering voice from the doorway.

Woodend looked up, and saw Horrocks standing there.

'Is this the man you made the phone call with, Helen?' Woodend asked.

The girl nodded.

'I can't honestly say I wasn't expectin' you to turn up,' the chief inspector told the man from London. 'Even so, it still feels a bit like bein' told by the doctor that the rash you've developed is the pox.'

Jack Horrocks scowled. 'We need to have a long serious talk!' he said. 'Now!'

'No, *you* need to have a long serious talk now,' Woodend contradicted him. 'Me an' Helen, on the other hand, need to finish our little chat while we're waitin' for a WPC to arrive to take care of her.'

'Maybe I didn't make myself plain,' Horrocks said. 'I've just given you an order.'

'An' maybe I didn't make myself plain, either,' Woodend countered, a smile playing on his lips. 'I've already laid out one of your lot this mornin', an' nothin' would give me greater satisfaction than to go for my double.'

Thirty-Three

The WPC had a matronly figure and a kind face, and as she led Helen Dunn to the front door, she draped her arm over the girl's thin shoulder.

On the threshold, Helen stopped and turned around. 'It's been nice talking to you,' she said to Woodend.

'It's been nice talkin' to you, an' all, lass,' the chief inspector replied. 'An' I meant what I said earlier. You're welcome at my house any time you feel like droppin' in. The rabbits'll be waitin'.'

The girl smiled, and allowed the WPC to lead her to the waiting car. Woodend watched her until she'd climbed inside, then turned towards the living room where, he suspected, the man who called himself Horrocks was waiting to have their long, serious discussion.

He was not wrong. Horrocks was indeed in the living room, sitting on a perfectly normal sofa, which made up one third of a perfectly normal three-piece suite. Looking around the room, Woodend saw that it also contained a sideboard, a cocktail cabinet and a television, just as any ordinary living room might. But appearances could be very deceptive.

'I suppose this is what you call a "safe house", is it?' the chief inspector asked.

'It's a house, and we have the use of it when we need it,' Horrocks said cautiously.

'An' how many more of them have you got scattered around the Whitebridge area?'

'That's none of your business.'

'No,' Woodend admitted. 'I suppose it isn't. But your Miss Beale is. She *was* your Miss Beale, wasn't she?'

'Let's just say that both Miss Beale and I were working for the same side,' Horrocks replied.

'Meanin' that you're Special Branch, an' she was MI5?'

'I'm not prepared to go into the details.'

'Maybe you're not. An' maybe I can even understand *why* you're not,' Woodend said. He sat down in one of the armchairs, and lit up a Capstan Full Strength. 'But if you want me to co-operate with you – an' you must do, or you wouldn't still be here – I'm goin' to expect you to answer at least a few of my questions in return.'

'I don't think you quite appreciate the position you're in,' Horrocks told him. 'You injured one of my men.'

'He'll live,' Woodend said indifferently. 'Besides, he started it.'

'He was only doing his duty – a duty which you tried to obstruct.'

Woodend smiled. '*Tried* to obstruct?'

'Which you *did* obstruct, then,' Horrocks corrected himself. He glowered. 'You think you're very clever, don't you, Mr Woodend?'

'For a simple, provincial bobby, I'm not half bad,' Woodend said. 'So do we have a deal or not?'

'If that's what you want to call it, then, yes, we have a deal,' Horrocks said grudgingly.

Woodend took a deep drag on his Capstan Full Strength. 'I've always pictured the spyin' trade as bein' both glamorous and professional. But there was nothin' glamorous about what Verity Beale was doin' here in Whitebridge, and from what I've seen of the way your organisation works, it's my opinion that the Boy Scouts could run the secret service a damn sight better.'

'VB was a highly effective operative,' Horrocks said, stung.

'An' what *was* her job, exactly?'

'I don't have to tell you.'

'Then I'll tell you,' Woodend said. 'Her job was to mix with people who had the *potential* to be security risks, an' try an' sniff out the ones who actually *were* risks. I imagine she was only one of a series of "operatives" you've got in the district. Am I right about that?'

'No comment,' Horrocks said.

'That's a comment in itself,' Woodend said. 'This wasn't VB's first job of that nature, was it? Before she came to Lancashire, she was based in Woolwich, tryin' to make friends with some of the fellers who had a connection with the Arsenal.'

'How the hell did you know that?' Horrocks demanded.

'It was a careless move on your part to put a Woolwich address on her fake drivin' licence,' Woodend told him.

Horrocks gave him a slight, superior smile, as if he was glad to snatch a small victory from wherever he could.

'The driving licence was genuine,' he said. 'It was only the information on it which was false. We don't need to forge official government documents – we work *for* the government.'

'Anyway, after she was rumbled in Woolwich, she moved up here, so she could see what dirt she could dig up on the airmen an' the fellers who work at the plane factory,' Woodend continued. 'She needed a cover, so you got her a job in the grammar school. An' she needed an excuse to come in contact with the people she was meant to be investigatin', so she jumped the teachers' waitin' list, and was given plum classes at the base. Tell me, was she under orders to sleep with the people she was investigatin'?'

'Of course not!' Horrocks said, outraged. 'This isn't Russia! We don't order our people to do things like that.'

'But she wasn't exactly *discouraged* from doin' it, either, was she?'

'Our operatives are all engaged in a war to protect this country from the enemy within, and they have the discretion to do whatever they think is necessary to get results. We're not ashamed of their activities.'

'Maybe not, but you certainly wouldn't want some of those activities to become more widely known. An' you were quick to appreciate that that's exactly what would have happened if you'd allowed the local police to investigate Verity Beale's murder,' Woodend said. 'The problem was, you couldn't really stop us without tellin' us the truth – an' tellin' the truth is somethin' you're not very partial to in your game. So you needed an excuse to take us off the Beale murder, an' some bright spark who works for you came up with the idea of fakin' a kidnappin'.'

'Local police always panic when they've got a kidnapping on their hands,' Horrocks said smugly. 'Besides, *you* were in charge.'

'An' what's that's supposed to mean?'

'According to your record – which you won't have seen but I have – you had a similar case back in '48.'

'Ellie Taylor,' Woodend said.

'I forget the girl's name. Anyway, you took it very badly when she turned up dead. For a while, your boss was quite concerned you might have a nervous breakdown.'

'I think it was the old feller – her grandfather – who really got to me,' Woodend said reflectively. 'He'd been through so much in his life. He shouldn't have had to spend his last few days mournin' for Ellie.' The chief inspector shook his head, as if trying to shake away the past. 'Anyway, what made you choose Squadron Leader Dunn an' his daughter for this particularly nasty little job of yours?' he asked.

'There weren't too many suitable candidates *to* choose from,' Horrocks said. 'Besides, according to his file, Dunn is a first-class chap – a true patriot.'

'It's a pity you didn't bother to tell Verity Beale that,' Woodend said, in disgust.

'What do you mean?'

'She set his own daughter to spy on him.'

'That does appear to have been an oversight,' Horrocks said, sounding slightly uncomfortable. 'It's not always easy, when your business itself is secrecy, to make sure that everyone is fully briefed about everyone else. But it was certainly a mistake on VB's part to ever consider Dunn a security risk.' He glanced at his watch. 'Time's pressing. Can I say what *I've* got to say now.'

'Aye, go on,' Woodend replied.

'The offer I'm about to make was originally intended for your Sergeant Paniatowski – that's the main reason she was allowed on to even the periphery of my investigation – but now you've found out so much for yourself, I suppose I'd better make it to you.'

He stopped, and looked questioningly at Woodend.

'I'm still listenin',' the chief inspector said.

'Since I was never really officially here, I can only take the murder investigation so far myself before I'm forced to hand it over to others to tie up the loose ends. Which is a lucky break for you, Mr Woodend.'

'Is it? Why?'

'Because I've done all the work – and you'll get all the glory.'

'You sound like you've made an arrest already.'

'Nobody has actually been arrested as such, but I do have the guilty parties under detention.'

'An' they are?'

'Martin Dove and Roger Cray.'

'The Latin teacher and the bureaucrat!' Woodend said, disbelievingly. 'Have they confessed?'

'Not as yet. But they will.'

'What was their motive?'

'They were planning to steal some secret documents, and VB was on to them. The only way to silence her was to kill her.'

Woodend shook his head. 'As a motive, that really doesn't hold water, you know,' he said.

'Why not?'

'Because of somethin' that's been botherin' me from the very start of this case – the way the killer chose to dispose of the body.'

'What do you mean by that?'

'If you'd told me that Cray had killed her because he'd found out she was not only sleepin' with him but with Dove as well, I'd probably buy it. At a push, I might even accept the idea that they both knew she was sleepin' with the other, but then they discovered she was havin' it off with a third man, an' that's what pushed them over the edge. But if they'd killed her because she'd learned about their spyin' activities, they simply wouldn't have disposed of the body in the way they did.'

'So how do you think they *would* they have disposed of it?' Horrocks asked sceptically.

'Any number of ways. Left her where they'd killed her. Buried her in the woods. Maybe even tried to burn the body. But what they *wouldn't* have done is risk drivin' her twenty miles just so they could dump her in a pigsty. Why should they? There's nothin' personal in the kind of murder you just described. They'd have killed her simply because she was a threat to their security, an' they'd have wanted to be shot of her body as soon as possible.'

'Perhaps they did it in the way they did *precisely* so you'd come up with just the kind of theory you're producing now,' Horrocks said – but his voice was starting to lack any real conviction.

'In the real world – a world which you seem to know very little about – people simply don't think like that,' Woodend said.

'And I suppose that because you – as you see it – *do* live in the real world, you know who actually *did* kill her, do you?'

Woodend closed his eyes, and put his hands to his forehead – an indication, to anyone who knew him well, that his brain was going into overdrive.

238

'I thought that would throw you,' Horrocks crowed. 'It's all very well for you to criticise my methods, but it's not quite so easy to come up with a solution of your own, is it?'

A pained look crossed Woodend's brow. 'It'd be easier to think in the middle of a bloody monkey house than it is sittin' next to you,' he said. 'Why don't you just shut up for a minute, an' let me work it out.'

It was more than a minute – possibly as many as three – before Woodend lowered his hands again.

'Well? Do you have a theory – or don't you?' Horrocks demanded.

'You asked me if I knew who'd killed Verity Beale,' Woodend said. 'An' now I've finally managed to clear my head of all the distractions that the Helen Dunn case has been fillin' it with, I rather think I do know.'

Thirty-Four

It was that time of day when the workers were at work, the children were in school and the old people were just letting their lunches go down before setting out on their gentle afternoon strolls. So the two men walking towards each other at the top end of the Corporation Park had the place pretty much to themselves.

'It was very good of you to make the time to see me, Mr Barnes,' Woodend said.

'You were lucky to catch me during my free period,' the history teacher replied. 'I've only got half an hour before I'm due back in the classroom. Will that be long enough for what you want?'

'It should be. I've only got a *few* questions I need to ask you.'

'About Verity?'

'Naturally. I'm almost at the point of makin' an arrest, but before I actually go ahead with it, there are one or two matters I need to clear up. An' I think you might be just the man to help me with that.'

'I see,' Barnes said seriously, as if he were aware of the heavy responsibility, which was being laid on him. 'What is it you want to know?'

'Why do you think Verity Beale showed an interest in goin' to your church?'

'I thought I'd already explained that.'

'Then explain it again.'

'She wanted the chance to get to know God better.'

'Did she? Or was it just that she wanted to get to know some of the *congregation* better?'

'People do use their places of worship as a basis for their social lives. There's nothing to be ashamed of in that.'

'Is that what you do?'

'No, but . . .'

'How long it did take Verity Beale to become acquainted with Captain Tooley?'

'I think I introduced her to him the first time she attended the church, but I couldn't say for sure.'

'In other words, Tooley had been a member of the congregation for longer than she had?'

'Yes, he appeared shortly after Christmas, which was when, I assume, he was first posted to the Blackhill base.'

'Did she specifically ask be introduced to him?'

'Not that I remember.'

Woodend pulled his packet of Capstan Full Strengths out of his pocket, and offered it to Barnes. When the teacher shook his head in refusal, he lit up one for himself.

'Could you do somethin' for me, Mr Barnes?' the chief inspector asked.

'What?'

'Could you close your eyes?'

'All right,' Barnes agreed, still mystified.

'Try to picture that first meetin' between Verity an' Tooley in your mind. Was it like she was bein' introduced to a complete stranger, or do you get the impression she already had an idea who he was?'

'She . . . she called him Captain Tooley,' Barnes gasped.

'Go on,' Woodend said encouragingly.

'He wasn't in uniform at the time. I introduced him as "*Wilbur* Tooley", but when she shook hands with him, she said, "Pleased to meet you, *Captain* Tooley." Why didn't I notice that before?'

'Because you're not trained to,' Woodend said.

The sound of a heavy vehicle distracted them both. They

turned to see a police tow-truck labour its way up Park Road and then turn on to the Eddie's staff car park.

'What's that doing here?' Simon Barnes asked.

'My lads need to check over one of the cars, an' I thought it would be better if it was taken away, so they could do it somewhere the pupils can't see what's goin' on,' Woodend explained.

'Whose car are we talking about, here?'

'We'll come on to that later,' Woodend said easily. 'Let's get back to Miss Beale. When did you first fall in love with her?'

Barnes jumped. 'I beg your pardon?'

'You heard,' Woodend told him. 'You're surely not goin' to deny it, are you?'

'No,' Barnes said thoughtfully. 'I'm not going to deny it. I probably fell in love with her the moment I saw her. But it was not until we started going to church together that I was really sure of my feelings.'

'In other words, you realised that you were in love with her when she seemed to be startin' to take an interest in you,' Woodend said. 'For a while back there, you must have considered yourself the luckiest man in the world, Mr Barnes.'

'I did,' Barnes agreed. 'I'd never had much success with women. And looking at me, you can easily understand the reason for that, can't you? But, you see, I thought Verity was different. I thought that she could see beyond the surface trappings to the real me.'

'But she soon lost interest in you, didn't she? Or rather, she transferred her interest to other people.' Woodend paused again. 'Yesterday, when we were swoppin' quotes in the playground, you said somethin' about us all actin' – from time to time – like "the jewel of gold in the swine's snout". You were makin' a general point yourself, but that's not how it's used in the Bible, is it? In Proverbs, Chapter 11, Verse 22, it's much more specific.'

'Yes, it is,' Barnes agreed.

'So what's the full quote?'

'You already know.'

'I'd still like to hear you say it.'

Barnes closed his eyes again. '"As a jewel of gold in a swine's snout, so is a fair woman which is without discretion."'

'Why don't you tell me exactly what happened on the night Verity Beale died?' Woodend suggested.

Barnes sighed, as if keeping up a front had suddenly become far too much of an effort. 'I had my suspicions about how she was betraying herself, but I didn't want to condemn her out of hand,' he said.

'An' so you followed her?'

'That's right. While she was on the base, I parked in the woods. When she'd finished her class, she got into her Mini again and drove past my hiding place. A minute or so later, Tooley the Fornicator followed her in his car.'

'An' you followed them *both*.'

'Yes, I did. There's a secluded lay-by about three miles beyond the woods. They pulled into it, and I drove on.'

'But you didn't go far?'

'No, not far at all. I parked a little way up the road and walked back on foot. When I reached the lay-by, Verity's car was empty, and they were both in his. Tooley's is a big car – a heavy car – yet it was rocking! Rocking! Because inside they were . . . they were . . .'

'Makin' love?'

'Making *lust*! I loved her with all my heart, yet had never even so much as touched her. But Tooley, a man married in the eyes of God to another woman was . . . was . . .'

'How did you feel?'

'How do you think I felt?' Barnes demanded angrily. 'Tooley isn't handsome! He's not built like a Greek god. He's gangly and awkward. Just like me! He could . . . he could almost have been taken for my brother.'

'An' just as Cain was jealous of his brother Abel, because God seemed to prefer him, you were jealous of Tooley. Did you want to kill Tooley, just like Cain killed Abel?'

'Of course I did. I wanted to kill them both.'

'What stopped you?'

'I thought if I could only talk to Verity alone, I could make her see the error of her ways.'

'So you went back to your car and waited?'

'Yes. When they had finally finished their fornication, they drove off again, and I followed them to the Spinner.'

'You didn't go in?'

'No, I parked my car where it wouldn't be noticed, and waited for them to come out again.'

'Somebody *will* have noticed, you know,' Woodend said. 'With all the forensic evidence my lads will find in your car, we probably won't need any witnesses to make our case – but they'll be available if we want them.'

'Does that really matter now?' Barnes asked.

'No, I don't suppose it does,' Woodend replied. 'Why don't you go on with your story?'

'The American left the pub first – driving home to the family he had chosen to betray. The landlord locked the door at a quarter past eleven, but there still people drinking inside. At about twenty-five to twelve, Verity came out. If there'd been someone else with her, I'd probably have put off confronting her until the morning. But she was completely alone – almost as if that were the way God had intended it to be.'

'What did you say to her?'

'That she was not irrevocably lost. That there was still hope for her. She laughed in my face. "Hope for *me*?" she said. "What you really mean is hope for *you*, isn't it? Hope that I'll turn into the kind of woman you've always wanted – and could never have!" It was cruel – so very, very cruel!'

Yes, it was cruel, Woodend thought, but he could understand how it might have happened. Verity Beale had been playing an unnatural, stressful role for months – maybe even for years. She must, during that time, have done things which, even though she thought them necessary for the good of her country, still made her despise herself. That very evening she had made love to the American airman, not because she wanted to, but because she needed to keep a hold on him while she completed her investigation. When she had seen Simon Barnes standing in the car park, looking both condemnatory and pathetic, it must all have seemed like the last straw, and she had lashed out at him with words, just as Woodend himself had lashed out with his fists at the spy with the droopy moustache.

'She was right, of course,' Simon Barnes said sadly. 'I had been a fool to even dream I could ever have a woman like her. But did she really need to *say* it? Did she really need to tell me that she'd only been using me? That I was – and these were her very words – "nothing more than a station she'd had to pass through to get to where she was really going"?'

'An' that's when you hit her?'

'The flower border was made of bricks. I'd noticed that earlier. You notice all kinds of things when you're standing, waiting. She turned her back on me – contemptuously, oh, so contemptuously! – and bent over to open her car door. I picked up a brick and smote her. I hadn't planned it, but that's what I did. I was surprised when she collapsed. I stood looking down at her, wondering what would happen when she came round again. Even if she didn't report me to the police, she'd be bound to tell other people about it, wouldn't she? And not just what I'd done – but why I'd done it. They would have felt the same contempt for me that she so obviously felt. I'd have been Simon Barnes the coward – the man who struck a woman from behind. Simon Barnes the poor lovesick fool – who couldn't even get from her what she seemed to be giving everybody else so freely. I think it was at that point that I decided I'd have to kill her.'

'An' when was it you decided where to leave the body?'

'Later. When I'd bundled her body into my car. At first I thought of just leaving her by the roadside, a few miles from the pub. But that would have been too good for her, wouldn't it?'

'Would it?' Woodend asked.

'Of course it would. Whoever found her would have seen her as nothing more than a poor, innocent victim of a murderous attack. I didn't want that. I wanted them to see her as she *truly* was – as a Jezebel. Do you know what happened to the Biblical Jezebel?'

'She was thrown to the dogs of the field, so they could lick her blood an' eat her flesh,' Woodend said.

'But there are no dogs of the fields in Lancashire. So I did the next best thing. I left her among the unclean swine – where she belonged!'

Thirty-Five

DCC Ainsworth sat behind his desk, his face cloaked in an expression which it would have been totally inadequate to describe as rage.

'You just can't keep your bloody big nose out of anything, can you, Chief Inspector?' he demanded.

Woodend, who had not been invited to sit down, and hence was standing, gave a shrug.

'I found the missin' girl, just like I was instructed to, didn't I, sir?' he asked.

'But you weren't supposed to *find* her – you were only supposed to *look* for her.'

'I'm not a mind-reader, sir,' Woodend said, in his own defence.

'Yes, you are – but only when it bloody well suits you to be!'

Woodend sighed. 'If Special Branch had decided to trust us – instead of just trustin' *you* – we'd never have had to go through this kidnappin' pantomime in the first place, an' we'd probably have arrested Simon Barnes a lot earlier.'

If there was one thing worse than bloody Cloggin'-it Charlie thinking he was right when everybody else thought he was wrong, it was him thinking he was right when everybody else was forced by circumstances to agree with him, Ainsworth decided.

'Inspector Rowe has filed an official complaint against you,' he said, attempting to snatch some small personal victory from the jaws of defeat.

247

'An' who's Inspector Rowe, when he's at home?' Woodend asked.

'He's the member of DCI Horrocks' team you assaulted.'

'Oh, the Mexican bandit!' Woodend said. '"Assaulted" isn't the term I would have used for what I did.'

'So what would you have called it?'

'I flattened him,' Woodend said. 'I well-an'-truly *flattened* the bugger. My knuckles are still a bit sore from it.'

'I'm amazed you can take it so lightly,' Ainsworth told him. 'Aren't you worried about the consequences at all?'

'Not really, sir,' Woodend admitted. 'Why should I be, when I've got somebody like you in my corner? You'll handle it so there are no come-backs, won't you?'

'You're being very presumptuous, Chief Inspector,' Ainsworth told him.

'Am I? Sorry again, sir. It's just that I've always thought of you as the kind of boss who stood behind his men.'

'Like hell you have!'

'Besides, as things stand, we can probably come up with some story to explain away what happened to Helen Dunn. Of course, the officers actually involved in the operation will know it's all cock-and-bull, but they're good lads, an' they'll keep quiet if I ask them to. On the other hand, if I was brought up on a charge, I'd have to tell the truth, wouldn't I? I'd be forced to explain how all other police work in Lancashire virtually ground to a halt while we investigated a crime that you already knew *wasn't* a crime at all. I shouldn't think it'd do your standin' much good with the men you command. An' once the press got hold of the story, well . . .'

'That's sounds suspiciously like blackmail,' Ainsworth said.

'Does it? Sorry, sir, it wasn't meant to.'

Ainsworth slammed his hand violently down on the desk. 'I'll want a full report on this whole bloody mess by tomorrow morning at the latest,' he said.

'I'll get started on it the moment I come back from the railway station,' Woodend promised.

'And why, pray, do you feel the sudden need to go the railway station?' Ainsworth asked.

'I'm goin' to say goodbye to somebody,' Woodend told him.

The porters on Whitebridge Station waited until all the passengers had climbed on board the train before they wheeled the coffin out of the luggage office and loaded it into the goods' van.

'Where are they sending her?' asked Rutter, who was standing with his boss near the ticket barrier.

'They'll be sendin' her home – wherever that is.'

'Does she have a family, do you think?'

'Verity Beale doesn't, because Verity Beale never existed. But I expect there's some family with a surname beginnin' with B who've been spun a story about their daughter's tragic accident, an' are waitin' for their Vera, or their Valerie, to come home in a box.'

The coffin had been loaded, and the doors of the guard's van securely closed. The guard on the platform waved his flag, and the train began to chug out of the station.

'I don't think that I've ever learned so little about the victim in one of my cases as I've learned about the victim in this one,' Woodend said reflectively. 'We know some of things that Verity Beale *did*, but we've no idea what she was *like*. Did it not bother her at all to order Helen Dunn to spy on her own father? Was she really as hard and heartless as she seemed, when she told Simon Barnes that she'd just been usin' him to get what she wanted? Or was that nothin' more than her trainin' an' experience comin' into play? Is it possible that beneath that tough shell there lurked a woman who was vulnerable, frightened an' as unsure as the rest of us are?'

'I suppose we'll never know,' Rutter said.

'No, we won't,' Woodend agreed, with a regretful sigh. 'I wish I could believe that her death hadn't been totally pointless – that through it, a few people in her business might begin to see that it's no good sayin' the end always justifies the means, because that can often do as much damage as whatever those means are tryin' to prevent.'

'Like people who threaten to blow up the world in order to save the world?' Rutter said.

'Exactly,' Woodend agreed. 'Khrushchev will feel more secure if he gets his missiles on to Cuba, and Kennedy will feel more secure if he doesn't. I'm not sayin' they both don't have a point, an' I'm not sayin' they're wrong to care about the people they're supposed to be protectin'. But neither of the buggers is goin' to feel secure if, between them, they turn everythin' into no more than a smoulderin' pile of ashes, now is he?'

'We're both getting a bit philosophical for this time of day, aren't we?' Rutter suggested.

'Aye, you're right,' Woodend agreed. He glanced down at his watch. 'Still, I suppose there's nothin' wrong with the quest for moral certainty an' universal truth – especially when you know exactly where to find it.'

'And where might that be?' Rutter asked, smiling.

'In the public bar of the Drum an' Monkey, of course,' Woodend said. 'It's remarkable how much better the world starts to look after a couple of pints of Thwaite's Best Bitter.'

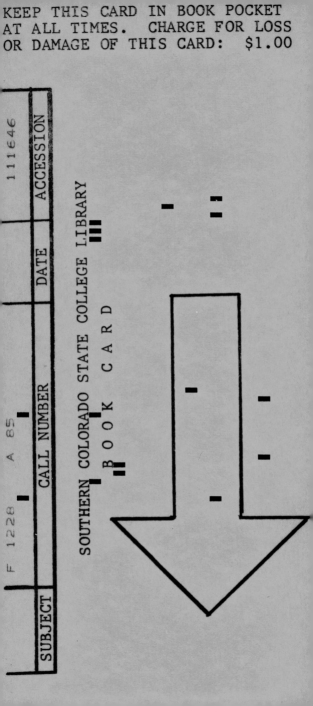